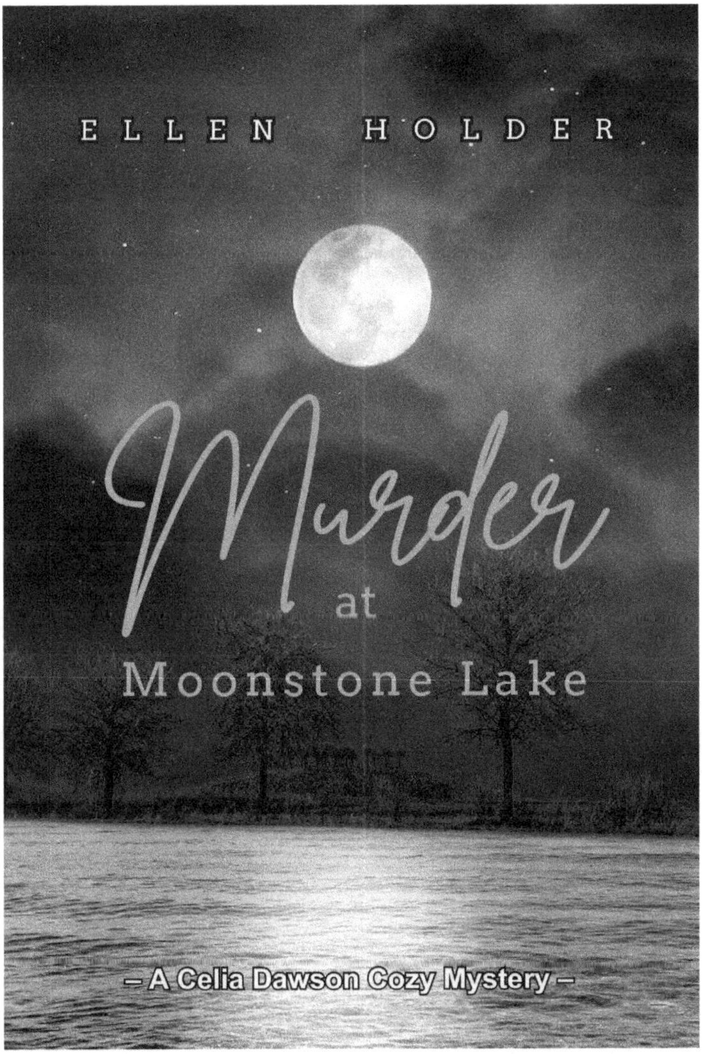
ELLEN HOLDER
Murder
at
Moonstone Lake
– A Celia Dawson Cozy Mystery –

Murder at Moonstone Lake

Ellen Holder

HOWLING WOLF PRESS

ISBN: 978-1-961703-09-4

Acknowledgments

My greatest support is my husband, Dave Holder. He's my biggest fan, eagerly reads every word I write, and never resents the time I spend on this passion. Fellow writers have encouraged me, including close friends Kim Smith Browning and Michelle Fulmer, who cheered for me every step of the way. Beta readers have been super, and my publisher (Howling Wolf Press) has kept me motivated and inspired. I must mention a writing buddy, Jeremy Homan, who suggested the premise for *Murder at Moonstone Lake*. It began as a lark but, without his idea, I might never have written this novel.

Chapter 1

Before ever touching her, I knew Marge was dead. She lay sprawled on the wood floor in her living room near an overturned table lamp. The wide-open eyes, slightly parted lips, and blood-matted hair said it all. Some of the blood had trickled onto her face, now drying and thick. A fly crawled undisturbed, already drawn to the sticky feast.

I glanced around, listening for the sound of footsteps or a creaking floor, but all I heard was my pounding heart. If someone had attacked and killed Marge, could they still be in her house? A killer with a speck of sense wouldn't hang around to be discovered . . . unless it was some deranged psycho waiting for another victim.

Maybe there *was* no attacker. Maybe Marge simply fell and hit her head on one of those end tables by the couch. But the gooey blood on the base of the lamp suggested a different scenario. My senses screamed, *This was murder!* And my sixth sense screamed the loudest.

I looked closer at the lamp, which was missing a shade and a light bulb. The cord was wrapped around the slender neck near the light socket. The base was heavy brass, shaped like a fat jug. How odd that it was in the living room, unused.

Squatting next to Marge, I felt her neck, then her wrist. Her skin was pale and icy, with no pulse at all. I probably shouldn't have touched her, but I had to know if she might still be clinging to life, perhaps in a coma but still alive.

I stood and dug out my cell phone from a pocket in my jeans, took a deep breath to steady myself, and punched in 911. I pictured myself getting knocked cold by the murderer while making my call. The hair stood up on my arms, and I bolted back out the front door I'd left standing open. I turned back to watch the doorway and kept my voice low.

"I'm calling to report a dead body. At least I think she's dead––I can't find a pulse."

The voice in my ear was equal parts ho-hum and concern. "Give me the address where the body is located. And I need your name."

The house number was on the front of the house and I read it into the phone. "One twenty-two North Lake Drive here in Conroy . . . yes, that's Moonstone Lake Retirement Village . . . My name is Celia Dawson."

Stepping farther out into the shaded yard, I sought relief from the mid-morning Florida heat. I tried to act casual so as not to draw attention to myself. I didn't want nosy neighbors crowding around and drifting into Marge's house. It would probably start a stampede. I said to the operator, "I'm outside now. And I'm pretty sure no one else is in the house. She looks like she's been dead a few hours."

"Help is on the way. Stay on the line please, until police or an ambulance arrives."

Holding the phone face-up, I moved back into the doorway. I felt protective, like I needed to stay with Marge, as if she were likely to sit up and ask for a glass of water. That wasn't sensible, I know, but I wanted to keep her in sight.

I was stunned, maybe numb. But the fact that Marge had been killed began to sink in. Why were my cheeks wet? Had I been crying?

I raised the phone to my ear. "Just checking in. I'm still here," I said. The phone was silent. I looked at the display. The battery power was at zero. I slipped the useless phone into my pocket and went back to my musing.

Death wasn't pretty. But my eyes kept straying back to her perfectly still body. No rise and fall of the chest, no sound of breathing. Her pink, flowered housecoat was snapped up the front but had popped loose above the knees. One foot still wore a pink slipper, while the other was bare.

Marge was not a close friend. But my best friend, Rosanna, worked for her in the retirement village office. I had merely come to check on Marge that morning when I found the office still closed at 10:15.

Our retirement community is for fifty-five and older. I don't like to think about how often people around here die. But Marge's death was different. Violence lingered in the air, nearly as tangible as the blood that lay on the floor. The room gave me the creeps, but my curiosity was stronger.

My analytical side kicked in. Wiping my cheeks, I thought about the time frame and how things might have happened. Marge closed the front office around 5:00 every afternoon. Yesterday, she probably walked straight home to her bungalow by the lake, maybe fifty yards from the community center and management office. She might have changed into her nightclothes before having dinner if she wasn't expecting a visitor.

I wondered if she ever got to her meal. That could indicate when her visitor had arrived. The killer could've shown up in the early morning hours before people were stirring and awake. Either way, the medical examiner would determine the time and cause of death.

Not yet hearing a siren, I had time to check out the kitchen. Surely I'd be safe, slipping from the doorway back inside the house. Who would be fool enough to hang around this long after they'd killed somebody? Almost in a crouch, I tiptoed toward the kitchen, careful not to touch anything.

Now, this might've been a foolish thing for me to do. But, with a shocking crime scene right before me, I couldn't resist looking for details. I might see something the cops would miss.

The kitchen smelled faintly of tomatoes and garlic. On a table against the wall, I saw a half-eaten plate of spaghetti and a nearly empty wineglass. The tang of Italian dressing lingered in the air from the smear left in her salad bowl. A chair pulled out from the table sat cock-eyed, abandoned.

I turned away from the table, back toward the living room, startled to see the silhouette of a man filling the front doorway. He didn't notice me in the shadowy kitchen, and with the sun behind him, I couldn't make out his face.

He stepped into the living room, his eyes riveted to the sight of Marge's body sprawled on the floor. A high, pitiful moan escaped him, sounding young and vulnerable. But his hair was white, and I recognized Howard, a long-time resident of the retirement village. Like me, he was in his sixties.

Since I'd moved there a year earlier, I'd heard yelling and arguments several times between Howard and Marge. At least I heard raised voices behind her closed office door; I never made out their actual words. How strange to hear him openly grieving over her dead body now.

I spoke quietly, not wanting to startle him. "Howard?"

He jumped at the sound of my voice, and his face darkened. "What're you doing there, lurking in the kitchen? What have you done?"

I barely knew Howard, but I found him annoying, and I didn't care for that tone in his voice. "What on earth are you talking about? I found her like this, I called 911, and they're on their way."

Howard stared at me, and his face crumpled. He sank to his knees next to Marge and reached for her.

"No, don't touch her!" I yelped. "This might be a crime scene." I heard a siren in the distance, growing louder and closer, and I suggested he go outside and flag them down.

But he ignored me. He wrapped his arms around his middle and rocked back and forth, still crying but quieter.

The siren was right outside now, and the noise finally shut off. The entire neighborhood would be there soon.

"God almighty," I muttered, as I hurried through the living room and out the front door. I might have looked like a murder suspect fleeing from the crime scene. It didn't cross my mind at the time; I was simply glad to see somebody arrive who knew what they were doing.

A male and female dressed in white uniform shirts and dark pants stepped carefully from the ambulance and looked around the area. They'd arrived ahead of the cops at a potential crime scene, one that could still be dangerous.

I waved them over. They gathered their equipment and walked toward the house. "She's there in the front room," I said and stepped away to give them plenty of space.

A few minutes later, the female driver came back out the front door with Howard in tow. "Sir, you need to wait outside," she told him. He looked stunned and raised his hands to cover his face.

I stepped closer to him. "They'll do everything they can for her, Howard. We need to stay out of the way."

He turned on me with a snarl. "What happened to her?"

It was like a slap in the face, but I didn't raise my voice. He'd lashed out at me like I was the enemy. "I have no idea," I told him. "She wasn't in her office, so I came to check on her. She might have been ill."

"Oh God. I'm afraid she's dead." His voice had gone from angry to a hopeless wail. He opened his arms and pulled me to him.

What a surprise! We'd never been fond of each other, and that's putting it mildly. Still, I softened a little and patted his back. "Yeah, it looks that way. Maybe they can revive her."

I didn't want to give him false hope, but I wanted him to stop blubbering. I know men hate to see women cry. But a bawling man is so much worse.

Other residents had gathered around to see what the uproar was all about. An ambulance was not an uncommon sight in a retirement community. However, this one was parked in the driveway of the owner and manager, Marjorie Coleman. They all called her "Marge in Charge." But not to her face. No sir, she would crawl down your throat in a heartbeat.

Two sisters walked toward us, Tammy and Darlene. They had recently moved to central Florida from West Virginia. "What's going on?" Tammy asked. Their faces were alight with excitement, their eyes large and curious.

They seemed appallingly delighted to see Howard's arms around me.

"Marge has been hurt," I told them, disentangling myself from the man. "I came to check on her and found her . . . unconscious." I was hesitant to mention death, not wanting to see these ladies lose their cool. They needed to hang onto every scrap of cool they had.

Another blaring siren drew our attention to a police car heading down the long drive that leads into the park from the highway. Our conversation halted as the siren grew louder. The black-and-white parked next to the ambulance, and a cop got out and headed for the house. He'd been inside a short time when the EMTs came out, returned their equipment to the ambulance, climbed back in, and began backing away.

Darlene, the shorter of the two, blurted, "Why are they leaving without Marge?"

"I guess there's no point taking her to the hospital." Tammy's matter-of-fact voice was tired and resigned.

"My word! Is she dead?"

"That appears to be so," Tammy told her. Tammy was tall, her short, dark hair sprinkled with gray.

Howard reached for my hand and squeezed it like he was hanging from a cliff. His tears started up again, and it sounded like he was choking. Where was all this emotion coming from? If he'd been sweet on Marge all this time, it sure never came across that way. In fact, most people at Moonstone Lake were convinced he was gay.

The officer emerged from the house and raised his hand. "Back," he said to the crowd. "This is a crime scene." He was joined by a new arrival who attached crime scene tape to trees and shrubs, encircling the yard and house.

Sighs arose from the onlookers, and they shuffled back a few feet. A dozen or so people filled the street, with only four of us in Marge's front yard.

"Dawson! Celia Dawson!" the first officer called out.

I stepped forward, and he motioned me to follow him toward his car. Being singled out in front of all my neighbors, I must have looked like a suspect.

His partner finished taping off the entire yard, and Tammy and Darlene had to join the neighbors in the street. Darlene rolled her eyes at her taller sister, as if Tammy could overrule the officer.

He addressed the gathering once more. "Has anyone else here been inside the house in the last twenty-four hours?"

Howard lifted his hand in a half-hearted way. "Me. I was in there."

"Anybody else?" When no one moved or answered, the cop continued. "Okay. You can return to your homes now." He motioned for Howard to join us.

The gathering stood rooted in place, not budging. "There's nothing else to see here," he called. "The Medical Examiner is on his way. We got things under control."

People began to murmur and whisper. They glanced sideways at each other and acted miffed, gathering across the street and lingering in smaller groups. How could they go home already? Nothing much ever happened around Moonstone Lake. Who wanted to be shut out now?

The approaching roar of a lawn mower sounded rude and invasive. The riding mower came into view with its familiar driver, Russ, who maintained our lawns. With a startled look, he pulled across the street into Tammy and Darlene's backyard and shut off the motor. His mouth hung open and his eyes grew wider, while a dark maroon Crown Vic with a flashing light on the dash pulled up next to the police car.

I stood with Howard beneath a towering oak tree, with the young blond officer standing near the front fender of the police car. He introduced himself as Sergeant Stan Sloan, but he paused as he saw the tall man climb from his car. The dark-haired man with serious brown eyes headed in our direction, drew near to Sergeant Sloan, and acknowledged him with a nod.

The officer turned back to Howard and me and gestured to the tall man. "This is Police Detective William Hendrix. Detective, these are residents, Celia Dawson and––" Sloan turned to Howard, extending his hand as if he could pull the name right out of him.

"Howard James. I live right over there." Howard pointed to the house across the street and to the right of Marge's front yard.

The detective shook our hands, then asked to speak with Sloan for a moment. They stepped a few feet away, and we waited. I wondered which one of them would be back to question us. Apparently, the detective needed to examine the crime scene and see the victim before the M.E. got there. He had no time to question us right then and had to leave that to Sloan. He strode away toward the house, his face solemn and his open sport coat flapping in the breeze.

Sloan joined us again and pulled a pen and pad from his shirt pocket.

"Ms. Dawson, I understand you called this in. Were you the first one to discover the body?"

"I think so. Her door was unlocked, so someone could have been there before me. But nobody else was there when I went in her house."

"You knocked and no one came to the door?"

"Right."

"And you felt free to walk in anyway? Were you close friends with Ms. Coleman?"

I stopped and considered my words. I needed to be precise with this guy. "No, I wouldn't consider myself close friends with her. She owns this park, and we're all acquainted with her. I had been to her office, which is always open by nine each morning. It was after ten, with no note on the locked door. So, I was concerned and thought maybe she was sick.

"I walked over here to her house and, when she didn't come to the door, I turned the knob, and it opened. I was going to call out to her, but there she was in the middle of her living room floor."

The officer's pen scratched on his notepad as fast as I talked. He raised his head and looked at my face. At that moment, a mockingbird started chattering in the branches above us. We must have been closer to her nest than she liked, and she made quite a fuss.

The officer took off his hat and waved it in the air, muttering, "Get outta here." Which resulted in the bird dive-bombing his head.

I rubbed my nose and stared at my shoes, trying not to giggle. The solemn, tense situation made it harder than ever not to laugh.

Sergeant Sloan suggested we move to the other side of his car, and the tall detective joined us. He introduced himself again and sent Sloan to help secure the building.

Hendrix asked us the same questions, making notes on his own pad. Then he asked me, "Did you touch the body?"

"Not at first. Then I thought about checking for a pulse. She looked dead, but if there was a pulse, I knew the ambulance people would need to know when I called it in."

"So, you touched her wrist?"

"Yes, and the side of her neck."

"And why'd you go to her office this morning?" He looked up from the pad directly at me.

My mouth fell open. I drew a blank and scratched my head, stalling. For the life of me, I couldn't think why I had gone to Marge's office. Too much had happened that morning, and I was lucky to even be coherent. I knew I looked guilty, like I was trying to make up a convincing lie. And I had absolutely nothing to hide.

My foggy brain cleared, and I slapped my forehead. "Oh, of course. It was about the microphone in the community building. It hasn't been working, and tonight's bingo night. I wanted to ask if she got it fixed." I studied his face, looking for a reaction. He was expressionless.

"After you discovered the body, did you see anyone else in the house?"

"Well, no. I only glanced around the room, but I listened and didn't hear anybody moving around. It was creepy, so I went outside to call nine-one-one."

Then I hesitated. I didn't want to say I went back in the house, but I *was* back inside--in the kitchen when Howard came in. I had talked myself into a corner, and now I had to admit it. Howard would mention it if I didn't.

"I shouldn't have gone back in the house," I told the officer. "But I wanted to see if she'd had dinner before she died. Or, if she got interrupted in the middle of dinner . . . I was still in the kitchen when Howard walked in through the open front door."

"That was a risky thing to do. Had you been cautioned to leave the house when you called nine-one-one?"

"Yes."

"Did you touch anything in the kitchen?"

"No, nothing."

Hendrix turned to Howard and asked, "You're Howard James?"

Howard nodded. "That's me."

"Mr. James. What were you doing at Ms. Coleman's house this morning?"

"Yesterday, the last time I saw her, she seemed upset. She wouldn't say what was wrong. I called her this morning, and she didn't answer her cell phone or her office phone. I even left a voice message, and she didn't call back."

His voice had become shaky, so he paused for a second and ran a hand through his silver hair. "I couldn't get her on the phone, so I went to the office. Like Celia, I found the office closed and walked over to her house, thinking she might be having a bad day." His eyes brimmed with tears again. He cleared his throat and rubbed at his eyes. "I was never so shocked. Never in my life."

The next question was quick and direct. "What is your relationship to the deceased?"

"My relationship?" Howard stared back, open-mouthed. "Marge is my sister."

Tears filled his eyes again, and I tried not to fall over from the news. *His sister?*

The detective paused, as if he was studying Howard's facial expression. "Can you think of anyone who had reason to kill Ms. Coleman?"

Howard looked past the tall man and stared at the lake. His eyes narrowed and his lips thinned. "No. I cannot. But I'll think on it. You can be sure I'll think on it."

"And you, Ms. Dawson. Can you think of anyone who might want to kill Ms. Coleman? Was anyone angry with her?"

I pondered the detective's question and didn't answer him right away. The only one I could think of who was often angry with Marge stood there next to me. But I couldn't imagine Howard wanting to kill her.

"No," I told Will Hendrix. And I said no more.

But I, too, would keep his question on my mind. Marge's killer was still free, possibly walking among us in our retirement village. Could any of us feel safe until this person was found and arrested? I vowed in my heart that I would not rest. Not until I discovered who killed "Marge in Charge."

Chapter 2

Detective Hendrix took our phone numbers and addresses, in case he needed to question either of us further, then gave us both a business card with his cell number and his phone number at the police station. The medical examiner had arrived, and a team of investigators were going over the crime scene.

People drifted away as the day wore on, and growling stomachs called them to lunch. Russ and his lawn mower disappeared; I heard the droning motor somewhere nearby in the neighborhood. Life moved on.

Howard and I walked back to the street, nodded awkwardly to one another, and headed in different directions.

"One more thing," I heard from behind me. Howard and I both turned to see Will Hendrix following with his pad and pen. "Other than yourself, Mr. James, can you tell me her next-of-kin?"

"She's been divorced a number of years," Howard said. "Her ex-husband is Daniel Coleman. She has two grown children, Jason Coleman and Jennifer Coleman Hughes, both in the Tampa area."

Hendrix nodded and put the pad back in his shirt pocket. "Thank you. You've been very helpful." Howard lumbered away.

Hendrix rubbed his chin, causing the scent of his shaving lotion to drift in the air, and spoke to me. "You do know what this caution tape means, don't you?"

"Of course."

"Well, just be sure you stay out of that house--and yard. We'll handle the investigation from here. Okay?"

"Of course." I hoped my cheeks weren't red.

As he turned away, Tammy and Darlene attached themselves to me and peppered me with questions. Their last name was Jessup, but I'd long ago dubbed them the Gossip Sisters. Darlene was the chatterbox, while Tammy only added a wry comment now and then with lots of eye rolling.

"Could it have been an accident?" Tammy asked.

"I doubt it. She wouldn't have hit herself in the head with a lamp."

Almost breathless, Darlene fixed me with her wide blue eyes and asked, "Since you found the body, are you and Howard murder suspects now?"

"I don't think so. But, yeah, maybe."

"Leave her alone, Darlene. She needs time to herself after all this hullabaloo."

I smiled my gratitude at Tammy. "Actually, I need to get home and call Rosanna. If she's still shopping, she won't even know about all this."

Rosanna worked part time in the office, helping Marge with phone calls and paperwork. As far as she knew, Marge was working in the office right now, not on her way to the morgue.

"My heavens! That's right, we don't have a manager anymore. Will we all have to find another place to live?" Once again, Darlene was all aflutter, her white wavy hair blowing in the breeze.

Tammy's hand closed around her sister's shoulder. "Let it be. Don't go borrowing trouble. Rosanna will know what to do."

She got Darlene headed back to their place across the street from Howard. The homes were in sight of Marge's Spanish-style bungalow, which sat on the shore of Moonstone Lake. Both Howard and those sisters could have witnessed who came and went from Marge's home last night, if they'd been peeking out a window at the right time or sitting on either of their screened porches.

Howard had already been questioned. I planned to ask the Gossip Sisters about it later. But a part of me knew, if Darlene had any information, she would have already prattled to the police or the detective, enjoying her time in the limelight.

I longed for the cool comfort and quiet of my home.

Lake Drive loops around the retirement village, from the entrance straight down to the tennis court and shuffleboard on the lakeside. Then it curves left by Marge's house, the clubhouse and office, and beyond that, the pool and picnic area which overlooks our small marina and dock. Then it curves left again and heads back toward the entrance.

I live near the entrance. Milo Delaney lives on one side of me, closest to the lake, and my best friend, Rosanna Russo, lives on the other side.

The street to the left was a few steps closer to walk back home, but I wouldn't be bombarded with as many questions if I took the quieter street to my right. I would arrive at my back deck and quietly slip inside.

The stroll eased my tension, even with the noonday sun bearing down and heating the air. I walked as if in a dream; nothing seemed real. Death was always shocking and upsetting, but this was a murder, close to me. A woman I saw almost daily. Others could be in danger.

As I drew closer, I saw Milo in his usual folding chair, relaxing under a palm tree with a Miller Lite in his hand. He wore denim shorts, a sleeveless T-shirt, and rubber flip-flops. And that day, he needed a shave.

"Looks like you're right in the thick of things," he said to me.

I could never see his eyes. He wore tinted glasses most days, might even wear them inside. I'd never been inside his home, so I wasn't sure about that.

"I didn't see *you* in the crowd."

"Nope. But news travels fast. So, is Marge really dead? I hear you found her."

"I'm afraid so." The finality of what I said suddenly hit me, and I trembled. Milo, for all his gruffness, jumped up and offered me his chair. I didn't especially like being that close to him, but I sank into the woven chair, considering it offensively warm.

"Sorry," I said. "I need to sit for a moment."

"Take your time." He sipped his beer. "Want one of these?"

"No thanks. I'll get some cold water when I get home." I nodded at my neat little home, only steps away.

Milo opened the cooler next to his chair and handed me a bottle of water. I reached for it and chugged half of it down, closed my eyes, and relaxed.

As I rose to my feet, he gave me a hand up. He usually looked like a beach bum, but he wasn't so bad. I had a feeling I could count on him in a pinch.

I told him I felt steady again and could make it home on my own, but he walked beside me to my door.

Inside, I hurried to the front of my house and peeked out the window at my short driveway right next to Rosanna's. I could see she still wasn't home. I put my phone on its charger, and I punched in her number.

She'd left for town earlier that morning, had a hair appointment to touch up her roots, then planned to stop by the pharmacy, then the supermarket. I couldn't wait another second to talk to my buddy.

She answered her phone with, "What's up, Celia?"

"A whole helluva lot. Are you driving?"

"I'm pulling into the park now. You sound strange."

"You're almost here. We'll talk in person."

Weak all over again, I knew I needed to sit. I moved to the front porch and settled into one of my wicker chairs, thankful for the soft cushions. Rosanna's little red Kia headed my way.

As soon as she swung into her drive and shut off the engine, she jumped from the car, her face all frowns. Despite the gravity of the moment, I couldn't help noticing how great her hair looked.

We're basically the same age. However, I make do with naturally gray hair, while Rosanna keeps hers dyed dark brown and looks ten years younger. Her Italian heritage sparkles.

She burst onto my front porch, threw herself into the chair beside me, and demanded, "Let's hear it."

I was suddenly tongue-tied. Marge was Rosanna's other "best friend." Rosanna had worked with her for three years or more and was close to Marge, though many residents didn't like her.

"What?" she asked.

"It's Marge. I found her in her living room this morning on the floor. She's dead, Rosanna. I can't believe it. Somebody killed her."

Rosanna's face went pale, and her mouth hung open. She was silent. Then she sputtered. "I'm gone for two hours, and everything around here falls apart."

I was so nervous and jittery, I almost laughed. She misread my face, because she grinned and said, "You're kidding, right?"

"No."

She stood suddenly and stared out through the screen toward Marge's house and the lake, her eyes welling up with tears. "When did it happen?"

I told her how I'd found Marge, the bloody lamp, everything I'd told the cops. She listened without a word, then turned back to me. "I'm too stunned to think straight. This can't be real." She paced back and forth across the small, enclosed porch, wiping at her eyes. "I know it's early, but I think I need some wine to calm my nerves."

Rosanna grew up in Brooklyn, New York. Her Italian accent was different from my southern drawl, and when she talked, her hands moved constantly. That day, her voice trembled with emotion. I thought wine sounded like a good idea, and I led her inside to the cool kitchen.

I poured two glasses of chardonnay and handed one to my friend. She stifled a sob and took a big sip.

Rosanna and I had met in college, where we took mostly the same classes, studying to become schoolteachers. She was witty, outspoken, and always positive about life. I was naïve and serious-minded, full of self-doubt. She helped keep me grounded when I thought everything was too much trouble to stick with. And we found in each other someone to spark laughter in every situation, someone to confide in, someone to trust. Our lives took different paths, but there we were, next-door neighbors in our retirement years.

I intended to be strong for Rosanna. Losing Marge hit her even harder than it hit me.

She swallowed the last of her wine and looked me in the eye. "We have to find out who did this to poor Marge." Her voice was soft, but with steel underneath. "Maybe we can't kill them back, but we can kick their butt!"

"That's what I'm thinking. When the shock wears off, we need to get on this."

A sigh escaped her. "I need to rest first."

Someone pounded on my door, and we both jumped like startled puppies.

Foremost in my mind was the knowledge that, a few hours earlier, some person had swung a brass lamp and bashed in the head of our neighbor; I hesitated to open the door.

A voice thundered from outside. "It's me--Howard. Open up."

I pulled the door open and came nose to nose with the man.

He glared at me. The old Howard was back. I knew how to deal with this Howard.

"I lost that business card already," he said. "The one the detective gave us. Henley or something like that."

"It's Will Hendrix," I said. "I'll give you his number, but you're not getting my card. You'll lose that too."

"This is the saddest day of my life, Celia. Why do you have to be so bitchy?"

I raised my hands in a calming gesture. "Come in and have a seat. We're all a little edgy." He shuffled in and remained standing.

"Why is this the saddest day of your life?" Rosanna asked.

Howard's face hardened, and he turned away from us, glaring out the window. He was fit and trim and looked a little like Sean Connery, except Howard had a full head of hair, thick and white. He didn't seem inclined to answer her question.

"Ask Celia. I'm sure she'll enjoy something to chatter about," he muttered.

I was sad for Howard, but I wouldn't let him get to me. "Rosanna, were you aware that Howard was Marge's brother?"

She raised her eyebrows and studied Howard for a moment. "She never mentioned it. Is that a big deal?"

Howard stared at the floor. "We both agreed not to mention it. People don't have to know all your business. And Marge didn't want folks to think they could come to me with problems about the park."

"Well, when people don't know all your business, sometimes they get the wrong idea. We all assumed she was your girlfriend." Rosanna's voice was gentle.

"It was Marge's idea to keep it secret. Do we have to talk about this now?"

"Howard, you brought it up," I told him. "You said this is the saddest day--"

"Yes, I know what I said; I apologize. I'm out of sorts and I don't feel like baring my soul. It's already raw."

I dared to speak again. "It always seemed to me you didn't like each other."

"There's a thin line between love and hate," he said. Without another word, he turned and stalked back out the door.

Rosanna shook her head. "He didn't get that phone number."

"I guess he'll have to come back and ask me nicely," I muttered. Or he could simply call the police department and ask for Detective Hendrix.

With her head hanging, Rosanna turned to leave as well. "I need to go check on my cat," she said. "Call me later."

She usually came back from the hair salon in a jolly mood. But the murder of our friend was a sad and sobering reality. We both walked under a cloud of gray.

Howard had come for the detective's phone number, and he'd left without it. I had Howard's number (we'd recently served on a committee concerning the clubhouse) but I didn't want to talk to him again. On this day, he had seen the murdered body of his sister in a pool of blood. I would be kind and text the name and number of the detective to him.

Now, what could be his reason for calling Detective Hendrix?

Chapter 3

I awoke from my nap with a start, like waking from a bad dream. Though safe and sound in my home, something felt off. Then it hit me: We'd had a murder at Moonstone Lake! And I had so many troubling questions.

When I was five years old, my mother began reading Nancy Drew mysteries to me. She bought me the entire series of books. I almost knew them by heart by the time I started reading them myself. Nancy Drew was my hero, pure and simple. I had wished daily for a mystery to solve.

One evening my parents had a fuss about something--who forgot to pay the light bill, maybe. In the end, Mama got so mad she threw a glass against the wall. Their argument didn't bother me too much. I slipped into the kitchen later when everything had settled down. A chunk of glass under the edge of the cupboard caught my eye, a piece the broom had missed. I picked it up and said aloud, "Evidence!" A smile spread across my face as I tucked it into my pocket.

Now I had that feeling all over again, but I wasn't smiling. The sunlight grew weaker outside as my urge to find clues and evidence grew stronger.

Marge's house was taped off. I wondered if the big, important detective had checked to see if her bed had been slept in. I itched to get inside––but I knew better. If I befriended him, rather than ignoring his orders, I'd end up with more information.

There was nothing wrong, however, with an evening stroll that ended up near her backyard.

I tucked my phone into a front pocket and waited for darkness. I folded a zip-up plastic bag and slid it into another pocket. A light jacket would shield me from mosquitoes, and it provided more pockets for a pair of rubber gloves.

Heading out the back door and across my deck, I realized I might run into Milo again. No time to stop and chat, and I didn't want to be noticed. So, I trekked back through my house and out the front, checking to see if Rosanna was anywhere around. She wasn't outdoors, but she might be watching me through her window. So could everyone else on my street, but I took walks all the time. I strolled down the street toward the lake, knowing I'd have to pass Howard's house and the Gossip Sisters.

Lucky for me, everyone seemed to be watching TV. A colorful glow flickered from windows and glass doors.

Marge's dark, lonely house was surrounded by yellow tape. I paused in front and shuddered. Suppose a serial killer were hanging around who got off on killing senior citizens. I was out in the darkness, alone and vulnerable. I shook off the uneasiness. Maybe I was being paranoid. Whoever killed Marge would take pains to stay away and avoid being noticed.

Streetlights glowed at regular intervals, but the shadowed areas could give me cover if needed. Not that I was doing anything wrong. But I didn't like nosy neighbors watching me and starting gossip about me poking my nose into the investigation.

I followed my usual walking path, then veered off to the marina and ventured onto the dock, only steps from Marge's backyard.

Standing in the evening breeze, I stared across the lake and imagined a boat motoring in my direction. That could have happened last night, I thought. The killer might have come by boat, tied up at the visitor space at the marina, and entered through Marge's back door where no one would notice.

A concrete seawall separated Marge's backyard from the marshy lakeside. The wall was meant to keep alligators from crawling up the bank into residential areas, and it kept the backyard drier. In the middle of her seawall, a walkway led to her small, private dock. A boat could have tied up there, but it would be obvious someone was visiting this house.

No, I was sure they would have docked at the marina, close to where I now stood. That is, if they were planning more than a visit. If they had murder in mind.

My skin prickled, like I was a real detective. I didn't need a badge, merely needed to think straight and pay attention. Retracing my steps across the marina's dock, I strolled toward the silent house. The clubhouse next door was empty. Bingo had been canceled, and someone had lowered the flag in front to half-staff.

I edged closer to Marge's backyard, as the killer might have done, and halted at the crime scene tape. My senses were so alive, I almost saw waves of evil shimmering in the darkness. *I must not cross this barrier.*

The shrubs that encircled her backyard stopped at the seawall. I stood outside the bushes with my back to the clubhouse, in the parking spaces for golf carts, but away from the glow of the streetlights. Something caught my eye, something out-of-place in the greenery of one bush. I edged closer.

It looked like a pair of glasses dangling among the leaves. I used the light on my cell phone to get a better look: glasses with heavy black frames. My breath caught, and I reached for my rubber gloves. Glancing around to see if anyone was in sight, I turned my back to the street and houses and pulled on the gloves. I unzipped the plastic bag, pulled the glasses from the bush, and dropped them in.

Before I called the police, I intended to have a close look at those glasses. It was a bit sneaky, but I was pleased with myself. Grinning, I slid them into my roomy jacket pocket and scuttled back home. *Evidence!*

The shortest route back was right by Milo's back door. Maybe he'd be inside watching TV and wouldn't notice me. No such luck. I tried to slip past his patio, but I heard his teasing voice.

"Out for your evening constitutional?"

"Had to make it a short one. Mosquitoes are after me," I said.

"Wanna stop and have a brewski?"

I paused long enough to look his way. I was curious to see if he still wore those dark glasses. Nope. But he wore a ball cap and sat in a patch of shadow, where a palm tree blocked the streetlight. I still couldn't see his eyes.

"No thanks, Milo. I need to get in and make some calls."

"Okay, okay. Enjoy your solitary evening."

"You, too." Why did everyone have to rub it in when a woman was single? I could enjoy peace and quiet, just like Milo, a single guy.

I crossed the deck and unlocked my back door. *Home free!* I closed all the blinds, flipped on the light, and took my discovery to the kitchen table.

Technically, I might have been tampering with evidence. But I would take every precaution not to *destroy* evidence or alter it in any way. Plus, these glasses might not have a single thing to do with Marge's murder. I pulled the rubber gloves back on my hands, opened the bag, and removed the glasses. I held them under the light fixture above the table, looking for details. They were like new.

Carefully, I turned them to see inside the arms. One side displayed a tiny label from a discount store. The other side showed "1.0," a weak strength for reading glasses. I wore 2.75 myself when I read novels.

Someone had recently bought these glasses. They must have dropped them by mistake. If the intent was to discard them, they could have tossed them into the lake. I decided I'd call Detective Hendrix in the morning.

Rosanna had been tearful and pleading when she said we needed to find Marge's killer. *Well, I'm on it, Rosanna.* I returned the glasses to the plastic bag and slipped across the driveway to her door.

She might be in her nightclothes already. And she might be trying to relax, read a book, cuddle with her cat. But I knew her well, and I figured she was still in turmoil over Marge's death. Rosanna probably needed someone to talk to as much as I did.

We'd been best friends for many years. Soon after graduating from college, Rosanna married Antonio Russo. Her parents were thrilled she married a fellow Italian. Rosanna and Tony had a happy, stable marriage for thirty-eight years. They raised a beautiful daughter and built a spectacular home in Atlanta. Her husband died in a car crash soon after he turned sixty-two. When she retired from teaching two years later, Rosanna moved here to Conroy at Moonstone Lake. Her daughter, Bella, lives in St. Petersburg, which is what brought Rosanna to this area.

I met my husband in the late sixties at the college we both attended. He also became a teacher––Drew Wyndham. I think I loved him almost instantly.

We both loved books, we both played guitar, and we laughed at the same movies. He was like my twin, but we looked nothing alike. My hair was light brown then, and his was blond. My eyes are blue, his are green.

We both took teaching jobs in my hometown, Savannah, Georgia, where we were married. And we lived happily-ever-after for two whole years. I was so crushed when he divorced me, I have never let myself grow close to another man.

I reverted to my maiden name, Dawson. And I clung to my best friend, Rosanna. When, as a widow, she retired to Florida, she let me know a home was available right next to hers.

Now here we are, both of us sixty-three, older and wiser, and still as happy as Lucy Ricardo and Ethel Mertz.

As we sat at her dining table, she agreed with me that the glasses were new. "Now all we have to do is think about possible suspects who wear reading glasses. Easy-peasy," she joked.

"A lot of people around here wear glasses. But I can't see a reason to wear reading glasses down at the dock."

"Maybe they weren't wearing them," Rosanna said. "Maybe they fell out of a shirt pocket."

"That makes me picture a man. Women don't usually have shirt pockets. A woman would either wear them or carry them in her purse . . . or perch them on her head."

"Not if she was driving a boat, y'know? They could blow off into the water."

Rosanna was right. Sometimes it takes two heads to think a thing through.

"By the way," she said to me. "Why'd you go for a walk, snooping around all over the place without taking me?" Her elbows were on the table, but she waved both hands in the air.

"I was antsy to go as soon as it got dark when I wouldn't be noticed. Plus, I thought you might still be upset or resting."

Rosanna heaved a sigh. "Yeah, I get that. But I want to help all I can . . . I have an idea. You should come with me when I open the office in the morning. Y'know, it might be our last chance to search Marge's office for clues before the detectives show up again."

She rose and strolled to her kitchen sink. I'm only five-four and she's even shorter. I wondered how she could reach all her upper cabinets.

"I can cover the front desk while you search Marge's office," I said. "With her gone, you'll be needing help, anyway."

"We could go now, but it would attract attention." She filled her coffeemaker with water and spooned in some ground decaf. "We better wait till morning. Let's make a plan, though, or I'll never sleep tonight."

The smell of hot coffee began filling the room, and I pulled up a chair at her kitchen table.

Bitsy appeared and rubbed against my leg. Her purring enticed me to reach down and rub her calico fur. I missed having a cat but contented myself with sharing my best friend's feline. The responsibility of caring for a pet and dealing with a litter box did not appeal to me.

Rosanna set a cup of steaming coffee before me, and I was grateful for air conditioning. Since the day I turned forty-five, any kind of heat sets off a hot flash in me. I stirred in creamer and took a sip.

"We need to get there early and look through everything. We'll leave it all like we find it, because I know the police will search it too."

Rosanna sipped her coffee. "If someone comes in, we'll hear the door jingle. You can buzz me if you need me at the front desk." She set her cup aside and drummed her fingers. "Did the police ask you about Marge's attorney or next of kin?"

"Why would they ask about her attorney? Detective Hendrix asked about her relatives and Howard told him about her two children and ex-husband. Ever since the cops left, I've been wondering who'll inherit this place, and who'll run things until the estate is settled. Someone has to keep the business going, write checks, and so forth. Right?"

Rosanna nodded. "You're so right. Holy cannoli, I can't appoint myself the new manager. Maybe the cops have called her attorney already."

"How would they know which lawyer to call?"

Her eyes brightened. "They'll check with City Hall, or property records. When Marge bought this place, there would be legal documents with the attorney's name."

"Of course! That makes sense." I smiled. "You're a good sleuthing partner."

"I give you stability," Rosanna said, trying to sound pompous.

"Oh yeah?"

Rosanna chuckled and Bitsy flicked her ears. The cat tiptoed over to lap from her water dish. No one had offered her any coffee, but I think she would have liked some cream.

Long-time friends, both of us still grieving the loss of a third friend, relief and peace settled over us. Because we had a viable plan to search for Marge's killer. And who knew what tomorrow might bring?

Chapter 4

Wednesday morning dawned fresh and hopeful. I met Rosanna in my driveway, and we walked together to the office. She carried a box of brownies.

"When did you find time to bake brownies?" I asked.

"I got these at the bakery yesterday."

"You didn't offer me any last night."

"The caffeine in the chocolate would have kept us awake."

"I still would have eaten a brownie, if you'd offered one."

"Yeah, I know. And I would've hated watching you eat it," she said, giggling.

The Conroy police detective was back at Marge's house. His car sat in her driveway, but no one was in sight. No doubt he'd be at the office later.

We hurried past and unlocked the office door. Rosanna tucked the box of brownies in her desk drawer, and I made a pot of coffee. When the detective came poking around, he could have coffee, and we might even share the brownies.

"I never thought they'd be back this early," I told Rosanna. "You better get in Marge's office and find out what you can, *while* you can."

Rosanna darted down the short hallway and called back over her shoulder, "Could you bring me a cup when it's ready? I like it black."

Like I didn't know that already.

I returned with both our coffees and watched Rosanna rifle through stacks of paper, search desk drawers, and scan through the old-fashioned Rolodex full of names and phone numbers. She was more familiar with where records were kept, so I took notes, jotting down information about Marge's children, her ex-husband, and her attorney.

Rosanna understood the financial information and was used to the office. I left her with it, took my coffee back up front and flipped through some folders. Most things were kept in computer files and on thumb drives, but Marge never got rid of the file cabinets. They were mostly files on residents, vendors, plumbers, and repairmen.

I found a file on the marina, showing which residents kept boats there. All the slips were occupied except three spaces for visitors. Short canals connected us to two other lakes, so we often had visitors by boat. Didn't sound like tight security, but no big surprise. There was no security at the front gate, either.

Movement outside the windows caught my eye. A tall skinny boy, walking stiff and uneasy, headed our way from the direction of the marina. He looked like a fourteen-year-old who'd had a growth spurt and needed bigger clothes. The door chimed when he walked inside.

"Is Ms. Coleman here?" he asked.

"No. I'm sorry," I said, not sure how much I should tell the boy. "Can I help you?"

"She said I had to, like, come to the office to get my check."

Rosanna had heard the door and strolled to the front desk. "And what's your name?" she asked him.

"Riley Atkins."

She consulted a folder behind the counter for items to be mailed or picked up and shook her head. "Sorry. I don't have anything for that name."

He hung his head. "She told me Monday night she'd, like, have it ready for me today." He heard our gasps and jerked his head up. I was about to offer him a brownie to soften the bad news I would have to give him but, at that precise moment, the detective walked in. The boy turned, ready to slink out the door.

"Wait," Rosanna said. "If she promised to pay you, tell me how much. We might have enough cash on hand."

He turned back to Rosanna but sidled away from the tall man who eyed him so closely.

The detective turned to me and nodded. I blurted out, "We just made coffee." His eyes twinkled, but he didn't respond. I liked his warm brown eyes.

Noticing Riley's unease, he asked, "Son, do you know Ms. Coleman?"

"I trimmed some bushes for her last week and I, like, bagged up some trash from her garage. I know Milo Delaney, and he told me she was, like, looking for help."

"When did you last see her?"

Riley's eyes darted back and forth from Rosanna to the detective. His voice was hesitant. "It was Monday night. She told me she didn't, like, pay in cash, but she'd have a check ready for me this morning."

"Well, Monday night someone, like, killed her," said Hendrix.

Color drained from Riley's face, and his freckles stood out like ink spots. "You don't think it was *me* who killed her?" he stammered. "She was acting mean, after all that stuff I helped her with. And it made me, like, mad and all, but I didn't kill nobody. I wouldn't even know how!"

"Simmer down," Hendrix told him. "I only need to ask you some questions. We can step outside."

"I'm not gonna get paid? I need my thirty-five dollars. It's, like, owed to me."

Rosanna spoke up. "I remember Marge having some yard work done last week. We have money in petty cash."

She counted out the money while the boy scribbled his name on the receipt, and the detective nudged the boy outside. After a brief conversation, Riley left, and Detective Hendrix came back inside.

The detective wore a sport coat and open-neck shirt. He introduced himself to Rosanna. "My name is Will Hendrix, detective with the Conroy Police. I need to speak with you about Marjorie Coleman."

"I'm Rosanna Russo; I was Ms. Coleman's assistant. I'll help you all I can."

He smiled, then turned to me. "Do you also work here, Ms. Dawson?"

"No, I'm volunteering today, answering the phone, giving Rosanna a hand."

Hendrix nodded. "We've contacted Ms. Coleman's attorney, Grant Phillips. He'll be in touch with you today, Ms. Russo, with instructions for keeping the office open."

He turned his attention back to me. "I'm glad you're both here. I have a search warrant to look through Ms. Coleman's office, but I won't ransack the place. Just looking for possible information about any problems she might've had with any business or individual."

"Has her death been officially ruled a homicide?" I asked.

"It has." He watched me closely, like he questioned my interest.

"Was it the lamp, and do they know the time of death?" He was silent, perhaps considering my questions, so I continued. "I can't help being concerned. I don't like thinking the rest of us could be in danger."

"The greatest danger would be getting too involved, possibly becoming a threat to a person with something to hide. I mean no disrespect, Ms. Dawson, but you should take care. And leave the investigation to us."

"I beg your pardon. I was only curious." I wanted to stalk away from him, but I tried to seem indifferent. I'm pretty sure I sounded like my usual snarky self.

He turned to Rosanna, who showed him to Marge's office. I went back to searching through papers and files at the reception counter.

I had never worked in that office. When teaching, I'd done enough paperwork, stuck inside a building, to last me forever. I retired to do things I enjoy, not more work. But crime solving was something I always wanted to do. This was my chance, and nothing was going to stop me from trying. Nothing except a quiet, authoritative detective like Will Hendrix. I'd have to stay below his radar.

I had mentioned coffee when he first walked in, so I moseyed a few steps down the hall and stuck my head into Marge's office. "Are you ready for that coffee yet?" I asked the detective.

He gave me a pleased grin, as if he thought I couldn't stay away from him. "Not quite. If it's okay, I'll have a cup before I leave."

"There's one other thing I need to mention," I said. "I'd already planned to call you about it this morning, and now here you are."

Hendrix raised his eyebrows and waited, like he was trying to be patient. Which I found irritating, and I changed my mind.

"Don't let me interrupt you. We'll get to it before you leave."

I was relieved to get out of that office. One minute he acted stern and formal with me, the next minute he sent little signals with hearts and arrows attached. Maybe he enjoyed thinking he was a chick magnet. Well, my chickie days were far behind. I was more like a wet hen.

It would take more than a detective's badge to impress me. Let Rosanna deal with him.

Back at the reception counter, I put away the file on the marina. I didn't know how many people the cops might have questioned so far. But had anyone been questioned about boats arriving at the marina?

I thought of "Miss Glory Bea," as she was called, who lived around the corner from Marge. Her house was closer to the marina than most. She and her husband were elderly and always enjoyed company. I'd have to stop by and see her, maybe later that day.

The drone of the riding mower interrupted my thoughts, and the lawn man roared up and parked beside the office. Rosanna was occupied, so I would have to deal with him, whatever it was. He trudged around the corner, wiped his feet on the doormat, and pulled open the swinging door. He wore long pants, a long-sleeved tan shirt, and a safari hat with khaki material sewn on the back, providing a cover for the back of his neck. Russ Evers was a freckled, fair-skinned man, so I knew he had to protect his skin, working in the broiling sun at least five days a week.

"I guess Rosanna's here today?" he asked.

"Sure, but she's with Detective Hendrix right now. Anything I can do for you?"

"I'm checking to see if paychecks will go out on Friday as usual." He often clowned around when he saw me. Today he had more important things on his mind.

"She's probably deciding things like that right now. After tomorrow she'll know how much authority she'll be given, with Marge's sudden death."

Russ went pale for a moment, then scratched his chin. "I hope somebody has enough authority to sign my check."

"I'll ask her to call you when she's free. How about that?"

He nodded and gave me his number, watching as I wrote it on a notepad. With a small salute, he started to leave but paused and turned back to me. "You work in the office here regular-like?"

"Oh, no. I'm only helping today until other arrangements can be made."

"Good," he said, giving me a wink. "I like watching you prance around the neighborhood." He pushed the door open and disappeared around the corner. The noisy mower chugged away leaving welcome silence in its wake. I was glad to see him leave. I knew he was a married man, and his remarks didn't sit well with me.

An occasional low chuckle followed by Rosanna's trill of laughter drifted down the hallway. Rosanna had little interest in men, but most of them were interested in her. I had little interest in Will Hendrix, but jealousy still popped its head up.

With her full, voluptuous figure, Rosanna's face was plump enough to smooth out any wrinkles. I thought of her dark curly hair and warm olive skin, then stared at my arm resting on the counter. It was pale with a stray freckle here and there.

Later in the day, I might change into my swimsuit and visit the neighborhood pool. Catch some rays! A little tan might look good with my silvery hair.

Hendrix and Rosanna came strolling back into the front office. "I need to have a look at her computer," he said. "But I need to get the passwords from her daughter. I can come back tomorrow and check things out."

Rosanna was now standing next to me, and Hendrix continued. "I think Ms. Coleman's daughter, Jennifer, will be calling you today. She'll have power of attorney, and she can arrange with you ladies to keep the business running."

I'd already told him I didn't work there, but I kept my mouth shut.

"Well, I hope you have a smooth transition, working with the daughter. We may be pestering you for a few days, too. Can't let this case go cold." Hendrix nodded at me. "I'd enjoy a cup of that coffee now, if you don't mind."

I poured the coffee into a Styrofoam cup and reached for a lid, then paused at the cream and sugar. "Black," he assured me. He could almost read my mind. Yikes!

Coffee in hand, he trooped outside to his car. As he pulled away, my brain woke up and I realized I still hadn't mentioned those eyeglasses I'd found the night before.

Oh well, I still had his phone number.

The office was quiet once again. Rosanna informed me Will Hendrix had a cute sense of humor. "I like that dark, slicked-back hair and his intense brown eyes. He must be old enough to retire, but I see very little gray," she said. "But I have no time for men. I'm too busy already."

She showed me her notebook, where she had jotted down some numbers Hendrix had found under Marge's desk calendar. They looked like odds for a horse race. Under the numbers, Marge had printed *J. Yancey*.

"Was Marge into gambling?" I asked her.

"Maybe. She mentioned several times going to Tampa Bay Downs to see the races. As far as I know, she went by herself. Her daughter lives in Tampa."

I drummed my fingers on the countertop, letting my imagination run wild. Did people still have bookies? We'd need to check her contacts and Rolodex again for someone named Yancey.

The front door chimed again, and Whitney, another resident, burst into the office. Her trim, muscular husband was right behind her.

"I think Devon can fix that buzzing microphone down at the bingo table," she announced. "Life must go on, and we got things to do. Don't y'all think we need to have a memorial service for Marge? We can't do that without a good mic. And, on top of that, I don't want to cancel bingo again next week. Lots of people here really look forward to that."

She was a beautiful woman in her fifties, African American with glowing skin and long hair arranged in intricately designed corn rows. Devon hung his arm around her shoulders and grinned, flashing perfect teeth. He had been a fullback with the Miami Dolphins before retiring.

"I studied electronics before I went with the Dolphins," he told us. "It's no problem for me to service that sound system."

"I don't have any authority," Rosanna said. "I'm keeping the office open till Marge's daughter shows up and takes over."

"You care if I go down and take a look? I'll tell you what I think needs doing. I won't work on anything without a go-ahead."

Rosanna shrugged her shoulders. "If I knew how to fix it, I'd do it myself. Go ahead, then, and see what the problem is. I'll clear it with the daughter."

They smiled, waggled fingers at us in a goodbye-kind-of wave, and they were gone.

I turned to find Rosanna writing on a sheet of paper with a thick black marker. *Temporary Office Hours: Monday thru Friday, 9 am to 12 noon. Until further notice.*

I slipped four brownies into a small plastic bag. It was almost noon, and I planned to see Miss Glory Bea on my way home.

"What about the call we're waiting on from the attorney? And what if Jennifer calls you?" I couldn't help fretting over details. (After all, Marge was no longer in charge.)

"I'll forward the office calls to my cell phone. I'm tired of hanging around this place. The phone will ring all day, and it's depressing answering the same questions over and over about Marge. Everybody wants details, y'know?"

"I almost forgot." I handed her a slip of paper with Russ Evers' name and phone number. "The lawn man stopped by, worried about his paycheck. You were busy, but I told him you'd call him back."

Rosanna sighed and tucked the paper into her front pocket. "I'll call him from home. Right now, I need to get out of here. Marge's spirit is still strong in this office."

"Want to go with me to deliver these brownies to Miss Glory Bea?" I asked her.

She considered my offer while her forehead wrinkled into a tiny frown. "I don't think I can. Glory will have questions about the murder, and I'll end up crying. I loved Marge like an older sister. Half the time, she got on my nerves. But I think I understood her and her quirky personality. Most people never saw her good qualities."

Her eyes were bright and wet, and she reached for a tissue.

We both liked Marge, despite her ill-tempered moods. She was coarse and brash, and either laughing or ticked off with somebody. We would miss her, and we were incensed that someone had taken her life.

Whether they planned it with a cool head, or killed her in a sudden flash of anger, they had no right to take her life.

The Conroy Police might, or might not, find her murderer. But I would never give up until the killer was revealed and brought to justice.

Chapter 5

As I left the office, the first house on my route belonged to Miss Glory Bea and her hubby, both in their eighties. I fell into the local habit of addressing an older lady as "Miss," along with her first name. It's a sign of respect, and not as formal as calling her "Mrs. Golding."

She says her mother named her Gloriana Beatrice, thinking the names were so beautiful she wanted to use them both. But it was a mouthful. So, she called her daughter "Glory Bea" instead.

Today, I had a few questions for her, and I hoped she would talk freely. She had several windows on the street side of her house with a partial view of Moonstone Lake––and Marge's bungalow. Glory and Harvey were both pretty much house-bound, close to being invalids. They would surely have been at home on the night of the murder. Maybe she had noticed activity at Marge's house or at the marina.

I knocked at the door and waited. Neither of them could move quickly. A voice called out, "Come on in. It's open."

I peeked around the door and spied Harvey in his easy chair, TV remote in hand. He had a scrap of white hair brushed across the top of his balding head, and his watery blue eyes stared at me through smudged wire-rimmed glasses.

"It's me––Celia. Did you say to come in?"

"I sure did. Good morning." He gave me a distant look, obviously having a problem remembering who I was.

I heard the scrape and clump of Glory's walker as she made her way down the hallway. Her face lit up when she saw me.

"Celia, it's good to see your smiling face! I mostly look at Harvey, day after day." Her face was full and cheerful, with a wide grin and plump cheeks. "Have a seat here at the table and I'll get you a cup of tea."

Their living room and dining area were all one open space, with a work island separating it from the kitchen. I pulled out a dining chair and took a seat. "Please, no tea for me. But I brought you some brownies."

Glory laid her fingertips against one cheek and her mouth formed an "O." I handed her the plastic bag, which she immediately set on the table and began unzipping. When she pulled out a rich, dark brownie, she closed her eyes and breathed in the aroma.

"My favorite!" she said. "Harvey, you want a brownie with your tea?"

He turned from the TV and gave her a questioning stare. He turned loose of the remote and cupped his hand behind his ear. "Speak up, woman. I can't hear when you mumble like that."

She rolled her eyes and poured a cup of tea. I didn't know how she would manage carrying it to him, so I rose from my seat. "I'll take it to him. Pour one for yourself."

I placed the hot tea on the table next to Harvey's chair. Looking right into his face, I spoke clearly, "You want a nice brownie with your tea?"

"You bet your boots I do. If you got plenty, I'll take two." He finally had a smile on his face. You know what they say about the way to a man's heart. His had come alive.

Glory Bea sat in her chair at the dining table, chuckling at the change in him. I took him a couple of brownies, then joined her at the table.

"I'm always happy to see company," she said. "We don't get out much. But I have all these here big windows with a nice view, and people coming and going. I'd rather look out the window than watch TV all day. I got chores to do, and it takes me a long time to get around with this walker. Still, I do better than Harvey does." She paused to study me and munch on a brownie.

"I helped Rosanna at the office this morning. On my way back home, and I decided to stop and visit a bit."

"Wondered what brought you by. Been a lot going on around here, and I already talked to that detective. What's this world coming to? We supposed to have security around here, and then Marge goes and gets herself killed, right here under our noses! It's the end times, that's what it is."

She paused to slide her glasses back up the bridge of her nose, and her eyes were solemn. "If somebody stopped here to kill me and Harvey, they'd have a field day. I keep the door unlocked, except when we go to bed. Don't get much company, but when we do, neither one of us wants to struggle to the door. I still got my husband, but I can't count on him to protect me."

I glanced back at Harvey, glued to the TV and shoveling brownies into his mouth. A walking cane leaned against his chair.

"How's he doing, Miss Glory?"

"Well, he's eighty-nine, not getting any younger. He's not in good shape, and that's partly my fault. I been a Southern cook all these years, frying near 'bout everything, and he loves all the wrong stuff. He's been riding the gravy train all over Cholesterol City, and it's headed for the Sweet By and By.

"But why should he live his last years eating soup and Jell-O? He should enjoy his life." She brushed some crumbs from the table into her hand, then deposited them on her napkin. Her eyes brightened. "So, what's up?"

"I was thinking about the view from your windows. Maybe you noticed someone around Marge's house on Monday night, or someone coming from the marina. It wouldn't necessarily look suspicious or make you think anything wrong was going on."

Her eyes were thoughtful. "What time would you be talking about?"

"Sometime after five o'clock."

"I'm not usually looking out my windows after dark, but it don't get dark now till around eight."

"Maybe you were at your kitchen sink while it was still daylight. Maybe you can think back two days ago and remember something," I said.

She rolled her eyes and rubbed her forehead. "I'll have to think about it. Write your phone number down on this pad, so I can call you if I remember anything. I don't usually pay attention to who walks down the street, one way or the other." She slid a pad and pencil across the table and struggled up from her chair. "You got time to come look at my new outfit?"

"Sure!" I left the pad with my number on the dining table and followed her to her bedroom, which was the next room past her kitchen, on the same side of the house. With her walker, she shuffled rather smoothly into the room and slid open a closet door. I noticed the large bedroom window with a view of Marge's front yard, right across the street.

Glory pulled out a hanger with a pantsuit of pale blue and yellow. She laid it carefully across her bed and looked up at me with shining eyes. "What do you think?"

"It's lovely. What's the occasion?"

"Nothing special. When I go to bingo next week, I want to look nice. Now that I think about it, if we have a memorial service for 'Marge in Charge,' I could wear it then too."

I thought it odd Glory would use that slightly cynical term for Marge in the same breath she was mentioning a memorial service. Then again, older seniors don't worry much about what they say. They blurt out what they think and don't exactly measure their words. Now my curiosity was piqued.

"Some people have mentioned Marge's abrasive personality. Did she ever treat you disrespectfully?" I asked.

"Me? Not that I recall." She raised her eyes from the new outfit and looked out the window toward the home surrounded by yellow tape. She shuffled and pushed with her walker a few steps closer. "You know what? I do remember something. I was in here getting ready to put on my gown for the night. I like to have that done early, before I get sleepy. And ole' Marge's front porch light was on already. Somebody was going in her front door."

"A man or a woman?" I asked, almost holding my breath.

"Could've been either one. I saw short grayish hair, a dark jacket, and long pants. Not fat, not skinny, not tall or short. Just . . . somebody. And I didn't see their face. My Lord, I could've seen the murderer!"

"Do you have any idea what time that might have been?"

She leaned on her walker and looked at the ceiling, like she was gathering her thoughts. "Every night, when the evening news is over, I come back here to put on my gown and robe. That's around seven o'clock." She looked so earnest, with her round blue eyes and her thin white hair, I couldn't help giving her a hug.

"Thank you, Miss Glory. If you remember anything else, like some idea of who that person was or anything at all, please call me. Of if you merely want some company or need my help, call me."

"Well, I do get lonely. But I'm not helpless yet. You're a sweetie for offering, though." She looked back at her outfit lying on the bed. "And you like this pantsuit?"

"Yes, I do. The colors are great. Where did you find this?"

She looked perplexed for a moment, then her mind seemed to clear. "Um, one of my nieces came by and took me shopping. I don't remember the name of the store."

We walked back to the living room where I told them both goodbye and saw myself out. She was lowering herself into an easy chair as I pulled the door shut.

I headed up the street toward home, thinking about this new wrinkle. Glory Bea could have seen the murderer. If I could nail this down, we might have a suspect.

I turned to look back toward the elderly couple's home and saw movement at a rear window, a window some distance from their living room. A white egret flew toward the lake, drawing my attention upward. From the corner of my eye, I saw Glory at the window, watching me. I hoped my expression of rapt attention for the bird would convince her she had not been noticed. If she had anything to hide, I wanted her to feel secure with her secret.

***

Three raps on my front door, followed by two short dings of the door-bell, woke me from my nap. I had dozed off reading a novel. I yawned, set the book aside, and struggled up from my recliner. Rosanna always used a special knock, so I'd know it was her. I opened the door and motioned her in.

"Did you just now get home?" I asked.

She settled on the couch near my recliner. "Yes, I stayed a little longer after you left. I had paperwork to do, but I didn't want people popping in and out with all the same questions." She looked a little guilty and raised both hands. "I know it was a good opportunity to question people, but at the same time, I have a responsibility to keep the place running. And now, I'm not simply helping Marge; I'm doing it all myself."

"I should have stayed. I thought you were about to close up and go home."

"No," she said. "I was glad you were going to question Glory. I'm not up for that sort of thing. I want to find out who killed Marge, y'know, but I think you're more suited for all this detective stuff. So, tell me how it went; I'm dying to know."

"She didn't remember seeing anyone. And then she did. We were in her bedroom, and she looked out her window. It seemed to trigger her memory. Rosanna, she saw someone going in Marge's front door on the night Marge was murdered. They had short gray hair and wore dark clothes. But she only saw their back and can't say if it was a man or a woman."

"Most men wear their hair short, and most older women do too. But it would certainly eliminate a woman with longer hair."

I chewed my thumb nail and thought about her comment. "Yeah, the description is specific in some ways, and vague in other ways. Like: they weren't tall or short, fat or thin. 'Average,' she said. But, Rosanna, something else bothers me."

Her brow wrinkled; I had her attention. "Glory can hardly get around with her walker. But when she led me into her bedroom, she moved quickly and easily for a step or two. Then she went back to heavy breathing and dragging herself around.

"When I left, I happened to look back at her home. She was watching me from a room down the hall, peeking out the window, only minutes after I'd seen her lowering herself into her chair with obvious difficulty. How could she jump up and dash down the hall that quickly? She wanted to watch me, for some reason. She might not know I saw her. Why would she be acting so strangely?"

I could see the distress on Rosanna's face. She was so soft-hearted, especially about the older seniors in our community. She spoke cautiously.

"I think Miss Glory gets extra help from the county. They send people around to deliver food, to help her and Harvey keep up with medications, help with house cleaning and so on. She even gets some disability income. Um, well, she might not be as helpless as she seems."

"She also might be sharper than she seems," I said.

"She's a good woman, though," Rosanna assured me. "Y'know, her husband was a minister for many years. Please don't hurt her feelings."

"I promise I'll tread softly." I drummed my fingers on the arm of my chair. "Did you ever hear from the attorney, or Marge's daughter?"

"Oh yeah. The attorney called to say that Jennifer is executrix of the estate. He didn't mention the son, Jason. I know he's the older of the two, but I also know he has problems with drugs and alcohol. Marge would have wanted her daughter to take care of things.

"I also had a call from Jennifer. She works for a marketing firm in Tampa, y'know, but she'll be at the office in the morning to discuss the responsibilities at the office with me."

I nodded my head and waited for her to continue.

"Here's the thing," she said. "I was Marge's assistant, and only part-time at that. Now it's all on me, and I didn't ask for this. Unless Jennifer plans to come here and run the office herself, I need help. If she lets me hire some temporary help, would you be willing to fill in?"

"Oh, Lord. Maybe it won't come to that. Maybe she's ready to jump right in and take over."

"Well, think it over tonight. I need you to be with me at the office when she comes. You can watch her closer than I can, y'know. I'll need to think about *what* she's telling me, and you can watch for underlying meanings or whatever. You're good at that. And you need to be there. We need to find out who did this. And sometimes it's family members, right?"

"I guess it could be anybody. Anybody with a strong enough motive or deep enough hate . . . Marge didn't get along with people very well. She's not exactly the kind of person––well, she *wasn't* the kind of person who catered to people's needs. Everywhere I turn, people tell me they found her rude and offensive."

Rosanna laughed. "You and I managed to be her friend. I had no idea what I was getting into when I applied for that part-time job with her. She was insufferable. She would explain something to me one time only, and I was supposed to absorb it all, like I had a photographic memory.

"I'd finally had enough, and I exploded. I told her what she could do with her job, grabbed my bag, and started for the door. Then she burst out laughing, asked me to sit down. Somehow, we talked it all out. I saw she was human and needed someone she could rely on. I learned to talk back to her instead of taking her crap. We knew where each one stood, y'know? She could be so infuriating. But it's like having a dog that barks at everybody. You wish they'd shut up, but you still grow to love them."

I looked at her in wonder. "You take in every stray. Did I seem like a stray when you helped me have enough backbone to finish college?"

"You never seemed needy to me," Rosanna said. "I do like to help people. But you helped me as much as I helped you. Now I'm more outgoing and self-confident. I think our personalities have always worked well together."

"You may have the only personality that worked well with Marge's. I always had fun, just the three of us going out to eat or to the movies. Her cigarettes always bothered me, but she had some good qualities––when she wasn't angry. But someone took her life away from her, and I *will* find out who did it." I stood, ready to go home and relax.

"So, are you going to the office with me in the morning when I talk with Jennifer?"

I looked at the dark brown eyes she rolled up at me. If she could, she'd keep me busy every day. If she could, she'd oversee my investigation into Marge's murder. But I needed plenty of time to investigate on my own.

"Yes, I will. But if I become an employee of Moonstone Lake Village, it will be temporary and only part-time. I already have a job on the weekends. Okay?"

"Sure, fine." Her eyes flickered with impatience, but she sighed and composed herself. "See, I work well with people."

"Yes, you do. But you didn't learn it from Marge."

Chapter 6

Second morning in a row, I had to go to that blasted office. I already resented my new part-time job. The upside was Marge's daughter, Jennifer, would arrive and take charge. I hoped to learn more about their family dynamics and get some ideas about who might have wanted to harm Marge. It might save time to look for who *didn't.*

I knew I was being snarky but, so far, Rosanna and I were about the only people I knew of who even liked Marge. I never even thought Howard liked her until I saw him cry, standing over her body.

When we unlocked the office and walked in, the first thing Rosanna did was check the office phone for messages. While she jotted them down, I started the coffee maker. When residents stopped in, they expected and enjoyed complimentary coffee. I made regular and decaf. With elderly residents, some had to avoid caffeine altogether. Too much for the old ticker.

Around midmorning, a black BMW pulled into Marge's parking space, and a petite blond climbed out, teetered on her six-inch heels till she got her balance, then marched to the front door, head held high. She wore a black suit (as important people in authority should) with a short, tight skirt which promised to make men salivate as she wielded her power.

The chiming door announced her arrival as she breezed into the room. I smelled expensive cologne, lavishly applied, and my eyes watered. She whipped off her sunglasses, pinned me with her gaze, and said, "Are you Rosanna?"

"No, I'm Celia Dawson. This is Rosanna Russo." I gestured to the nearby desk where Rosanna sat smiling. She rose and headed our way.

The blond brushed past the front counter where I stood and on toward Rosanna. She tucked her shades into her shoulder bag and extended her right hand. "I'm Jennifer, Marge's daughter. We have things to discuss."

Rosanna grasped her hand and spoke gently. "I'm glad to meet you, Jennifer. And I'm so, so sorry about your mother."

Jennifer lowered her head and looked uncomfortable, tucking a strand of hair behind her ear.

Rosanna continued, "I'm sure you'd prefer to sit in your mother's office. Do you mind if Celia sits in with us? She's been helping me here."

"Fine with me." Jennifer stepped past Rosanna and headed for the office.

I rolled my eyes and followed Rosanna down the short hallway behind Jennifer, who immediately settled into her mother's chair and looked at the untidy stacks of paper across the desk. "What's all this?" she asked Rosanna.

"I've left it like she left it, y'know? A Conroy police detective has been here and looked through things, but I made sure nothing was rearranged, in case that matters to you."

Jennifer sighed heavily, and her strictly-business face crumpled into weariness. "Oh, I don't really care," she groaned. "I'm responsible for taking care of things, but I already have a demanding career, a husband, and a daughter. My heart's not in this." She looked sadly at the clutter, pulled open the middle desk drawer and peered inside. "I need to see Mom's checkbook and her online bank account."

"I don't know where she keeps her personal checkbook, but the business checkbook is in the bottom left drawer. And I don't have the password to her bank accounts. I can get you into her computer, but not into specific accounts. She probably has those numbers recorded somewhere," Rosanna said.

Jennifer finally acknowledged my presence. "I haven't properly introduced myself. I'm Jennifer Hughes, Marjorie's daughter."

"Pleased to meet you. And you have my condolences on the death of your mother," I told her, trying to muster up all my pleasantness.

"I don't mean to be abrupt, but my time is limited, and I have a list of issues to discuss." She reached into a folder and withdrew a sheet of paper. "First: Rosanna, I want to make you temporary manager of Moonstone Lake Retirement Village, if you're willing to accept and we can agree on your compensation." She nodded at Rosanna.

"Second: the family will have a memorial service for my mother this Sunday morning, April eleventh. Please post this notice around the village inviting any of the residents to attend." She handed the sheet to Rosanna and continued. "If you can give me an estimated number by Saturday of how many to expect, I can let the caterers know. A meal will be served after the service."

"I'll be glad to do that for you," Rosanna said. "We're also planning a memorial for your mother here. We haven't set a date yet, but I'll let you know. And we'll make it a convenient date for you, so any of your family can attend."

Jennifer nodded. "Next, I have been appointed executrix of the estate with power of attorney. I've written up some guidelines we need to go over. I'm not sure what's stated in Mother's will, but if I have any control, I'll be selling this business and property. I have no interest in running the place, and no time to do so. Mother's attorney has already been approached by an interested buyer.

"As for passwords, Mom gave me a list of them a few weeks ago, when she was visiting Tampa. I'd call that perfect timing, but she couldn't have known she'd lose her life this soon. I'm glad she did something so practical. She wasn't there to visit me or her grand-daughter, mind you." Jennifer grinned, obviously well-acquainted with Marge's idiosyncrasies. "She was there, as always, for the horse races."

Rosanna listened quietly, and I did a good job of keeping my mouth shut. When I was tempted to talk, I sipped my coffee. *Oh Lord, where were my manners?*

"Jennifer, can I bring you a cup of coffee?"

"No thanks. But I could use some cold water."

"Coming right up," I said and slipped out the door. I returned with a bottle of chilled water and offered it to Jennifer. The look of horror on her face stopped me in my tracks.

Her eyes were glued to the computer screen and her mouth hung open. "What happened to the money? This bank account shows a balance of $53.16. My mother was broke!"

Her eyes shifted to Rosanna, who looked equally stunned. "I wrote lots of checks for your mother. But I never signed any of them. I only paid the invoices she authorized for payment."

"I might have to get a short-term loan to keep this business afloat. Maybe there's another account somewhere. I'll call the bank. Maybe she has some savings." Jennifer made notes frantically, and Rosanna fanned herself with a big envelope.

Jennifer looked up from her notes. "Before I forget," she said to Rosanna, "I need to give you the passwords to access this same information. I don't know when the Conroy Police Detective will be coming by, but he'll need to get into these accounts. I don't want to give him that information over the phone or by email." She retrieved a sheet of paper from her shoulder bag and handed it to Rosanna. "Keep this with you until you turn it over to him. Okay? I think he'll be here later today."

Rosanna spoke in her soothing way. "Oh, I'm sure he wants to talk with you in person."

"Well, I hope he shows up before I leave. I have appointments later in Tampa."

I bit my lip, but it was time to speak up. "Rosanna, remember that piece of paper you and the detective found? The name 'J. Yancey' and the numbers that looked like gambling odds?"

"Yes, we made a copy for the detective and left the paper in the middle desk drawer. Do you know that name, Jennifer?"

Marge's beautiful daughter shook her head but searched for the paper. She glared at the numbers and her lips pressed together. "Mom's been doing too much gambling. That might be the whole problem."

"I know next to nothing about gambling," I said. "Do people still use bookies?"

"I think it's mostly done online," Jennifer said. "But some people don't like using computers. I believe you can still find bookies to assist you. And plenty of shady characters who'll loan you money to cover gambling debts."

The front door chimed, and I went back to the reception desk. Howard stood glancing around the room, craning his neck toward the hallway.

"You working here now?" he asked me.

"Just helping Rosanna. She has it all on her now, a lot different than her former part-time job." Something about Howard always made my hackles rise.

"This car out front, is that Jennifer?"

I had to remind myself that Jennifer was his niece. "She's in Marge's office with Rosanna."

"I don't want to interrupt them. Will you let her know I'm here?" He shifted his weight from one foot to the other. The whole situation appeared to make him uneasy.

I turned away from the front desk and met Rosanna strolling into the room.

"Howard. I thought I heard your voice." Her eyes lit up with a softness I hadn't witnessed in some time.

He walked to her and took her hand. "I hope this isn't a bad time. I need to see Jennifer before she leaves."

"Sure, come on back." Rosanna turned, and they both headed for the heiress of $53.16. (Well, 26.58, if she split it with her brother.) I followed with my eyes fixed on the water fountain, like that was where I was headed.

I was not invited to this gathering and did not go with Howard into the office, but hung back two feet from the door, convincingly close to the water fountain, and listened.

"Uncle Howard. Nice to see you," Jennifer said. Sounded like they paused for a hug.

"You, too," he said. "Can you stop by my house before you leave?"

"Sure. I need to leave in an hour, so I'll see you on my way out. By the way, does the name J. Yancey mean anything to you? That's the initial 'J,' not J-A-Y.' It could be John, Joe, Jim--whatever."

"Doesn't ring a bell. Is this person connected to Marge or the business?"

"I'm not sure." I heard paper rustle. "Those numbers look like gambling odds, don't they?"

"Could be. She did love the horses--I'll see you in a bit then. Take your time."

I stepped into the restroom as Howard came out of the office, like I had just arrived in the hallway.

When the front door swung shut, I joined Rosanna and Jennifer. They were still searching for another bank account. Savings, they hoped.

"Howard's a nice guy," Rosanna said. "But he pretty much keeps to himself. Is he helping out with all this mess?"

"He's the one who made an offer on this property," Jennifer said.

Rosanna gasped and looked at me, incredulous.

"I already know I'll inherit this place. Maybe only half, but Jason will want to sell it too. As soon as we're legally able, we'll gladly sell to Howard. His offer is generous." Jennifer sipped from her water bottle and glanced at the time on her phone. "Now, let's take a look in the safe."

"What safe?" Rosanna asked, her eyes wide and her mouth open.

Jennifer grinned at us and rose from her chair. She removed the bulletin board from behind her mother's desk, exposing the safe. It was sunken into the wall, so the dial could not prevent hanging something flat in front of it.

She spun the dial back and forth and then opened it with a satisfied smile. From inside, she removed a crystal paperweight.

"Mom did have it after all," she exclaimed. "Dad always accused her of stealing his paperweight. She swore she had no idea where it was. It's so like her to keep it hidden, just to annoy him." She set it on the desk.

"I can vouch for the fact this belongs to my father, and I'm taking it to him. You are both my witnesses. Sherry will be happier to get it than Dad will. She despised my mom."

We knew Sherry was her father's second wife. The one he met *before* he divorced Marge. If Sherry hated Marge, the feelings would've been mutual.

"Sorry," Jennifer said. "I guess I'm saying too much. There's only one other thing . . ."

She reached back into the safe and drew out a leather-bound journal, and her eyes teared up. "It's my mother's private journal. I'm taking it with me. After I've read it, I'll decide if I think the police need to see it." She stuffed the journal into her large shoulder bag and looked at Rosanna, as if daring her to challenge her decision.

I was itching to get inside that journal, and I knew the police had every right to see it. But I would give Jennifer her private time with her mother's journal and not make a fuss about it quite yet.

"Whoa, and here's another checkbook." Jennifer had looked back inside the safe. "I'm running out of time, but I'll put this in her desk so the detective can look it over. I'll try to come back in a few days, Rosanna."

She closed the door and spun the lock. "Howard's expecting me. I'll call you tomorrow."

Jennifer nodded at Rosanna and hurried to her car. I ran after her and caught up before she closed the car door. She whirled and looked at me, startled.

I extended my hand. "You forgot the paperweight."

I trudged back inside, glad it was almost time to close the office.

Rosanna met me, giggling. "I can't believe she was running off without that precious paperweight. Who knew Marge had a safe in the wall?"

"Yeah, who knew? I wish she'd had a bundle of money in there. What will keep this business running?"

"Jennifer said she'd call tomorrow," Rosanna said. "I've assured her we take in money daily, for HOA fees and from some who pay rent on their property . . . As for my salary, she's offered me a generous amount, saying the *new owner* might make other arrangements in the future. Beyond that, maybe Howard will advance some money."

Before Rosanna could answer me, the front door chimed. Devon and Whitney breezed through the door, all smiles.

"I fixed that microphone, easy as pie," he said. "The cord had a short. I repaired it with electrical tape. Whenever you like, I can order a replacement cord, to be on the safe side."

Whitney beamed at her husband, obviously proud, then shifted her gaze to us. "I want to know if you need some help, Rosanna. This must be a big load on you, with Marge gone. Maybe Celia's going to help. But if not, you can count on me."

I nearly collapsed with relief. Rosanna raised her eyebrows and smiled at Whitney, who had worked as a paralegal before retiring. "I'm sure Celia's happy to hear that. I'll appreciate your help. Marge's daughter will have to authorize your pay, and I'll talk with her about your hours. In the meantime, can you start in the morning at nine?"

"Girl, you know I'll be here!" She flashed us a brilliant smile. "Right now, I got to go home and feed my starving, electrical-genius husband."

Devon hooked his arm around her neck and kissed her cheek. They waltzed out the door, and I threw my arms into the air in a silent cheer.

Now Rosanna wouldn't need me, at least not regularly. I could do my own investigating, no longer tied down in the office.

"It's almost noon," I told her. "You leaving now?"

"I need to make a few phone calls first. You go ahead. But thanks for keeping me company and helping me deal with Jennifer." Rosanna tilted her head back and chuckled. "All that bluster at the start. Holy cannoli!"

"Yeah, I think it was all nerves and insecurity. And grieving over her mother. When she settled down and apologized, I started to like her. She's not much like Marge, is she?"

"Nope. Must be like her dad, right? I never met him." She glanced at the small purse I had hung over my shoulder. "With Whitney helping me, you can get right on this murder. I can't wait to nail the dirtball who did it."

"Anything I uncover, you'll be the first to know." I waved and headed for home.

Chapter 7

Early afternoon, plenty of sunshine, and I had finished up a day in the office with Rosanna. I changed into a sky-blue swimsuit and made my way to the pool behind the clubhouse. I wore a big T-shirt coverup with flip-flops and carried a mesh bag slung across my shoulder with my phone and a towel inside. It was a short walk from home, but I rode my bike so I wouldn't have to stop and chat with anyone on my way. Why was I wasting time at the pool, when my priority should be looking for Marge's murderer?

On the other hand, everyone I'd been running into had asked me questions about finding her body, and my ears stayed tuned to catch any offhand remarks that might give me a lead. My main purpose today, however, had more to do with vanity.

On Friday night, I had a gig coming up, and I liked the idea of working on a tan and having a healthy glow for a change. I love bright colors, but they didn't look as good with my fair complexion as they would with a tan. Frankly, nothing much looks good with this pale skin. Living in Florida, getting a tan should not be a problem.

Nearly every weekend I sang at the Midnight Blues Bar & Grill. I called it the "Booze & Blues," which makes it sound like a dive, but it's actually a cool place. Aside from the usual bar, the tables have dark-blue linen tablecloths and crystal globes with chunky white candles. The wait staff wear black pants and crisp white shirts. With old, polished wood and tall arched windows, that's classy enough for me.

Each night I stood next to a polished, baby grand piano where my accompanist, Neil, played anything I asked for. With my platinum hair (okay, it's gray) and milky skin, I always wore black. And Neil, with his rich brown skin and black hair, usually wore all white, right down to his shoes. You can wear white shoes year-round in Florida without getting funny looks.

My milky white skin seemed totally out of place. I had to stop hiding in the shade. It was time to do some sunbathing.

The pool wasn't crowded, with only three people in the water and a couple seated under an umbrella with their books and water bottles. And next to the building, in a shaded area, Candy Freeman sat on a lounger in her white bikini and white-framed shades.

If Moonstone Lake Retirement Village had a beauty contest, Candy would wear the crown, no doubt about it. She was almost too young for our fifty-five plus community. She'd been married and widowed a couple of times and was currently on her third husband. If she could be called a trophy wife, all three husbands could also be considered trophies, because they'd all been loaded with money. It made me wonder why she lived here with us retirees, when she could afford an estate with her own private pool. Maybe she enjoyed an audience when she swam and sunbathed. With her golden tan and honey-colored hair swinging around her shoulders, she attracted a lot of attention.

I plopped my bag into the chair next to hers, mine in full sunshine, right next to the line where the shade began.

"Hi, Celia," she said, raising her sunglasses for a moment. "I don't ever see you here."

"Yeah, I rarely take time to lounge by the pool," I told her. "But I need some tan. Why are you in the shade?"

"The sun's too hot and direct right now. I don't sunbathe after eleven. I like to tan slowly, so I don't get skin damage and wrinkles."

She looked me over with a critical eye and I braced myself.

"Gotta be careful, Celia. You'll burn easy, as pale as you are now. Got any sunscreen?"

"A little," I lied. "But the whole idea is to get some tan, not to use sunscreen and stay white."

I could have stayed home on my back deck to sunbathe in peace. (Well, no, I couldn't. There were too many spectators around there, and they'd think I was putting myself on display.) Or I could choose a lounger on the other end of the pool, by myself. But I needed to stay put and talk with Candy. She might blurt out something that would help with my investigation.

No one knew I was investigating. Well, I hoped they didn't. I had no authority to investigate, except for my natural-born curiosity which had a right to be satisfied. So, I drew a slow breath and made up my mind to be patient with Candy. My new friend.

"Take it slow," she said, "so you don't burn and peel. That's all I'm saying."

She rubbed me the wrong way with her free advice and pushy opinions. I'm a grown woman and I think I can decide how long I want to sit in the sun. Time to change the subject.

"Candy. If you keep wearing bikinis like that one, you'll have all the old men around here drooling over you."

"They were drooling already," she said.

I giggled and adjusted my lounger to face the sun more directly, settled in, and closed my eyes. I basked in the sunshine and enjoyed a cool breeze whispering in from the lake. The scent of orange blossoms drifted around me, and the gentle splash of people moving and paddling in the pool soothed away my tension. A nap was slipping up on me.

Candy's voice jolted me fully awake. "I bet you wet your pants Tuesday when you found old Marge dead on the floor."

I squinted at her and shaded my eyes, wanting to tell her off. But I also wanted her to keep talking, so I kept my cool. "How do you know she was lying on the floor?"

"It's what people are saying––I wasn't here. I was at the gym with my trainer. I didn't know about it till later in the day."

"You didn't like her much, huh?"

"Nobody did," she shot back.

"Marge was one of Rosanna's closest friends, and I got along with her just fine. She couldn't have been all bad." I sat up and rummaged in my bag for sunglasses. I didn't want *owl eyes*, but I couldn't keep talking with Candy with my eyes squeezed shut.

"Marge treated me like crap, I'll tell you that. I think she was jealous, and that's not my fault. She should have taken better care of herself."

"The two of you had issues?"

"Hey, don't go getting any ideas. I'm not saying I hated her. But I can't work up any grief for a bitchy woman who never had a pleasant word for me."

I shook my head. "I'll admit, she could be irritable. But when you see a helpless, lifeless body, it's shocking. I'll never hear her sassy voice again, and I'll miss her."

Candy started to speak, but she bit her lip and looked away. What was she about to say? Something like "good riddance" or that she wasn't one bit sorry for Marge? Candy had grown edgy. I needed to know more, but now was not the time to push her further.

I heard the lawn mower again, sat up, and leaned toward Candy. "You know the lawn guy?"

"Sure. Everybody knows Russ."

"Has he ever come on to you?"

Candy lowered her voice a notch. "He comes on to every woman he can stare at without gagging. Of course he's flirted with *me*."

"I wonder if his wife knows," I said.

"Nancy doesn't pay him much attention. Maybe that's the problem." Candy stretched out and reached for her romance novel.

"Time to cool off," I said. "I'm baking in this sun." I slipped off my sunglasses and splashed into the shallow end of the pool, sinking into the cool water. Below the surface, I listened to the peaceful, gurgling bubbles, then bobbed back to the top for air.

Swimming to the other end of the pool and back, I heard Candy's remarks play over again in my mind. Her attitude had surprised me. She felt free to speak her mind with me, and I wanted to keep it that way. I was determined not to let her see my disapproval.

I climbed out of the pool and went dripping back to my chair in the sun, toweled off and sat again. The bag at my side had been packed hurriedly, and I muttered aloud, "I forgot my water."

"I have an extra bottle. Here, you don't want to get dehydrated." Candy handed me the water and went back to her paperback novel.

I had already grown tired of her drivel and complaining, but my curiosity was taking over again. "Hey, how long have you been here, Candy?"

"You mean at the pool?"

"No," I laughed. "Here––at Moonstone Lake."

"About six months. We moved in last November."

"Yeah, I thought you were fairly new. It's nice to have you and Mr. Freeman here."

She bent her head and closed her book. "I've had to place him in a nursing home. It's more than assisted living. It's round-the-clock care. He doesn't even know me anymore."

"I had no idea. I'm so sorry, Candy."

"He's a lot older than me. And I do love him, but he has dementia. Our life together is over. I'll be there for him to the very end . . . but I'm lonely."

"If there's anything I can do––"

"No, I mean I'm lonely for a man. Don't think bad of me, but I'm ready to see other men. I know Vince wouldn't want me to sit at home and worry about him. I visit him every day, for all the good it does. But I don't want people saying I abandoned him."

I sipped some water while I struggled for what to say. How could I muster up some empathy for this beauty queen who was looking for a new boyfriend before she got husband number three in the ground?

When my teeth unclenched, I said, "Got anybody in mind?"

"As a matter of fact, I do. Can you keep a secret?" She leaned toward me with a grin that looked shy but was probably fake.

"Sure, I can." I wasn't lying. I *could* keep a secret, but I didn't promise to keep hers.

"Howard James is a good-looking man. He's older than I like, but I've let him know I'm available. So far, I'm not getting any response from him."

"Maybe he's gay," I said, watching for her reaction.

"Oh, I can tell when a man's gay. Howard is *so* not gay." Her laugh had a phony trill, like a talking doll.

"Most men would turn cartwheels at the chance to ask you out," I said. "What if he's already interested in someone else?"

Candy didn't answer me right away. She pretended to examine her nails. Maybe she thought I was her competition, since Howard and I had been interviewed together after we found Marge dead.

"Even if he was married, I could get him if I wanted him." She looked me right in the eye, almost daring me to disagree.

"Go for it, then! You'd make a handsome couple."

I nearly choked on my words. Part of me would enjoy watching from afar as Howard struggled to hold onto "the single life" and fend off Candy's perfectly manicured clutches.

But if Candy was right, if she had power over men like she claimed she did, if she could break up marriages with her manipulations . . . well, I wouldn't wish that on my worst enemy.

I would need to lend a sympathetic ear when Candy wanted to brag, bitch, or complain. It might be hard to keep my mouth shut, but I would listen all I could and find out more about this woman.

If she'd tried to manipulate Marge, she wouldn't have had much luck. It would be like manhandling a bulldozer. No, Candy would find someone like Marge completely infuriating, because Marge was as hardheaded as they come. And the feminine wiles Candy relied on would have no effect on most women, certainly not Marge.

Somehow, I needed to find out where Candy was on the evening of the murder.

"Candy, I have an idea. Something that might help you with Howard."

Her eyes sparkled, and she moved her head closer to hear every word.

"When you visit Vincent every day, is it a specific time?" I asked her.

She frowned and squinted at me. "What does that have to do with Howard?"

"Well, he and his cousin Tate usually come to the club where I sing on Friday nights. And I'm thinking, unless you visit Vincent every night, you could show up at the Midnight Blues and casually run into Howard. He pretends to have good manners, so he'll ask you to join them. That'll give you time to chat and get to know each other."

"So, you'll be there this Friday night?" she asked. Her eyes looked slightly unfocused, as if she were already scheming. "Are you any good?"

"Well, they *pay* me every week." I tried to hide the irritation she provoked in me.

"Why is he hanging around listening to you sing love songs? Are you after him too?"

"If I were, would I be inviting you over there to flirt with him?"

"Okay, that makes sense. But I didn't know you and Howard were such close friends. Maybe he likes you more than you realize. Not that it'll make any difference. I can change his mind."

She gave me a superior smile, like I was nobody. I hadn't realized how hard it would be to keep acting friendly with someone you'd rather strangle.

"Howard and I can barely tolerate one another," I said. "I don't know what it is about him. Arrogance, maybe. I call him out on his attitude, and he resents me in return. But he loves his cousin like a brother, and Tate loves blues. So, Howard takes him out to hear blues every weekend. They always have dinner there, at the grill, then stay a couple of hours for the music."

"Wonderful! I try to see Vince in the mornings, when he's rested and more likely to recognize me. Only been at night a couple of times, like Monday night when he was acting up. I'll be sure to see him Friday morning, so I can see you that night. Sing something that'll make Howard feel romantic when he looks at me."

I chuckled and gathered up my things. Maybe I should sing, "You Must Be Gold, 'Cause She Really Digs You." I'd have to write the song first. Could it be Howard was loaded? I never would have thought so. I would have to do some digging of my own.

My skin was flushed, and I was ready for a shower. As far as I could see, Candy now thought she had a new friend and cohort. She didn't quite trust me yet, but she would use me as much as I would allow. She'd made a point of telling me she was in town visiting her husband on Monday night. The night Marge was murdered.

I would find a way to check on her alibi. The one she rattled off so smoothly.

Chapter 8

I was finishing my evening walk, near enough home to have my mind on dinner. Up ahead, next door to my small bungalow, sat Milo in his accustomed spot. He was always friendly and interesting, but his usual banter was like teasing and flirting. I was not averse to playful conversation, but I never wanted to lead a man on or play with his emotions.

And I'd never flirt with Milo, anyway. He wasn't my type.

Despite his air of self-sufficiency, he still struck me as a lonely man. I was drawn to lonely people. I thought they needed fixing, and it's part of my nature to fix things, make them better. If I ever saw a man who clearly did not want to be fixed or tampered with, it was Milo.

He sat on his patio not looking in my direction.

As soon as he heard my footsteps on the pavement, he turned his head and watched me moving up the street. He had ditched his usual sunglasses, and he wore a long-sleeved denim shirt, unbuttoned like a jacket, with a white T-shirt underneath.

I was prepared for some off-hand comment, something quick and witty meant to get a rise out of me. But he remained quiet, watching every step I took. I was one stride past him when I turned, hands on hips.

"What?" I said to him.

"I didn't say anything." He watched me closely.

"But you always do."

"You can't have it both ways. Sometimes I say hello and you act like I'm taking up your valuable time. So, tonight I keep my mouth zipped, and you want to stop and quarrel with me." His words sounded confrontational, but he gave me an easy smile.

"I know how to quarrel, and this is not quarreling," I insisted. "Was there something you wanted to say?"

"Now that you mention it––yes."

"What?"

Milo fiddled with the cuff on his sleeve and said, "What are you having for dinner?"

"I haven't really thought about it." Was he too lazy to cook, trying to weasel an invitation to dinner from me? After all, women are born cooks, right? "I might bake a potato in the microwave and have a small salad with it."

"Guess what I have bubbling on the stove?" He looked pleased with himself.

"How should I know? Chicken and dumplings?" I knew there was maybe one chance in a thousand he'd be cooking chicken and dumplings. The very idea made him lose that smug look.

"Vegetable beef soup made from scratch," he told me.

My mouth watered for that soup. I consider soup a healthy comfort food. Especially since rainy weather had ushered in a cool spell, and the evening was chilly and damp, unseasonably so for April in Florida.

"You made soup? You cook?"

"Yeah, I like cooking now and then. Plenty of time on my hands, and I get tired of pizza and burgers."

I sniffed the air. "It smells heavenly. Your kitchen window is open, you know."

"Part of my plan," he said. "You should come in and have a bowl of soup with me. I even made corn muffins."

For the first time ever, I was seeing his eyes. They were a startling, clear gray with dark brows and lashes. Eyes that could draw me in. And this was not a man I wanted to get something started with.

Milo saw my hesitation. "Hey, I'm not asking you to stay all night. What's the big deal about having a bowl of soup with your neighbor?"

I drew myself up, and I'm pretty sure I scowled at him. I wasn't going to turn him down, and I wasn't going to make him beg. Neither would I act weak and wimpy about being alone with him.

"I'm not afraid to go inside your house. I'd *love* to see inside your house. I can't think of anything I'd rather have tonight than home-made soup, and yours smells divine!"

He stood and gestured toward his back door. "After you."

His home was neat and spotlessly clean. Milo had no clutter.

He pulled out a chair for me from the round oak table between his kitchen and living room. The oven buzzed, and he turned off the timer, grabbed potholders, and lifted the muffin pan from the oven rack. This new aroma was buttery and salty, with a touch of sweetness.

"You better let those cool a little before you try to get them out of the pan," I told him.

"Yes, Celia. These aren't the first muffins I ever baked." He set the pan on top of the stove and turned to me. "I have beer, wine, coffee and sodas. What would you like?"

"A cola, if you have it."

"Hope you don't want diet. I never buy diet."

"And I never drink diet," I assured him.

We sat with steaming bowls of hearty soup and a basket of muffins. What a cozy scene. Still, it seemed awkward––until I had my first taste of his soup.

"This might be the best soup I ever had." I nearly moaned with pleasure.

"It's ordinary vegetable soup with chunks of beef."

"Whatever you did, it's excellent. I guess everyone has their specialties."

"You think soup is my specialty?" His wide grin displayed white, even teeth.

I didn't answer him. I didn't want to feel any attraction to him, and he made that difficult. He suddenly changed the subject. "Is this the same general layout as your place?"

"Mine is pretty much the opposite. Your kitchen is near your back door and mine is up front. You have a patio in the back, and I have a deck by my bedroom."

Well, I never meant to bring bedrooms into the conversation. I wanted to stuff the words back into my mouth.

"You want to see the rest of my place? I keep things fairly neat."

My bowl was empty, and the muffin reduced to crumbs.

"Yeah, Milo. Give me the tour. Then I'll help you clean up these dishes," I said, rising from my chair.

I'd already seen his kitchen, with everything white, stainless steel, and dark granite countertops. He'd paid for all the extras.

Milo led me into his living room, really an extension of the kitchen and dining area. The walls had built-in bookcases around a wall-mounted TV. His sectional sofa and recliner were dark brown leather, very masculine. And he had an aquarium with colorful fish.

"I might have guessed you'd like an aquarium," I said.

"Why's that?"

"Fish don't bark, meow, or yammer at anybody. They swim around blowing bubbles, not making a sound."

"Bingo." he said. "And they're also relaxing."

He pointed out the first bathroom, then led me down the hall to the first bedroom, neatly decorated in neutral colors and accented with green. A second bedroom was used as an office, with desk and computer, more bookcases, and a modest set of exercise equipment. Last of all was his larger bedroom with lots of gray and a touch of navy blue.

I complimented him on his housekeeping and headed back to his office. I'd seen a photograph on a shelf in his bookcase, and I wanted a closer look.

Something made me stop short of picking it up, but my fingers trailed along the brushed nickel frame. Three guys in combat uniform stood together, smiling for the camera. Milo was the guy in the middle.

"Old friends?" I asked.

"Dead friends," he said, in a voice that sounded lost and hollow. "I should have been killed with the same landmine blast. I was a few yards behind them. It still haunts me."

He realized his emotions were on display and said, "Sorry. I don't usually share bad memories."

We walked back to the kitchen, and I set our bowls in the sink. Milo insisted he could clean his own kitchen.

"You don't want to bump elbows with me?" I joked, picturing the two of us standing at his sink, washing and drying dishes.

"Having you here . . ." He must have changed his mind about whatever he'd meant to say. He patted my shoulder lightly, walked ahead of me and out the back door, holding it open for me. "I was honored to have you to dinner tonight. Shall I walk you home?"

His words were overly formal, and his eyes were slightly misty. Was this the time to joke with him, or should I be formal as well? I decided to be myself.

"Thanks for dinner, Milo. If you ever need to talk, you know where I live." I kissed his cheek lightly and walked the few steps to my back door.

***

Before I was even dressed the next morning, someone rapped on my front door. I put aside my toothbrush, rinsed my mouth, ran my hands through my uncombed hair, and headed toward the racket. I pulled my robe tighter and knotted the belt around my waist, then peeked through the curtain.

Milo stood there in the sunlight with his baseball cap pulled low over his eyes.

I swung the door open and gaped at him. He'd never been to my door in the two years I'd lived here.

"Did you make coffee yet?" he asked me.

"It's brewing now. Come on in."

"Thanks." He stepped into my living room, then on into my kitchen, where the wonderful aroma of coffee filled the air. "I didn't know I was totally out of coffee. So, I'm imposing on my good neighbor for a cup to get me going." He turned and faced me. "Besides, I need to apologize for last night."

"If you can stand to look at me with my bed-head hair and no makeup, you're welcome to have a seat." Truthfully, I thought it might be a good idea for him to see me in all my inglorious unadornment. If he was beginning to form romantic fancies, seeing the real-life version of me should put an end to that.

"You never looked more beautiful," he said earnestly.

I smacked my forehead and poured a cup of coffee, handed it to Milo, then rummaged in my cabinet for another mug. I poured more coffee and added creamer. Milo had sunk into my soft, blue recliner and removed his cap. He sipped coffee with a look of sublime contentment.

"I love this chair. And you make great coffee."

Who was this man? He'd always kept his distance, and we only spoke in passing. Now he was like "Mr. Rogers," the folksy next-door neighbor. And I thought he looked great lounging in my chair.

"What's this about an apology?"

"I hadn't really planned to invite you to supper. But when I made that soup and it turned out so good, it occurred to me that you passed my house about the same time every evening and might be passing by soon. So, it was a last-minute decision. I hope I didn't come on too strong or make you uncomfortable."

At that moment, my door flew open again and Rosanna stepped inside. "I knew I saw a man go into your house," she said, pointing at Milo. Her arm eased back down to her side, and she looked him over slowly. Her eyes widened when she took in my yellow bathrobe and tousled hair. Not to mention Milo's happy expression.

"Hold on," I told her. "You're adding two and two and coming up with five. It's not what you're thinking."

"I hope not," she hissed.

"He arrived early for the coffee klatch. Join the party. Mugs are in the cabinet. Excuse me while I get dressed."

I laughed and started down the hall to my bedroom. Things were falling conveniently into place for me. It was obvious Milo was lonesome, but I wanted to get his attention off me. I'd already thought of Rosanna and here she was, exactly when I needed her. Surely, he'd notice how gorgeous she was, even with her extra pounds. They'd probably chat, and she'd realize he was a nice guy after all. Like I did.

When I got back to the living room, Rosanna had ignored the coffee and headed on to the office. I asked Milo what he thought of Rosanna. That's me; I get straight to the point.

"What do you mean? I hardly know her, and I don't think of her at all. Mind if I refill my cup?"

"Help yourself."

"I'll have one more, then I'm off to the store. I don't like being out of coffee."

Milo came back to the living room with his steaming cup and settled again in my recliner. I perched nearby on the end of my couch, now wearing faded jeans and a T-shirt.

"I had hoped you and Rosanna would strike up a conversation and get to know each other a little better," I said.

"Why are you pushing Rosanna on me? Matchmakers usually make a mess."

"Rosanna's my best friend, and she's a wonderful person. She'd be good for you. I can tell you're lonely."

"Celia, you'll have to let me choose my own friends. I haven't had many. Long-term friendships haven't ever worked for me."

He sipped his coffee and glanced around my living room. "I like how I can see you all over this room. It's vivid with your personality. And this chair, it has your scent."

"I have a scent?"

"Jasmine on a fresh breeze," he said.

"My, my. You have a way with words. You should be a writer."

"I *am* a writer," he said, his voice calm and businesslike. "I write thrillers, adventures, espionage, and historical fiction. Did you notice all the books in my house?"

I stared at him, wondering if he was kidding around. Maybe he was serious. I remembered seeing his high-end office equipment, nothing dusty and outdated.

"Yeah, I noticed. I guess you read a lot as well."

"I read all the time. When I'm not writing. Or cleaning my house or cooking soup." He grinned again.

"You keep surprising me," I said. "I thought I had you figured out, but I don't. I do know you're looking for something."

Milo's eyes held mine till I had to look away. I flicked a speck of lint from the knee of my jeans. "You know I'm a singer, right?"

"Right."

"I sing almost every Friday night at the Midnight Blues lounge. Rosanna usually comes to hear me. She likes to sit with Howard and his cousin. They all have dinner, maybe dance a little to the music. Why don't you come tonight? You could ride with Rosanna."

Milo sighed and stared into his empty cup. "No, I don't want to ride anywhere with Rosanna. I'm sure you're a fine singer, but I'm not into blues. I've been sad long enough."

He rose and carried his cup to the kitchen sink. He was cynical Milo again, with that smirky little grin at the corner of his mouth. "Thanks for the coffee. What brand was that?"

"The generic store brand," I answered.

"It was terrific. Must be one of your specialties."

That made me smile. But when he replaced his cap, settled it low on his forehead, and walked back out the front door, my smile went with him.

Chapter 9

On the day I have a gig booked, I'm always antsy. I've been doing this for years and it has nothing to do with stage fright. It's questioning whether I'm fully prepared, going over my playlist, checking my outfit, and fiddling with my hair. Relaxing is not an option. I'd only sit and stew about the job ahead of me. So, my best recourse is to stay busy.

It was Friday morning, and I was scheduled, once again, to sing at the blues lounge in town that evening. I washed and detailed my car in the driveway, something I did every week with as much pleasure as if I were soaking in a tub full of bubbles, sipping champagne, and listening to great music. Only in this case, the bubbles were in my scrub bucket, I had iced tea instead of champagne, and the music blasted from my old boom box.

Florida is a great place for convertibles, and I had a silver Miata with a black top. Everything would match: My little black dress with black, strappy pumps and silver earrings. And of course, my hair was silvery gray, cut in a pageboy bob that touched my shoulders.

After rinsing the car, I dried it with a soft towel, admiring the metallic sheen of the paint. My back was to the street while I sang along to some favorite tunes on my radio, totally absorbed in the music. When a hand touched my shoulder, I jumped and yelped, then turned to see Darlene grinning at me.

"Good thing this carport roof isn't any lower," she said. "You'd-a bonked yourself in the head."

"Guess I was wrapped up in the music."

"Nice voice. Never heard you sing before."

"Warming up for tonight," I said with a smile.

"What's tonight?" Darlene's bright blue eyes were wide and curious.

I laid my towel aside and turned down the boom box. "On Friday nights, I sing at the Midnight Blues Bar & Grill. I'll be there tonight, as usual."

"Oh, I wish I could come," she said with a loud sigh.

"Why can't you?"

"Tammy doesn't like that kind of thing. She thinks it's not good for us."

"You could come by yourself."

"Tammy wouldn't like it. And she wouldn't let me drive her car, not at night." Her eyes drooped like a little girl who wasn't included in a game of jump rope.

"You know, I'm older than Tammy but she thinks she's in charge of me––all because she went to college and became a nurse. That doesn't mean she's smarter. Straight out of high school, I went to work in a bakery, because our family needed more money. I've spent my life baking cookies and decorating cakes. That requires a few brains, by golly."

"Maybe she worries about you being out alone at night," I said. "I have to go early, but I'm sure you could ride with Rosanna if you really want to go."

Darlene looked to the side and slid her lower lip between her teeth. I couldn't tell if my invitation gave her hope, or only added to her stress. I gestured toward my house. "Want to come in for a glass of tea?"

She was carrying a camera, which she clutched to her chest in delight. "Yes, I'd love some iced tea, if it's sweet."

"Always," I assured her. She followed me to the door, which I held open while she scampered straight to my kitchen. I set my empty glass on the table, added one for Darlene, and filled them with ice cubes. As I reached into the fridge for the tea pitcher, I heard her voice behind me.

"Are these my glasses?"

Did she mean the iced tea glasses? I turned and found her staring at the black-framed eyeglasses sealed in a plastic bag, lying on my kitchen table. I had left them there in plain sight to remind myself to call one of the police detectives. Her eyes sparkled.

"Could be," I said. "They were hanging in the shrubbery that surrounds Marge's backyard. You think you might've dropped them there?"

"Oh, I must have. I bought them this past week at the dollar store. They're only cheapos, but I hate losing something brand new."

I casually reached for the bag and turned it until I could read the label on the arm of the glasses, confirming what I already knew. They had, indeed, come from Dollar General.

"Why are they in a plastic bag?" she asked, taking them from my hand.

"I thought they might be some kind of link to Marge's death, and the police might consider them evidence."

"Not *my* glasses!" she snorted, flapping her hand. She slapped them onto her face, with a tap between the eyes to settle them on her nose.

"Darlene, they're reading glasses. Do you usually wear them outside?"

"Only if I'm taking pictures." She patted her camera. "I like to look for water birds behind Marge's house, near the lake. But my digital camera has lots of settings on the back and the print's too small. I'm not used to all the buttons, so I take along these glasses. You want to see some of my pictures?"

I nodded and poured our tea, relieved I'd forgotten to give the glasses to Detective Hendrix as possible evidence. I pictured him warning me again to stay out of this investigation. And now it didn't matter anyway; Darlene readily claimed them as hers. If she had killed Marge and lost her new glasses on the same night, she would never be claiming those glasses.

She thrust her camera in front of my face, showing me a small flock of ibises with their curved bills. She flipped to the next photo of an owl perched on Marge's boathouse at dusk. Next was a late evening shot of Marge's front yard where a pair of Sandhill cranes stood with a baby crane between them.

"Wait!" I sputtered. "Let me see that picture a little closer."

Her mouth dropped open a little, and she handed me her prized camera. I studied the photo.

"Darlene, did you notice the man in the picture? The one at Marge's door, with his back to the camera?"

She pulled the camera back and glared at the photo. "No! Who in the world is that?"

We both studied the picture: A tall, slender man in a ball cap, tan pants, and a blue short-sleeved shirt. "His head is turned to the side.

It doesn't show his face clearly, but nothing about him looks familiar. So, you weren't aware you were taking this guy's picture?"

"Lord, no. I don't guess he'd care--I was taking pictures of birds. This was a few days ago."

I noticed a small date stamp on the photo. "That was April fifth, Monday evening. The night Marge was killed."

Darlene took a big gulp of her tea, pulled a chair out from the kitchen table, and plopped into the seat. Her eyes were huge.

I joined her. "Let's look at all the recent photos. We might find more clues." I slid closer to her, and we looked through her pictures. She had a good eye for the wildlife and flowers she loved to photograph. We were seeing earlier dates now, like April third.

She even had a photo of Candy taking a walk with her miniature white poodle. Candy stood beneath a palm tree, holding the tiny dog next to her face, posing for the picture. Darlene grumbled, "I only wanted a shot of the dog, but Candy had to have her face in the picture. Typical."

I had taken Darlene for a bit of an airhead. She was, in fact, rather astute.

We found no more pictures with people in the background visiting Marge. At least it looked like he had visited Marge. For all I knew, he could have knocked a few times, then turned and left. Would there be a fingerprint on the doorknob or doorbell? The detectives would need to see this picture.

"Do you mind if I download this picture to my computer and print it out? I think the police need to see it."

"Really?" Darlene's face was filled with something like disbelief. "Mercy me! Are you sure you need this?" Her eyes drifted to the window in the direction of the lake. Her thoughts must have traveled there as well.

"It could help us find out who killed her," I said.

Darlene sniffed and her face lost its child-like expression. "I don't really care. Me and Tammy never liked her."

I made a copy of the photo while Darlene finished her tea. When I returned her camera, she was all smiles. "I'm going to call Rosanna on my way home. If I go with her tonight to hear you sing, I'll leave old Tammy here to twiddle her thumbs and watch TV."

Her grin was gleeful as she sailed out the door. Darlene should have a life of her own, I thought. But I sure hoped I hadn't stirred up trouble between the two sisters.

***

The business card for Detective William Hendrix was still in a drawer by my favorite chair. I called his number, and he answered on the first ring.

"This is Celia Dawson," I said, "from Moonstone Lake Retirement Village."

"Yes, I remember you. When I talked with you and Ms. Russo on Wednesday, you said you had something to tell me."

"Oh, that was about some glasses I found near the lake. I meant to give them to you, but it turns out they belong to a woman here in the community."

The line was silent for a moment. "First of all, Ms. Dawson, were you in the backyard of the deceased when you were near the lake? And secondly, why would you give them to someone else before we checked them out?"

This was not going the way I had planned it. "They only belonged to Darlene, a lady who lives here with her sister. She takes pictures all the time, mostly birds and flowers. She had lost the glasses down by the lake. And, no, I was not in the taped-off backyard of Marjorie Coleman when I found them."

"Then why did you consider giving the glasses to me?"

I struggled to keep my voice calm and even. "Because it occurred to me the murderer could have arrived by boat, entering the house through the backyard. And the glasses were hanging in a bush between the sea wall and her backyard."

"So, you went snooping. I thought I cautioned you about that."

I counted to ten. Fifteen, actually. "Do you even want to know what I'm calling you about now?"

"Certainly. What's on your mind?"

I explained about Darlene's camera, with the date-stamped photos. And the picture of a man apparently at Marge's front door the night of the murder. "I made a copy on my printer, and I can send it to you by email. Maybe you'll recognize the man, or maybe he left some fingerprints on the door."

"I'd prefer to come by and pick up the photo. Is this a good time?"

"I have business in town tonight and won't be here much longer."

"Then please tell me when you'll be available tomorrow." His voice had become overly formal.

"Any time after ten tomorrow morning," I told him.

"Ah, late riser," he said.

Now I really wished I had called Sergeant Sloan instead of Will Hendrix. I heard him chuckle.

"I'll call you before I come tomorrow. And thanks for letting me know about this. It could be crucial to the case."

I ended the call and noticed Darlene strolling back down the street, her cell phone pressed to her ear. Rosanna would have a companion for dinner tonight, whether she liked it or not.

Chapter 10

To begin singing at the Midnight Blues by eight, I'd leave home early enough to settle in and discuss the evening's selections with Neil. I'd much rather be early than to arrive five minutes late. But that night I got ready too early. Like I said, I was keyed-up all day, and my talk with Will Hendrix didn't help things.

So, at 5:30, all dressed up with nowhere to go, I decided to stop by the nursing home and visit Vincent, Candy's invalid husband. If I ran into Candy, I'd say I half-expected her to be there. But she was probably getting dolled up to come to Midnight Blues that night.

Settling into my convertible, I noticed Rosanna had left already. I zipped out of my short driveway, hoping she'd taken Darlene with her. No time to put the top down; that was for later when all the singing was over, and I was ready to relax. When the sun had set, and the air was cooler––and I wasn't concerned about my hair.

Silver Palms Care Center was only a slight detour on my route to Booze & Blues. When I parked in the visitors' section, I checked around to see if Candy's big white Escalade was in sight. The coast was clear.

I strolled inside, walked up to the reception counter, and told the nurse I'd like to see Vincent Freeman. She asked me to sign the register, and she'd go check on him. Sure enough, along with my signature there was a space for the time of my visit. When she marched down the hall, I flipped the pages back to Monday, April fifth and searched for Candy's name. She had signed in at 10:15 that morning.

Returning to Friday, I signed my name and looked around for a wall clock. When Nurse Judy returned to her post, I was filling in the current time and printing my name.

She told me he had just finished his dinner and would fall asleep soon, but I could visit for a few minutes. Room 133 on the left.

I had only met Mr. Freeman once, and I doubted he would remember me. My reason for coming had been accomplished, but I should at least stop in and say hello, especially since I had signed the register. The nurse would find it suspicious if I left without visiting.

I stepped into his room with a smile. "I'm Celia Dawson, a friend of Candy's. You may not remember meeting me."

He studied me for a moment. "Don't believe I do. But I'm proud to have such a pretty lady come visit me."

"I had some extra time, and you were on my mind. Candy mentioned you yesterday." I felt like an imposter and hoped I wasn't stammering.

"Well, if you've seen Candy lately, maybe you've seen our little Puff Ball. How is she?"

"You mean the little poodle?"

"Yeah! Candy calls her Princess, but she's Puff Ball to me."

"As a matter of fact, I saw a picture of her this afternoon. She's adorable."

"I miss that little dog. And I miss Candy, but I don't want her spending all her time here. She has lots of friends, and I don't want her to be lonely."

"Mr. Freeman, Candy tells me how much she loves you. I'm sure you know that already."

"I know a lot," he said. "But thank you for telling me that." He yawned, trying to cover his mouth. "I'm not bored with your company, but it's hard to stifle a yawn. After dinner I always get sleepy."

"I need to be going anyway." As I started for the door, I turned back to him. "If I can stop by again, is there anything I can bring you?"

A smile spread across his face. "I'd like a picture of Puff Ball. That'd brighten this room up for me."

"You got it." I saluted him and left the room. I wondered why his adoring bride had not already brought him a picture of their pet. Also, he was clear and alert. I wasn't buying the notion he no longer recognized Candy. Like he said, she had a lot of friends. And tonight, she'd be trying to make a new one.

***

The glare of the setting sun disappeared as I stepped into the dim interior of the blues bar. The much cooler air inside was refreshing, like plunging into the ocean in July. And I still had enough time to speak to a few people and get myself settled.

Rosanna sat at a table near the piano, looking at a menu. She wore a flowered sundress that looked great with her Italian complexion. Darlene sat across the table in a simple, cream-colored blouse and a conservative black skirt, not really her personality. Snow-white wavy hair framed her face and set off her deep blue eyes. She waved at me and fairly bounced in her seat, like a child at the circus. I had an uneasy feeling about Tammy, the sister left at home.

I walked their way, noticing the room was half-filled with dining customers. Some would stay for music; some would eat and go home. Neil sat across the room, still having his dinner, and he gave me a wave. I pulled up a chair at Rosanna's table and grinned at Darlene. "I see you made it after all."

"Yep! Rosanna was nice enough to offer me a ride. I left a note for Tammy and told her where I was going tonight. She'll probably have a fit, but who cares? I feel like I busted out of prison."

Rosanna reached across the table to pat Darlene's hand. "I sure hope Tammy doesn't get angry. I would have invited her too, but she didn't answer her phone."

"She never does, unless she recognizes the number. That's Tammy, for you." Darlene turned back to her menu. "What on earth should I order? A big martini? What does a martini taste like?"

"Honey, if you're not used to alcohol, you might just want to order dinner. We'll try a Shirley Temple later tonight, okay?" Rosanna tends to mother everybody.

Darlene ordered steak, Rosanna ordered a grilled chicken salad, and I ordered myself to take care of business with Neil. He had finished his dinner, and I joined him in his quiet booth.

His evening was always longer than mine. Soft, recorded music played during dinner until 7:00, when Neil began playing dinner music on piano. An hour later, I would join him to sing soft solos with a bluesy sound.

Neil had an accompaniment track with bass and percussion for the more upbeat songs. We did more than blues. The crowd favorite had to be our theme song, Melissa Manchester's "Midnight Blue."

Neil was in his early fifties, black, handsome, and still single. Women swooned when he sang "I Guess That's Why They Call It the Blues." He'd do the second hour solo, and I never knew what he might sing. But I knew it would be terrific. During the last hour, we sang duets, always ending with Eric Clapton's "Wonderful Tonight."

We looked over my list of songs for the evening, all of which he knew by heart. Once the music started, Neil never left the stage, except for short breaks. We made a great team, and I loved him like a brother. No one would mistake us as brother and sister; we were almost as black and white as the piano keys.

Leaving the playlist with him, I moved around the room to another booth and said hello to Howard and Tate.

"I wouldn't miss hearing you sing," Tate said. "What could be better than watching a lovely woman sing beautiful music while we sit back and enjoy a few beers?"

I'm not sure Howard would have been a regular customer without Tate's urging. They're like close brothers. Tate is a widower who lives with his daughter and her husband. Since Tate loves music, Howard delights in treating him every Friday night. Tate beams and claps, while Howard sits patiently, rarely ever looking my way. Who knows what goes on underneath that stately head of gray hair?

A sudden cloud of perfume wafted my way, and Candy appeared at my side. She looked exquisitely beautiful, and her eyes sparkled at Howard. He shot me a panicked look, like a man in deep water who couldn't swim. Almost sorry I had invited Candy, I moved aside.

"Oh, Howard. It's so great to see you here. Who's your friend?" she asked.

As I backed away, Howard introduced his cousin, then said to Candy, "Are Rosanna and Darlene expecting you?" If she realized he wanted to get rid of her, she ignored it.

Candy laughed, already charming Tate. She was good at reading men's faces and body language. Whatever made Tate happy, Howard would usually go along with it.

When he stiffly invited Candy to join them, she slid into the booth next to Howard, practically purring. Howard was her target, Tate merely a stage prop.

Rosanna's table seemed peaceful, so I pulled up a chair. I'd had a late afternoon snack before I got dressed, but I never ate before singing. Darlene's steak looked yummy, but I tore my eyes away from her plate and focused on Darlene. "Guess who I saw before coming here?"

"Not Tammy, I hope."

"No. I stopped by Silver Palms and visited with Candy's husband. You know Vincent Freeman?"

"I know what he looks like," she told me. "Why'd you go see him?"

Rosanna would get the full story later, but I couldn't tell Darlene everything I was digging into. "He gets lonely there in the nursing home, I'm sure. Candy goes to see him every day, but mostly he's there alone. So, I stopped by for a quick visit, and he asked me about their dog."

"You mean that little white dog in the picture with Candy?"

"Yeah, I told him I'd seen a picture of his dog, and he wants a copy to keep by his bed. Can you print one out for me?" I asked her.

"Sure can. I know how to use Tammy's computer, but she doesn't know I do."

"This won't get you in trouble, will it?"

"I'm always in trouble with Tammy. Big deal."

The front door opened, and Will Hendrix walked in wearing casual clothes, no tie or jacket. He looked different, less threatening. His smile was friendly, and he headed for our table.

"What are you doing here?" It was a dumb question, but he'd totally surprised me.

"What a lot of people do on Friday night after a long work-day––I'm having dinner and looking forward to some good music."

"All by yourself?"

"So far," he said to me. His eyes were warm and intense.

Rosanna spoke up. "You're welcome to sit here with us. Celia will shortly be onstage working."

"You call it work? I always thought singers were just having fun."

He was kidding around, but I still resented his making light of my efforts. "It's a lot of fun; that much is true," I told him. "But you'd know singing is work if you'd ever done it."

My indignation seemed to amuse him. Maybe he liked stirring me up. He turned to Rosanna and said, "You already have your dinner. I won't interrupt. I'll sit at this next table, maybe join you later."

I rose and strolled to the piano, making sure not to trip in my higher-than-usual heels. Neil was playing softly. I sipped from a water bottle and hummed a few scales, while the piano music drowned out my warm-up. With my side to the audience, I watched Neil's hands on the piano keys, effortlessly producing chords and melodies. When the tune ended, I turned around and reached for my microphone.

Someone vaguely familiar now sat at the bar, looking the other way and speaking to the bartender. I began singing "At Last," with lyrics about finally finding one's true love. As the first verse ended, he turned and smiled at me.

Milo.

Trying not to stare at him, I concentrated on the song I was singing. After telling me he didn't care for blues, here he was at the blues bar, hanging on my every note, my every move. He made my heart go pitty-pat, not always in time with the music.

My gaze shifted to Rosanna and Darlene, who were deep in conversation. Mostly Rosanna listening and Darlene chattering away. She seemed like a kid out of school, reveling in her freedom. They, too, distracted me.

Howard, Candy, and Tate snagged my attention. Tate gestured wildly as he told Candy something amusing. It must be, judging by the raucous laughter coming from her dainty lips. I wished she'd quiet down a little; my song was soft and tender. And Howard looked positively miserable, sitting next to her.

I almost lost track of my song lyrics. Glancing at a couple I'd never seen before, I recovered smoothly. As they danced by me, the lyrics flowed back into my mind: Something about a man smiling and casting a spell over me.

The words had new meaning, and I kept my eyes away from the bar, where Milo sat alone. All these people I knew, everyone there that night--maybe I shouldn't invite so many friends at the same time.

I pretended they were sleepy children sitting in their pajamas. They'd be going to bed soon. I relaxed and got into my music.

Time passed and my first break grew near. Neil would take the second hour, and I could visit with friends.

The door popped open, and Tammy marched into the room. She spotted Darlene and pinned her with a stern glare. I finished the last song, nodded to my audience, and stepped away from the microphone. Tammy and I reached the table at the same time. I expected trouble. Detective Hendrix must have been on the same wavelength. He rose and moved in our direction.

Tammy scowled at her sister. "I don't appreciate you running off like this." She stood over Darlene. They were drawing some curious stares.

"Please, Tammy. Have a seat," I said. She sat, reluctantly, and I took a seat across from her.

"I'm merely having dinner with a friend, and I left you a note." Darlene's voice was a frustrated hiss.

"We have a deal, Darlene, if you will recall. I think we should talk outside."

"Are we having a problem?" Hendrix towered over us.

"Sir, this is private business," Tammy told him.

"I'm not in uniform, but I am a police detective, and I won't allow any disturbance here tonight."

"I need to take my sister home." Tammy ground out her words.

"I'll be leaving with Rosanna later. Either be quiet or go back home!" Darlene now had tears in her eyes.

After a few beats of silence, Tammy sighed, seeming to wilt. "We'll say no more about it for now. I'll stay for the music."

"Whew!" Hendrix pretended to wipe his brow. "All I need is a cat fight on my night off." He grinned and invited me to his table for a drink. I went and sat with him for a moment, but I didn't accept a drink. I never drink, not even a sip of wine, when I'm performing. It might be relaxing, but I didn't want my voice to lose any sparkle.

I explained the awkward relationship between the two sisters. They'd lived together for so long they were bound to have disagreements now and then. Of the two, Tammy seemed more settled and mature. But I wasn't sure why she kept such a tight rein on Darlene.

"What brings you here tonight?" I asked him again. "I've never seen you come in, and I've been singing here nearly a year."

"When we talked this afternoon, you said you had business in town this evening. Later, I was looking through the paper and saw an ad for live music here tonight. It had your picture. I'm a sucker for pretty pictures."

Will Hendrix had a slender face with even features, soft brown eyes, and dark hair combed straight back with a little gray showing. His smile, steamy and intimate, threw me off balance. Was this really a good idea? After all, he was in the middle of a murder investigation. I had to keep things on a professional, business-only level. I changed the subject.

"Are you making any progress on the Coleman murder?"

"No promising leads so far."

"Well, I have some ideas. When you come by tomorrow for that photograph Darlene took, maybe we can talk. Right now, I should speak to the patrons and a few other friends." I rose from my chair. "Detective Hendrix, I appreciate you stopping by. I hope you'll enjoy the rest of the evening." I shook his hand and walked away, and I knew he still watched me.

Milo sat with his back to us, but I saw his face in the mirror behind the bar. I spoke to some regulars and a few people who were new to me. Then I slid onto the barstool next to Milo.

"I thought you didn't like blues."

"Just sulking when I told you that," he said.

"Hmm, I thought only women sulked. And besides, I don't sing strictly blues. I do a variety."

"I noticed your variety. One reason I'm not sulking now." His answers were usually short and cryptic. He kept me guessing.

"What're you drinking?" I asked. His glass held a golden liquid with bubbles.

"Ginger ale. After all, I'm driving myself home. Wouldn't want your buddy Hendrix giving me a hard time."

"Why would he do that?" I asked.

"Well, you left his table and now you're sitting with me. I wonder why?"

"I like you." It was as simple as that.

He turned and swirled his glass. "Can I buy you one of these?"

"My drinks are on the house," I said. "But I won't turn you down."

After all, buying someone a drink was a friendly gesture. My throat was as dry as a sand dune, and his ginger ale looked better and better. *He* looked better and better. He wore gray slacks and a crisp, white shirt, and smelled like spicy lemons.

Milo signaled for the bartender without ever taking his eyes off me.

***

Spending time with Milo had been relaxing and rejuvenating. He talked with his eyes more than his words. A current buzzed between us the whole time, and I was reluctant to pull away from him. My last hour of singing should be a breeze. I could handle singing, but I was not so sure anyone could handle Milo.

When I returned to the microphone, I noticed Howard and Tate preparing to leave. Candy did not look happy, but Howard seemed determined. She threw her arms around him and hugged him goodbye as if they were already a couple. Unsmiling, Howard held himself straight and tall. Tate grabbed Candy like he'd found the prize Easter egg. He followed Howard out the door but had trouble pulling his eyes away from Candy.

Her shoulders slumped ever so slightly, and her eyes strayed to Rosanna's table, with three women and one empty chair. Apparently, she was not interested. She strolled over and spoke to Will Hendrix. I was not aware they had ever met, but perhaps the fact I sat with him briefly made him fair game . . . and doubly appealing.

By then, I was singing a new song. I didn't notice if Will offered her a seat, but whether he did or not, she chose to move on to Milo, where I had spent more time. Candy was bored and playing now. The back of my neck prickled, and I wanted to throw her out the door. If I watched them any longer, it would get me rattled. My eyes shifted as I sang.

The night had worn itself out. When Neil and I sang the final notes of our last song, I felt worn out as well. The bartender switched to recorded music while I gathered up my belongings, and a few people began to drift out the door.

Darlene was determined to ride back with Rosanna, who promised to take her straight home. Tammy lifted her hands in frustration and stalked out to her own car.

Will Hendrix said he'd see me the next morning. I looked around for Milo, who had already slipped away. I was ready to put the top down on my car and boogie home, letting my hair blow wildly in the night air.

In the parking lot I turned my key in the ignition, punched a button, and watched the top slide back. Milo appeared at my car door and leaned close.

"I'd offer you a ride home, but you have your own car. I'll follow behind you, if you don't mind."

"Sure," I said. "You can escort me."

Milo's Land Rover sat close by. His headlights came on, as if he had offered his arm and his strength to lean on.

On the drive home with his headlights behind me, I thought about the people at the bar who had known Marge, many who didn't like her: Howard, who had argued with her so often; Tammy and Darlene, who openly acknowledged their aversion to her; and Milo, such a quiet, private man. I thought about Candy's lie, as to her whereabouts on the evening Marge was killed.

I had to wonder if her murderer had been among us all evening.

Chapter 11

I'm so wound up from singing on Friday nights, it takes a while to settle down when I get home. After showering and getting into some comfy nightwear, I pour a glass of wine and find myself a late movie on TV. Later, I come awake in my recliner and toddle off to bed. I hate being disturbed the next morning.

But there was the doorbell again. And again. My clock read 8:00, an hour earlier than I wanted to wake up. Sheesh! I stumbled to the door and looked through the peephole. *Tammy.*

"Hang on, I'll be right with you," I called out.

I hurried back down the hall and to the bathroom. I drank some water and grabbed a hairbrush. Back up the hall and to the living room, I pulled the door open and let her in.

"Last night wrecked my nerves. I have to talk to you." Tammy looked like she had slept very little. Maybe I was partly to blame.

"Have a seat, Tammy. You want a cup of tea or some coffee?" I was busy spooning fresh grounds into my coffee maker.

"If you're making coffee anyway, I'll have some. I need full-strength," she said.

While the coffee brewed, I left the kitchen, stood near her in the living room, and brushed my hair as she began.

"I shouldn't have caused a disturbance where you were singing last night. Darlene and I don't go to nightclubs and places like that."

"I see. Well, it's not a bad place. It's every bit as safe and respectable as our clubhouse here at Moonstone Lake. I invited her to come, but I didn't mean to stir up trouble between you two."

"People think I'm too bossy with her. But I have to look out for Darlene. She doesn't always use good judgment. And she's too trusting. I don't mean with you; I mean even with total strangers. She's not as mature as she should be." Tammy's face was a sickly gray, and she rubbed her forehead. There was a lot she wasn't telling me.

Laying my brush aside, I went to pour coffee. "Come on in the kitchen," I said. "I have cream and sugar if you want it."

The room was fragrant with the rich smell, and our eyes were brighter even before we took our first sip. We sat at the table with steaming cups. "Tell me what I can do," I said. "Darlene seems like a witty, outgoing woman. You're more reserved, and she's wide open. You think it's more than a personality difference?"

"Yes, she's more outgoing, but she's vulnerable. I think, most of the time, Darlene can hold her own. But I need to be there when she needs me. I never know when that will be."

"Can you be more specific?" I asked her. "Last night when you said, 'We have a deal,' what did you mean?"

"Some of that, I can't tell you without betraying a confidence. But she has agreed to yield to my better judgment, so I can protect her." Tammy lifted her chin and stared blankly at the top of my kitchen cupboards. I followed her gaze and saw a cobweb.

"Protect her from what?" I asked.

"From herself. That's all I can say." Tammy tucked her short hair behind her ear and toyed with the small hoop earring.

I sipped my coffee and pondered her words.

"I need to give her more freedom," Tammy admitted. "She's always been sociable. I'll need to come with her on her adventures. I'd rather sit home and read romance novels, but I'll take her out more."

Tammy finished her coffee. "If you ever hear her planning something behind my back, please, *please* let me know." Her eyes were desperate, and I nodded.

She rose to leave, and I slipped my arm around her shoulders. I'd always thought her reserved and haughty. But she was clearly hurting. "I never meant to cause you such stress," I said. "Thanks for talking things over with me. Where is she now, by the way?"

"I hope she's still asleep." She rolled her eyes and went back out the door.

***

My phone rang at 10:05. Sure enough, Will had waited till after 10:00.

"Good morning," I answered.

"Morning to you, sunshine. You up and ready to go?"

"Ready to go where?"

"Just a figure of speech. When can I come by and get that evidence?"

"I'm dressed and ready. The sooner the better."

"Heading your way now," he said, and we disconnected.

One thing I had learned about Will Hendrix: he was not a man for small talk. I liked that about him. He always got straight to the point, with few preliminaries. Probably a common trait among detectives.

My small, cluttered office was next to my bedroom, and I didn't plan on taking Will back there. Maybe I'd tidy it up after he left. I strolled back and located the printout of Darlene's picture and slid it into a manilla envelope.

With my avid interest in mysteries, I guess I considered myself a sleuth. Not that I had many occasions to practice sleuthing. But I loved to read mysteries and try to figure them out before the culprit was revealed.

Finding Marge's murderer was on my mind, day and night. Her death hadn't exactly left a gaping hole in my heart, and I knew the police detectives were working on the case. But it was an unsolved puzzle that nagged at me. My resourcefulness, persistence, and intellect were all challenged, and I was far from ready to accept defeat.

Back in the living room, I plopped onto the couch and fished the photocopy out of the envelope to study it again. I saw nothing familiar about the person in Darlene's picture.

My doorbell rang, and I motioned Will inside. He wore faded jeans, a gray Henley shirt, and running shoes. When I gave him the once-over, he explained, "Not officially working today."

Like antennae, his eyes swiveled right to the paper in my hand. I handed him the picture and we sat on the couch.

"I wish this actually showed his face; it's not definitive," he mumbled.

"Mainly it shows someone we don't recognize at her door on the night she was killed," I said.

He looked at my face, as if studying every detail. But I think his mind was piecing other things together. He slid the picture back inside the envelope. "Does this picture make you think of anyone here in the village?"

"Nope. The baseball cap is nothing unusual, and the shot was taken of the birds in the yard. The tall hibiscus bush hides the back of the head, so I can't see the hair color. But it makes me think of that note in Marge's office, the one where she had jotted down 'J. Yancey.' What if someone connected to her gambling has a mug shot that bears a resemblance, someone whose last name or alias is Yancey?"

Will gave me another thoughtful look, and I continued. "Would this guy have left fingerprints when he knocked or rang the doorbell?" I asked.

"Not if he was careful. Plus, an entryway collects lots of prints and they get smudged. It's not as simple as it sounds. I'm thinking about that name, though. I'll run it through our database and see what turns up."

"I've turned up a couple more things. They may not matter much, but I'll tell you anyway." Will nodded and gave me a smirky grin. "Are you patronizing me?" I demanded.

"Sorry if I gave that impression. See, you get this light in your eyes when you talk about the case, like it brings you alive and fires you up. You love detective work, don't you?"

Sighing, I calmed myself. "I like solving puzzles, finding answers to hard questions. And I'm determined to keep searching until one of us finds out who did this."

Will's face became serious. "I'm here today, more as a friend saying hello on his day off. But as a police detective, I have to caution you again--"

"I know, I know. Leave it to the professionals. You know, I'm going to come across *some* things in the course of talking with neighbors from day to day. If I stumble on something, shouldn't I share it with you?"

"Of course. Go ahead with what you have. Then I have a personal question."

Now he had me distracted. But I gathered my thoughts again. "Okay, two things. One, I stopped by to see an older, shut-in couple on Wednesday. Like everybody else around here, Miss Glory brought up Marge's death. One side of her home faces Marge's house and the marina, so I asked her if she remembered seeing anyone around either place on Monday night––from her windows, of course.

"She remembered seeing someone on the front porch at dusk, around seven; said it could have been male or female, only saw their back. This person had short grayish hair and wore dark pants and a dark jacket. That's not much to go on, but it's a different person than this picture Darlene took with her cellphone."

"Let me get this down." He reached into his jeans pocket and brought out a small black notebook with a pen attached. He jotted down a few notes. "What's the second thing?"

"The second thing is Candy Freeman. That's the woman who stopped at your table last night right before I finished my last song."

Will nodded. "The one who looked like a model and liked flaunting it?"

"Yes. I saw her at the pool Wednesday afternoon. She said something smart-alecky about me finding Marge dead. I asked if she'd had issues with Marge, and she seemed alarmed by my question. During our conversation, she made sure to let me know she'd been visiting her husband at the nursing home on the night of the murder. So last night, before I went to my gig, I stopped by the nursing home and visited Mr. Freeman. I stole a peek at the guest register, and it showed Candy had been there Monday morning, not Monday night. Plus, Mr. Freeman seemed perfectly lucid when I talked to him, not the empty-headed invalid Candy had described to me."

Will made a few more notes and looked up. "Anything else?"

"That's it. Now, what's your personal question?"

"Will you have dinner with me tonight?"

Like I said, he gets right to the point.

Will Hendrix was a fine-looking man. I decided he might be younger than me, but not much. His mischievous brown eyes had intrigued me from the start. And now, he wanted to take me out to dinner.

"Tonight?" I asked.

"Sure. I have the day off and I thought we could try the seafood restaurant downtown on Tenth Street."

Taken by surprise, I couldn't think of a reason to say no. "I might keep asking you about the murder case," I said. "Would that ruin your evening?"

"We'll talk about whatever you like. I want to get to know you better."

We agreed he'd pick me up at six for a casual evening together. No dressing up. When he drove away, I stood with my palms up and said aloud, "What just happened?"

Will could be charming and magnetic. He could also be aloof and intimidating. I couldn't resist spending time with him, learning more about his job and what he might be learning about Marge's murder.

But what appealed to me more was my quiet, unassuming next-door neighbor. Milo had been at the Midnight Blues for the whole evening after telling me he wasn't interested in the blues. He made me feel willing to be vulnerable. To stuff my reservations and hang-ups about relationships in a trash bin. There was still much to learn about Milo.

Chapter 12

At midday, the sun boiled down and turned our street into a hot griddle. But I needed a walk and headed for the lake. I would have dragged Rosanna along with me, but she was out grocery shopping again. Her job was full time now, and her Saturdays filled with errands.

The street took me past Howard's place, but I saw no sign of him or Tate. Tammy and Darlene lived across the street, and I glanced in that direction. Their car was gone; maybe they were shopping as well.

Their door swung open, and Darlene hopped down the steps, waving at me. "Celia! Wait up," she called out. I turned reluctantly. I had no intention of stirring up more trouble between the Gossip Sisters.

Darlene handed me a glossy photo of Candy holding her white poodle. It was Princess, the little dog Mr. Freeman had called Puff Ball. He would love this picture. I gave Darlene a wide grin and a quick hug. "Thanks!"

"I wanted to get this to you while I have the chance. Tammy thinks I don't know how to use her printer. Heck fire, I even found her photo paper and made it look professional. You like it?"

"It looks great. I'm going to frame this and take it to him today."

Darlene's eyes drooped. If I were going to the circus without her, she couldn't have looked more disappointed.

"Where's Tammy?" I asked.

"Gone to get an oil change. She won't be gone long."

"When she comes back, tell her I'm going to Silver Palms in a couple hours to see Vince Freeman. My car's a two-seater, but I have room for you. I know you'd like to give him the picture you took. After last night, I don't want to take you anywhere unless she agrees. Call me, Darlene, and let me know."

"She doesn't know I often use her printer. It's not that she would mind, but I don't have much else to do, other than try to outsmart her." Her eyes were bright with mischief and we both giggled. "I'll show her the picture on my camera and tell her we both want to show it to him, because he misses his dog."

With the photo in hand, I continued toward the lake. The caution tape had been removed from the front yard, but it still sealed off the front door. As I moved on around the house on the path to the marina, I realized the backyard tape was gone as well. In the backyard, Howard stood under a huge spreading oak, gazing at the water. I was hesitant to disturb him, but he turned toward me. The shade looked inviting, and I joined him. A breeze wafted in across the lake, bringing a light scent of swimming fish and sun-kissed water.

"What's that you're carrying?" he said, twisting his head so he could see the picture. "Oh, it's that woman from last night. She could not stop talking and she couldn't keep her hands off me. We had to leave early, she bugged me so much. Tate would've stayed and gawked at her all night."

"Come on, Howard, she's a beautiful woman. But let me warn you: If she's draping herself all over you, it means she's convinced you're loaded."

"You think I don't know that? I know her type. Hey, I get lonely sometimes, but that woman would be a continual headache. And why's she spending the evening with Tate and me when her husband sits up there in the nursing home?"

"She says Mr. Freeman wants her to be happy," I said, keeping a straight face.

"Well, she's not going to get her 'happy' from me, or my money either!" I'd never heard him mention his finances, and a guarded look suddenly replaced his indignant glare. He glanced back at the water, where small brown ducks swam among the reeds, bobbing for minnows and tadpoles.

"That's right. You'll need your money when you buy this place," I said.

"You know, I was content just to live here, my favorite place in the world. We came here when I was little, when it was a fishing resort. We'd spend a couple of weeks here every summer. Then I moved here, shortly after Marge bought it. She was so stressed all the time. I wanted to buy it from her then, but all we did was argue about it. I only wanted to help."

Listening to him, I pictured a little boy with his parents and his older sister, back in the forties, enjoying the fishing and canoeing. Then I remembered Marge, a week ago, sitting in her office, her face creased with frowns. Was she worrying over the finances, or wishing Howard would leave her alone?

All I knew for sure is she never seemed to like him. I wasn't buying his version. He didn't want to help her. He wanted the place for himself.

"She doesn't need your help anymore," I said. "How convenient that she's no longer in your way." My bitterness toward Howard boiled over. I was fed up with his arrogance.

His hard features returned, and he swore under his breath as I walked away. I would keep my eye on him. He could have been the person Glory Bea saw hunched over at Marge's front door. And here he was, standing in her backyard as if he couldn't wait to own it himself. Like they say, it's often a relative or someone close to the victim who turns out to be the murderer. As far as I was concerned, he had more motive to kill Marge than anyone I knew.

***

Darlene showed up around two to accompany me on my visit to Vince Freeman. Tammy had called earlier, assuring me she had no objections. She seemed to be happy Darlene was making friends on her own. She'd seen the picture on Darlene's camera, thought it was adorable, and she understood Darlene wanting Vince Freeman to see it.

How would Candy feel about us visiting her husband? Surely, she wouldn't mind. If I had a husband stuck in a nursing home, I'd be happy if he had lots of visitors. Still, I hoped Candy wouldn't be there when we arrived, or even show up before we left. She could be difficult. Almost always annoying.

We strolled into the lobby and both of us signed the register, Darlene looking as pleased as if she'd signed a congressional bill into law. With a solemn face, the nurse warned us, "This is not one of his better days." She escorted us to his room and invited us to stay, as long as he remained calm.

He was the same man, but with a totally different demeanor. I had seen him the day before, so I gave him a big smile and said, "Back again!" He showed no sign of recognition.

"Did you have an appointment?" he asked. "Where is my secretary? Jean?"

"Mr. Freeman, I saw you yesterday. I'm Celia Dawson. This is my neighbor, Darlene Jessup." He gave us a blank stare.

I took the photo of Candy and Princess, now framed, and showed it to him. His eyes softened a little. "Cute puppy," he said, but there was no light of recognition on his face. His room was larger than most, more like a cozy den. I placed the frame on a table beside a leather recliner, hoping he'd be thrilled to find it on a better day when he could remember his Puff Ball.

Disappointment showed in Darlene's long face, but she could see there was no use trying to communicate with Mr. Freeman. We left earlier than we had expected. Home seemed like a wonderful place to return to, where life held the same reality day after day.

Thinking of Candy, I softened a little. She might be shallow and greedy, but she had spoken the truth: At least part of the time, her husband had no idea who she was. And that had to be a lonely, desolate feeling, to have a husband still living who was already lost to her.

We drove home with the top down, our gray hair blowing in the fresh air. I was grateful to have a sound body and a clear mind. I had no idea what Darlene was thinking. But she looked my way and spoke loudly, wanting to be heard over the rushing wind. "I'm still glad we got to give him that picture."

She made me smile. There was something dear and sweet about Darlene.

Chapter 13

Saturday evening at the Saltwater Grill, Will and I sat sipping lemonade and poring over the menu. He had changed from jeans and sneakers to khakis, loafers and a cotton knit polo shirt. I wore a pink sundress, displaying upper arms that were only slightly flabby. I think we were pleased with ourselves, knowing we took a few pains to look nice.

We got the business of ordering our dinners out of the way, then settled down for a relaxed chat.

"I finally have you to myself," he said.

And suddenly, Candy was standing at our table. "Ooh, how cool to see you two," she squealed, still managing to keep the volume down. "You both know Neil," she said.

Her companion, with his hand tucked around her waist, was none other than my accompanist and singing partner. He nodded at us with an uneasy smile. Was he self-conscious? I'd always thought him to be confident and self-assured.

Candy looked at us as if she expected an invitation to sit and join us.

Will spoke up. "We all know where the good food is, don't we? Nice of you to stop and say hello. Enjoy your evening."

Neil looked relieved as they returned to the hostess for seating.

Will turned his plastered-on smile to me and let his features relax. His thoughts were so obvious, I wanted to laugh. He didn't want company, and he got rid of them, politely and graciously. How could two people such as us, so naturally attuned to one another, not already be in love? *Because it's not meant to be*, I reminded myself. *But he could be a great friend.*

As the evening wore on, Will filled me in on his life. He was ex-military, from the Air Force; he'd been married nine years, no children, when his wife left him for another man. For a while he had enjoyed the single scene. Now, many years later, he was still single and not enjoying it so much.

"I like making my own decisions, with no one to object. But it's lonely at night, on the weekends, holidays, that sort of thing. My parents are both gone, but I have a brother with a wife and kids. I enjoy spending time with them, but it makes me envious." He studied my face. "How about you?"

I slid my plate to the side and folded my arms on the table. "Drew and I met in college. We were studying to be teachers, hit it off right away. We both loved music, enjoyed the same kind of movies, the same humor. When we graduated and landed teaching positions in the same high school, we set our wedding date. We were married for two years, and I never noticed a problem.

"Except he wanted children so badly, and it wasn't happening. We went to fertility specialists. The problem was with him; he could not father a child. It went downhill from there."

"And…?" Will prodded me.

"He admitted he'd wanted to marry me to give him children to carry on his family name. He wanted kids around the table, the white picket fence, a dog, and a cat. It was not my fault we couldn't have that. I suggested adopting."

The rest of the story was hard to talk about, but I plugged along. "Drew said if he'd wanted to adopt children, he could have married a man. It was painful to hear, but I saw the truth in his eyes. He said if he couldn't raise his own children, he wasn't interested in children, that he would always love me, but not enough to remain my husband. Bottom line: he was bisexual, but preferred men. He had never told me till then. He'd been willing to devote his whole life to me, in order to have children. With that dream gone, he wanted to move on."

"That hit you pretty hard?"

"I don't know that I've ever recovered, not fully." Admitting that to him was not easy. I wanted to be stronger, not a weak victim consumed with self-pity.

"So, you never remarried."

"Not yet," I said, grinning at him. "I've had plenty of male friends. But I tend to keep them at arm's length. Who needs more disappointment?"

Will sighed. "I would say 'give yourself some time,' but I guess you've done that."

In the packed restaurant, the background buzz of conversation and laughter was oddly relaxing. Will had more questions.

"So, do you have any other family? Anyone close, besides Rosanna?"

"Parents passed on years ago. No siblings. And no children, although I could have had children." That's when I almost gave in to tears, but I held them back. "Rosanna has to serve as my sister and my cousin, all rolled into one."

"Well, this sure beats talking about the case," Will said with a chuckle.

"I'm a frustrated, wannabe detective. I have to talk about the case," I protested.

So, we did. Will admitted he hadn't turned up any new clues. The only thing he had so far was the photo I gave him, the report of what Glory Bea had seen, and the information I'd given him that morning about Candy's phony alibi.

I filled him in about Jennifer finding a second check book in the wall safe, plus Marge's personal journal, which Jennifer took home with her.

Will's face went on full alert. "I wasn't informed of a wall safe."

"It was the day after you were there. I guess you need to come back. Rosanna's the temporary manager and she has the combination, plus the access codes to the bank account."

"I need to get that journal from the daughter, as well. I should come back to the office in the morning," Will said.

"Oh no," I said. "Marge's memorial is in Tampa in the morning. Rosanna and I plan to go. I want to check out the family and see if I get any odd vibes."

"I should be there too. Ms. Coleman's daughter is not keeping me informed about things."

"She told us the journal was special to her, and she wanted to have a last visit with her mother——you know, reading the journal. She could bring it to the memorial and turn it over."

Breaking our chain of thought, our harried server stopped at the table and placed the ticket face-down next to Will. We smiled our thanks, and she rushed on to another table.

"One more thing: You should know I went back to see Candy's husband this afternoon," I told him. "When I saw Vince on Friday, I wondered what he was even doing in a nursing home. He seemed normal in every way I could recognize.

"But then today, he was a different man. I don't think he knew himself, or what planet he was on. Now I understand why she thinks it does no good to visit him. But his awareness seems to come and go."

"I can double-check that alibi," he told me. "She might have skipped signing in on Monday night. But we have no reason to consider her a suspect in the murder."

"I know. But I wondered why she would make up a story if she wasn't guilty of something, or afraid she'd be wrongly suspected." I rubbed my chin and tried to cover a yawn.

"I take it you're growing weary of my company," Will said. His eyes twinkled, but he seemed concerned.

"Not weary of your company––weary, as in 'I'm tired and I want my jammies'."

"We could both wear jammies," he said, his eyes warm and wistful.

He said that as if he took for granted he'd sleep with me that night. Then again, he might only be clowning around.

"What fun! A pajama party," I quipped. "As you know, I've had a few years' experience sleeping alone. I'm used to it now."

He grinned and gave me a wink. This was the same man who had been so gruff with me days earlier, warning me to leave the investigation alone. Now we were friends, sharing information. I appreciated his honesty and integrity. I even admired his good looks and trim build, but I knew I had to keep my distance.

Maybe it was my usual reluctance to let any man get close to me. And maybe my heart was already slipping away toward another man.

When we left the restaurant, I noticed Neil and Candy, still at their table, heads close together with dreamy expressions on their faces. He was with a married woman, and he probably didn't have a clue. I knew he'd be bothered when he found out.

We drove home through the dark, flower-scented evening, with orange trees blooming all around town. As we pulled into my driveway, I wondered about Will's age, but didn't want to ask him outright. We had already shared some personal memories, so I had the courage to pry a little more. "Will, are you anywhere close to retirement?"

"I could retire now; I'm sixty-four. But I don't know what I'd do with myself. I like my work. As long as I can stay fit and perform my duties, I'll stay on the job."

"Is there really enough in this sleepy little town to keep you busy?"

"Drugs and burglaries are enough to keep us busy. I'm thankful the homicide rate is fairly low."

"It might be low in town, but it's pretty high in my neighborhood," I said, hoping he knew my sarcasm was not directed at him. "Ever think about going it alone, being a private investigator?"

"I'll admit, it's crossed my mind. I could pick and choose cases, manage my own time. Wouldn't matter if I made less money." He grinned at me in the semidarkness. "Plus, you could get a license and be my sidekick."

"Now don't laugh, but that sounds interesting. Except I'd want my own agency: Dawson Investigations––how does that sound?"

"Sounds dangerous. God, I was only kidding."

Laughing, I covered his hand with mine. "Thanks, Will. I enjoyed this evening. Can't ask you in because I really am ready for my jammies." I released his hand and reached for my door handle.

Before I could open the car door, he asked me to hold on. He came around, drew me out of the car, and escorted me four steps to the front door of my house. I fumbled for my keys and unlocked the door, feeling awkward. "You're such a gentleman; I'm honored," I told him. "Thanks again for dinner."

"Let me know if you find more clues," he said, as his face drew closer to mine.

"You know I will." Looking downward and replacing the keys in my purse, I dodged the kiss.

Gently, he said goodnight. I stepped inside, relieved to be back home.

I planned to go to Marge's memorial service the next day in Tampa, but I didn't have to leave early. As much as I wanted to slip into a soft gown and robe, I changed instead into jeans, a T-shirt, and my walking sneakers. I had missed my evening walk and sometimes that walk was more important than other times. Tonight, it felt important.

Less than a week had passed since Marge's death. No suspect was in custody. The killer was still free. My phone and house key went into my pocket, and I picked up a small spray can of mace and headed out.

I usually left by the front door, made a circle around the block, then came back home towards the back of my house, which would lead me past the outside area where Milo often sat. Instead, I went out the back to be sure I wouldn't miss him. He had been on my mind since the night before, where he'd sat at the bar for three hours, watching me in the mirror.

Approaching his patio, I saw him in his usual seat. No beer and tinted glasses. He wore a ball cap, held a bottle of water, and had a blank expression on his face.

"You're home early," he said.

I took a couple of steps closer and sat in his other chair. "Doesn't take that long to have dinner."

"You wore jeans?" he asked.

"I wore a dress, but I changed as soon as I got home."

"Let's see, what's next . . . Did you have a nice time?" He scratched his chin.

"I guess. The shrimp were good. How did you know where I was?"

"I asked Rosanna. But I guess it's none of my business."

We sat quietly. The cicadas sang and crickets chirped.

Finally, he spoke again. "You didn't bring him in, and you avoided his kiss."

"What? You were spying on me?"

"Covert operations. I'm good at it."

I glared at him, and he spoke again. "You're not playing games with him, are you?"

"I don't play games––well, I kid around with you––but I don't toy with people's feelings," I said.

"Excuse me if I sound whiny, but you're always turning me away, trying to palm me off on Rosanna or somebody. Then out of the blue, you're off on a date with Mr. Police Detective."

"Well, I sent him home. And whose chair am I sitting in right now?"

We listened to a whippoorwill and more bugs chirping while Milo studied the darkness. Then he turned to me. "Did you ever read one of my books?"

"Not yet. This murder has been on my mind. In fact, that's why I agreed to go with Hendrix to dinner. I made it clear I wanted to talk about the case, which we did."

No reply from Milo, so I kept going. "I haven't taken time to find a bookstore or order a book online. Do you have any extra copies?"

"Sure. Come inside and pick one out." He got up, strolled to his back steps, and held the door for me.

His books were lined up on a shelf in his office/work-out room. I asked what he'd recommend, and he handed me his most recent, a suspense novel. I smiled my approval and looked at the cover: *The Fourth Vector* by Miles Delaney. Then he took that copy back and fished for another book from a box in his storage closet. "Here, take a new one. I've signed this one, too. A gift from me."

"Thanks, Milo." I smiled into his clear gray eyes. The soft light from his desk lamp illuminated every plane of his face. My heart woke up, even as I covered a yawn and clutched the book to my chest.

He must have found it endearing, because suddenly I was in his arms. Strong arms that held me captive and cuddled me at the same time. The book slid from my hands, and he crushed me against his chest. And then his lips, those beautiful lips, were so close to mine I felt the warmth from his breath. He nibbled gently at my mouth and my bones seemed to melt. A fingertip traced along my cheek, his mouth nudged my lips apart and we connected in a mind-blowing kiss. I don't remember how my arms got around his neck, but I hung on desperately.

If I had died right then, I would've died happy, knowing I had been waiting for that kiss all my life.

And then the rascal drew back, grinned, and said, "You think Will could top that?"

Still weak and limp, I stared at him. How could he shake me up like that and be so flippant about it?

He kissed me again––same earthquake. I pulled away reluctantly and tried to find my balance.

"Milo, I have to go home now. We need to talk about this, later. And . . . wow! But I need to go home now."

He handed me the book I had dropped, and he cupped my face in his hands, caressing me with his eyes. The smile he gave me was nearly as powerful as his kisses.

I walked home, a few inches off the ground. Milo followed closely and watched me from my back steps as I floated inside. Finally, I pulled on a nightgown and crawled into my lonely bed. I imagined resting my head on Milo's bare chest.

My breathing slowed, and I fell asleep.

Chapter 14

Sunday morning, five days after her body was discovered, we were on our way to Tampa to the memorial service for Marge. We'd left with plenty of time to get to the 11:00 service. Rosanna drove, I rode in front with her, Tammy and Darlene sat in back. Tammy didn't like to drive in larger cities where she didn't know her way around, so Rosanna offered them a ride. We'd be having our own memorial service at Moonstone Lake the following evening.

Rosanna had reported to Jennifer that eight of us would attend the service in Tampa, where Marge's children and ex-husband lived. I thought it was a respectable number, since most of our residents are elderly and would naturally choose the one at home on Monday night. Of course, Howard and Tate would be there. Also, Devon and Whitney, who were both active and helpful around the village. I took special note of who attended.

Why? Because I wanted to know the answer to everything. Police detectives could show their badges and question anyone to investigate an unsolved crime. I had no authority to walk up to any of Marge's relatives and ask them blunt questions, nor did I want to trouble anyone who might be grieving for Marge that day. But I had my own practical reasons for attending her memorial: I wanted to meet the rest of her family, to watch, study, and listen for any scrap of anything that might lead to finding her killer.

I hated to say much in front of the sisters in the backseat. There was no telling who Darlene might innocently blab to. Or Tammy, for that matter. They hadn't been dubbed The Gossip Sisters without earning the title.

Tammy spoke up. "I'll tell you, I'm only going to this thing out of curiosity. But *any* time Darlene can take a road trip, she's fired up and ready to go."

"And how!" Darlene blurted.

"Rosanna, I know she was your friend," Tammy continued, "but I could not abide the woman. She was hardly ever pleasant, much less friendly. Still, I can't imagine why anyone would go so far as to kill her."

Rosanna gripped the wheel of the car. "She was my friend, and Celia's too. I worked with her almost every day, so we grew a little closer. It was hard, at first, getting used to her bursts of anger and constantly changing emotions. But if you learn to take the bad with the good, you sometimes find out there's more good than you thought. See what I'm saying?" Her hand flapped in a dismissive way. "I learned to ignore her bad moods."

I pressed Rosanna a little further. "What made Marge tick?" I asked. "What made her so ill-tempered and volatile?"

Rosanna hesitated, choosing her words carefully. "Sometimes, when things were quiet and peaceful, Marge opened up about her past. She rarely mentioned her parents, and I never heard her mention brothers or sisters. We only knew about Howard when he told the cops he was her brother.

"But she was tired of making enemies everywhere she turned." Rosanna paused again, touched under one eye where a brimming tear was about to fall. "Marge went so many years, undiagnosed. Always being punished for her outbursts and suffering from frequent depression. When her marriage to Dan fell apart, she went for counseling and discovered she was bipolar. It made her furious, because it seemed to put all the blame on her for the failed marriage. Then she read up on the subject and began to understand her changing moods." Rosanna paused while she changed lanes, preparing to take the Tampa exit.

"She got quite a bit of money in her divorce settlement and impulsively bought the park during a hyper, manic stage, thinking she could do anything. Then the burden of running the place weighed her down and she'd become depressed and let things go. It all figures into her gambling habit, too." Rosanna drew a sigh.

"Marge really loved her two kids, but I'm afraid her son has some of her same problems. She ran out of patience with him. He always needed money, and she'd flat-out refuse him and send him to his father. Her life was tragic, y'know? And I feel bad talking about her."

I almost wished I had not asked Rosanna about it. But what else was there to do on the long drive? Talk about the weather or tell jokes? Marge was on our minds, and I was glad to know the whole story about her.

The sisters were strangely quiet. I glanced at Darlene in the rearview mirror, and her eyes were large and thoughtful. She and Tammy stared out the windows and made no more comments.

***

The memorial service was held in a large stone and stucco Episcopal church. Natural sunlight filtered through the stained-glass windows, casting a soothing glow across the polished pews. The smell of lemon wax and flowers filled the cavernous room. Huge arrangements of white lilies and pale-yellow roses flanked the pulpit. Front and center, on a table of carved wood, sat a beautiful urn filled with Marge's ashes.

We followed an usher to a long pew and filed in, one by one. Devon and Whitney sat in front of us, but I hadn't spotted Howard and Tate. Soft music played as I thumbed through the memorial leaflet we had each received at the guest register. I read where it said, "She is survived by her daughter, Jennifer Lynn Coleman Hughes; her son, Jason Alan Coleman; her brother, Howard Alan James, and granddaughter Alaina Margaret Hughes."

I turned casually and peered across the aisle. Howard and Tate were seated with the family. Looked like everyone had arrived.

The service began, and we heard brief eulogies given by her two children. Rosanna could have given a beautiful, moving eulogy, but had not been asked. No doubt she would have declined anyway. We came only to show our respect. And possibly glean some information.

The light meal afterward was served buffet-style in a large dining room which could have held several hundred people. Only thirty or so arrived and walked awkwardly to the grieving family and relatives to offer condolences. We spoke to Jason, Jennifer and her husband, their daughter Alaina, and Howard by turn.

I came to Jason first, who looked like he had a slow-burning fire in his chest, barely able to keep the smoke from coming out of his ears. When I spoke to him, he nodded dismissively, hardly giving me a glance. I wondered about his anger while I studied his face: fair-skinned with sharp features, blond hair like his sister.

When I reached for Jennifer's hand, she introduced her husband, Brandon. A slender young girl, twelve or thirteen, stood between them, her eyes red from crying. Jennifer slid her arm around the girl's shoulders. "This is our daughter, Alaina. She misses her nana."

I merely smiled and patted her arm.

Howard was last. I had recently spoken to him harshly, not sure he truly grieved for his sister. I offered my condolences awkwardly, knowing my words sounded formal and insincere. He accepted my handshake, but avoided my eyes.

However, he pulled Rosanna to his chest like a child clutches a stuffed animal. Anyone could gain comfort from Rosanna, and Howard seemed starved for her touch.

Rosanna and I, followed by Tammy and Darlene, walked together to the buffet, then settled at a round table with our hors d'oeuvres, tiny cakes, and iced tea. Whitney and Devon joined us. Howard and Tate sat at a table with relatives, so Devon was the only male at our table.

"Ladies, I'm so glad to be in such lovely company," he said, beaming.

"I'm glad to be in your company too, you handsome devil," Darlene said.

Tammy's mouth dropped open. "I never know what you'll say next," she muttered to her sister.

I rolled my eyes at Whitney, who hid her chuckles behind a napkin. As the subdued chattering continued, I glanced around the room, studying people.

Jason remained tight-lipped and solemn. He sometimes spoke briefly to his sister, but ignored everyone else at the table, even sad-eyed Alaina, who sat between her parents. Dark-haired Brandon chatted with Howard and Tate. To Tate's left sat a pretty redhead around fifty, and between her and Jason, sat a magnetic man in his sixties with streaks of gray in his brown hair, probably Marge's ex-husband. Far from grieving, the couple seemed bored and distracted, as if they'd sooner scrub toilets than attend this memorial. I knew they were there solely to support his children and grandchild.

Excusing myself, I stood and walked across the room, pretending to search for the ladies' room. On my way, I passed behind Jason and Jennifer where they sat. My walk was leisurely, as if unconcerned, but my ears were wide open. His head darted toward his sister, and I heard his terse words. "I am her firstborn, not you. Mom hasn't done right by me."

Jason's words still ran through my mind when I found the ladies' room down the hall. I entered one of the two stalls, put the lid down, and sat to think. I heard the door open, the sound of footsteps, then the sound of water running in the sink.

A voice spoke. "Did you see that young redhead with Daniel Coleman? That's Sherry, his second wife. Why is it wealthy men seem to ditch the mother of their children and look for a younger woman?"

"Oh honey, it's not just wealthy men who do that. They all want younger women."

"I heard it cost Dan a ton of money to divorce Jennifer's mother."

"Yeah, and it still makes his second wife furious. But they're rid of Marge for good, now. Sherry has always hated that woman. Alaina calls Sherry 'Gigi,' but she called Marge 'Nana.' Sherry wants to be the *only* grandmother. She looks grim today, but she's cheering inside."

"Marjorie Coleman was murdered. No one should be happy about that."

"I think Sherry is."

The door opened again and closed on the sound of retreating footsteps. I slipped silently out the door behind them while fishing in my bag for my phone. They went back to the banquet hall and to the serving table for more iced tea. I followed them and made a show of taking a picture of the table's centerpiece, then angled slightly toward them and snapped a second picture before anyone noticed.

Turning away, I studied the photo. It showed their faces well enough that Jennifer might be able to identify them for me. I wouldn't bother her with it today, certainly not today. But I would see her to-morrow night at our own memorial service. I hoped she could identify the women, who seemed to know intimate details about Daniel and Sherry Coleman.

As for the second memorial service on Monday evening, it would be a much different gathering. I had no idea how prophetic my thoughts would be.

Chapter 15

My cell phone rang its familiar jingling tune, and I dashed from my bedroom up the hall toward the living room where I'd left it. I had changed into some comfy denim shorts and a cotton knit shirt. I grabbed my purse and rummaged inside for the demanding phone. The screen displayed a number I didn't recognize.

"Hello?"

"Wanna take a nice, soothing boat ride to calm your frazzled nerves?"

"Milo!"

"Yeah, that's me," he said.

"Well, I just got home and haven't had a chance to catch my breath. Come on over and tell me what you have in mind."

It was close to four, and I was happy to be home again. I wasn't quite ready to go somewhere else. Milo's head bobbed along outside my front windows, and I opened the door.

His smile connected with me like a happy tune when he walked in. I gestured to my recliner, but he sat on the couch instead. "You look like you need the recliner––unless you want to sit here by me." He patted the cushion next to him.

The pull was strong, but I settled into the recliner, leaned back against the softness, and turned my head toward him. "I'm so relieved to have that trip behind me. Nothing about it was bad, really, but I've been tense from the time I left till the time I got back here."

"You need a change. We'll sit here as long as you want. But you might enjoy getting out on the lake, feeling the wind in your hair, smelling the fresh air."

"You have a boat?"

"I have a Bayliner down at the marina. Mostly use it for fishing, but it's good for cruising across the lake, seeing the sights." He studied my face. "I have some chilled wine and a few snacks in the cooler. It's all on ice. No rush."

"It sounds heavenly."

"Tell me about your trip."

"First of all, I still can't get used to knowing Howard is Marge's brother."

"I wasn't any secret," he said.

My eyebrows shot up. "How did you know? I've been here for two years, and I didn't know. They didn't exactly broadcast it."

"I make it my business to know things."

"You sure do. Maybe I need some lessons."

"I'd be happy to oblige," Milo said, reaching to squeeze my hand. "What else happened?"

"At the meal after the service, I picked up on a few things. Marge's son Jason seemed dark and angry, even rude to me when I was introduced. I met Jennifer's husband and daughter. An older couple was with them, probably Marge's ex-husband and his wife. I didn't meet them, but I overheard a conversation in the restroom. Two women gossiping about Dan and Sherry Coleman, saying Sherry hated Marge and was glad someone killed her."

"Did you speak to the women or recognize them?" Milo was alert and intense, his brow furrowed.

"No, they didn't see me or even know I heard them. But I got their photo with my phone when they weren't looking."

"Well, good for you, Nancy Drew!"

I chose to take his remark as a compliment. If he'd called me Miss Marple, it would have been a major blunder. I always thought movies from the Miss Marple era portrayed any woman over fifty as wearing pearls and a Sunday-go-to-meeting hat, even when wearing an apron, and they usually carried a walking cane. That was so not me.

"I was on the lookout for disgruntled relatives," I said, "and that would certainly include Marge's son, and maybe Dan Coleman's wife. I'm not saying either one should be a murder suspect, but it's something to consider."

"No wonder you're looking pale. Ready for some open water and sunshine?"

"Lead the way," I said, rising from my seat.

Milo stood and tucked a finger under my chin. My heart did a little tango, and I expected him to kiss me. But he only spoke softly. "It can get damp and chilly out on the water. You want to take a light jacket?"

Holding up my forefinger, I said, "Good idea." I scurried back to my bedroom for a zip-up sweatshirt, all the while wondering how Milo knew my cell phone number. We'd never needed each other's number, as close as we lived. But, like he told me, he made it his business to know things.

***

Milo helped me into his boat, handed me the small cooler, then hopped aboard. I'd seen the boat, never realizing it belonged to Milo. He kept it so clean and polished, it always looked new. We backed out of the marina into the lake, turned and headed straight across toward the other side. The breeze in my hair brought me back into the land of the living, and the sun warmed my skin.

We slowed as we approached the other shore. Milo turned the boat, and we moved slowly along the shoreline, looking at all the lovely homes built around the lake.

"A few of these lakes are connected by canals. We can check out Pineapple Lake and Lake Borden. Or we can putter around Moonstone Lake."

"You're the captain," I told him. "I'd like to see the other lakes. Right now, I'm enjoying seeing these houses up close."

Milo geared down to trolling speed and pulled the cooler closer. He opened the lid and gestured to the contents: a corked bottle of white zinfandel, a plastic bag filled with green grapes, and two small containers filled with cheese cubes and crackers. He also had clear plastic cups for the wine. "Help yourself," he told me.

"I don't think I'm ready for food. Can I pour you some wine?"

"Maybe half a cup. There's a shady area farther ahead where we can drop anchor and have a little picnic."

I poured wine for both of us and closed the cooler. We motored through the water, past cozy cottages with small boat docks, and past huge modern homes with elaborate swimming pools and fishing piers. Some of the boat docks had screened porches on the end, where you could view the whole lake as if floating in air.

We chatted about the scenery, the water birds along the shore. And, inevitably, we drifted back to the topic that stayed on our minds: Who killed Marge?

"They say people are often killed by relatives or close friends," I said. "That's why I watched Marge's children so closely. And I've wondered about Howard from the start. He was so upset when we found the body. But that doesn't mean he couldn't have killed her."

"You first thought they were lovers, didn't you?"

"At first, I thought he was gay. That was the rumor, anyway. So many women took food to him, thinking they'd win him over with their cooking. Tate was always there. But no one knew it was his cousin, so some folks thought Tate was his boyfriend. You know, women can find no other conclusion when their feminine charms don't work on a man." I grinned at Milo.

"Hope no one thinks I'm gay," he said. "Of course, I've kept most women away by sitting around looking like a bum. It sure turned you off for a long time."

I stared into Milo's eyes. He had that little smirk again, like he was full of secrets. "I know so little about you," I said. "You've changed before my eyes, but you're still the same man. I want to know everything about you."

"Hell, I don't even know everything about me." He shrugged his shoulders.

We were approaching a long pier where a man stood, leaning against the railing. As we drove by, we both raised a hand in greeting. He stared back at us and took a puff on a short cigarette pinched between his thumb and forefinger. He did not wave or acknowledge us, but pushed his sunglasses to the top of his head and watched us pass.

I didn't think he could have recognized me, since I was wearing sunglasses, but I recognized him. I turned to Milo. "That was Marge's son, Jason, still looking sulky. Was he smoking pot?"

"Looked like it." Milo was steering toward a canal, which would take us to Lake Borden. "What do you think he's doing here? Doesn't he live in Tampa?"

"Yes. And I saw him there, a few hours ago. Looks like he has friends on this lake."

"And?" He gave me a look that may have had the power to read my mind. Who knew, with Milo?

"And . . . this lets me know he could have been right here, on this lake, the night of his mother's murder. He could have come quietly to her back door by boat, unobserved. He could have visited her, argued with her, maybe high on something strong. And he could have killed her in a rage, then slipped back across the lake. But he would need a motive."

"If he was out of his head and furious that she wouldn't give him money, that's enough motive for some people."

"Rosanna says Marge had been threatening to take him out of her will," I said, watching Milo raise his eyebrows. I glanced back behind us. "I wonder who owns that house where we saw him on the pier."

"There are ways to find out."

"If I tell the police detectives, how can I even specify which house it was?"

"I'll get an address for you. I guess this means you'll be calling Mr. Detective, huh?"

"Not right away. Jennifer might come to our memorial service tomorrow night. I'll ask her about Jason, as casually as I can, and see what I can find out. I hate to cast doubt on her brother. He could be innocent, and the police questioning him would add more stress to the family."

"If he's innocent, he needs to be ruled out as a suspect," Milo said, his brows bunched together. "I get bad vibes from that guy. If he killed his mother, he wouldn't hesitate to come after you. And even if he didn't kill anybody, he could still come after you for raising an alarm on him."

I told Milo I'd be careful. What more could I say? It's not like I carried a gun or knew karate. I'm an amateur sleuth, not a police detective.

He spoke as if he'd read my mind. "If you were a licensed P.I., you'd have a gun to protect yourself." His forehead was creased with concern.

"I'm a wannabe investigator. I wouldn't know what to do with a gun."

We headed down a canal to Lake Borden, which was much smaller. On the side nearest downtown Conroy, Milo pointed out a modest lakeside restaurant called "Bistro on Borden."

"Ever eat there?" he asked me.

"Not yet. I've heard the food's good."

"I can vouch for that. It's not fancy or pricey, and I like the laid-back atmosphere. We should come here sometime, by boat, and park at their dock."

I nodded and smiled. I'd probably go with Milo anywhere.

We did a quick tour of Lake Borden and moved on to Pineapple Lake. This one was similar in size to Lake Borden, but on its south side grew a field of pineapple plants, where a plantation-style house stood on a hillside overlooking the field.

Most of the lakeside homes had boat docks. Marge's killer could have come from any of these docks. Her ex-husband could've had some reason to kill her, or his wife, Sherry. Anyone not wanting to be seen could have come across the lake after dark and tied up behind her house. As long as they didn't make noise and draw attention to themselves, they could slip away quietly, not needing a fast getaway.

Milo drove us back across the lake and slowly down each canal, arriving back at Moonstone Lake. He found a shady spot on the west side where the sun was low behind the trees, then cut the engine and dropped anchor.

We set the cooler between us like a table. He poured more wine. I found napkins and opened the food containers. As the day cooled down, the air turned heavenly, and a soft breeze caused the water to ripple and rock the boat gently.

"I'm already enjoying your book," I said, then popped a grape in my mouth.

"Oh yeah? Well, I sure enjoyed giving it to you." He moved his sunglasses to the front of his cap, and his lips curved upward. My cheeks grew hot, knowing we were both remembering last night's steamy kiss.

"I thought about how you came to the blues bar Friday night, staying the full three hours, then following me home like an escort. This morning, before we left for Tampa, I read a few chapters of your book while I had coffee."

A motorboat sped by in the middle of the lake and rocked our Bayliner. Small waves sloshed against its side. When it settled down, I took a sip of my wine.

"I admire your writing. I was drawn in from the first page. You write with authority and the scenes are vivid. Truth is, I get so involved in the story, I forget you're the author, and then it comes back to me: *I'm reading Milo's words*."

"I'm glad to hear it, Celia. And I gotta tell you, I stayed Friday night till you sang your last song because your voice held me captive. I connected with that voice. If I had walked in off the street, never having seen you before, I think it would have affected me the same way. I don't believe you were trying to be sultry or sexy, but it was there in your voice. And that short black dress–I couldn't take my eyes off you, so I watched your reflection in the mirror behind the bar."

"I felt that connection, too," I told him. "Like you were pulling the music from me. It's hard to explain."

"You explained it very well; there's a connection between us." He munched on a cracker while I studied his sharp eyes and intelligent face.

"You've never been married?" I asked him.

He shook his head. "The whole time I was in combat, I could've been killed on any given day. I didn't have time or opportunity to meet a woman and fall in love. And I wasn't *ready* to fall in love . . . I've been with a lot of women; they're not hard to find. But I always told them upfront not to expect anything long-term with me. I know I disappointed some of them along the way, and I'm not proud of that. I've always held something back. Sort of like you, Celia."

He was so open with me, I had to tell him about Drew and my short, disappointing marriage, things I had told Will Hendrix the night before. I hadn't planned to tell Will anything, but he had those detective skills that make you spill your life story. It was not an attempt to be close to Detective Hendrix. Not at all.

With Milo, however, I was drawing close despite my reservations. It just happened. And I shared more with him than I had with Will. Maybe part of me wanted to make up for not telling Milo first. Mostly, I wanted everything out in the open between Milo and me.

"So, do you hate the guy, or did you get over it?"

"Now that you mention it––no, I don't hate Drew. In fact, we've kept in touch over the years. He remarried––a man named Adam. They found a surrogate mother to carry a child for them. Technically, the child's father is Adam, but they're both happy with their little boy. I guess I'm still resentful, because he could've had a child with me, using a sperm donor. What's the difference? Either way, the child is not related by blood to Drew."

Milo watched me, his face expressionless. Intent, but giving nothing away.

"He cried when he left me. He said he'd always care for me, but he wanted me to have a full life with a man who could give me children. Me? I wasn't thinking about children. I wanted the man I loved to love me back, with or without children." My words were bitter.

"You still love him?"

"No." From Milo's silence, I wasn't sure he believed me. "He's like an old friend now. I remember the feelings and emotions when I *did* love him. I remember the heartbreak. But I haven't done myself any favors hanging onto my bitterness for so long."

Milo was still quiet, so my confession went a little further. "Every man I've met since Drew, good or bad, I've wanted to kick them in the butt." I slid my eyes back to Milo. He was grinning and blew me a little kiss, like he'd had me sized up from day one.

And I had to smile too, because he was right.

We pulled back into the marina, where Milo tied off the boat and gave me a hand-up onto the dock. He carried the cooler, and we strolled back up the short street to our side-by-side homes.

Reluctant to part, our goodbyes seemed awkward. We ended the day with a light kiss.

I unlocked my back door and went straight to the shower. The pounding water did not invigorate me but lulled me into a pre-slumber daze.

Dressed in a fresh nightie, I toddled to my bedroom and stared at my cold, empty bed. It was still too early to go to bed, and my recliner seemed more appealing, so I headed that way and tuned in to a mindless sitcom at low volume.

The only light came from the TV screen. Grabbing my afghan, I snuggled between the soft arms of the chair, all cozy. But I'm a realistic person, and the truth was, I was still alone.

So what? Big whoop-dee-doo. I would deal with that later.

Chapter 16

The three of us stood in Rosanna's bedroom where a brand-new Darlene stared at herself in the full-length mirror.

"How do you like it?" Rosanna asked me.

"Wow, I really do. Darlene, you look fabulous," I said.

Rosanna had decided Darlene needed a makeover. Her previously stringy hair had been trimmed and styled. It was parted in the middle and swept back on both sides, with waves touching her shoulders.

Darlene's face now had light makeup and rosier cheeks. Her dark blue eyes had a hint of soft blue shadow, and the once-gray eyelashes and brows were darker.

Rosanna had even coaxed her into a stylish summer dress with a scooped neck, cap sleeves, and a rather low-cut back. Darlene looked bright, happy, and years younger.

Her face glowed, and I asked, "How do *you* like it?"

"Are you crazy? I love it!" She stared into the mirror, touching her hair. "I haven't felt pretty in so long. Tammy says makeup is a waste of time and money. We are what we are, and that's that."

"Where'd you get that cute dress?"

"Rosanna took me shopping. We went to a discount outlet, so I wouldn't spend so much. But I really like this dress. I want to wear this next Friday night when I go with Rosanna again to the Midnight Blues place."

"She looks forward to seeing Tate," Rosanna said, lifting one eyebrow.

I half expected Darlene to protest, but she grinned and looked back at her reflection. The peach-colored dress was beautiful with her skin tone, and she puckered her coral lips as if she might kiss herself in the mirror.

"How shall I put this? You don't look phony," I said, "and the changes merely accent the good features you already have. But what a transformation––I never realized how attractive you were."

She stood and twirled the slightly flared skirt, then looked at Rosanna for more advice. "Is this too colorful to wear tonight? To Marge's memorial service? I bet Howard will bring Tate with him."

"Honey, tonight will be so different from yesterday's service in Tampa. We'll all be relaxed and informal. What you're wearing will be fine."

"I don't look forward to another sad meeting about someone who died, and I don't miss Marge all that much. I'm going because I know Howard will bring Tate. He's a relative, after all."

"I'm sure you'll get his attention," Rosanna said.

"Yeah, if prissy Candy can keep her paws off either one of them."

"Candy didn't like Marge," I told her. "Maybe she won't even come."

Darlene lifted her eyebrows at me. "If everyone stays home that didn't like her, we might have a small crowd."

Rosanna looked hurt but turned away so Darlene wouldn't see. Seven days had passed since Marge's death, and Rosanna still grieved. At least she hadn't had too much to do in preparation for tonight's memorial. Whitney had cheerfully taken that all on herself and had volunteers arranging tables and chairs for the meeting even as we spoke.

"Bet we have good attendance," I said. "Everybody'll be curious; they'll want to know about any new developments and any changes in how this place is run. People are already whispering about Howard taking over."

"You think her son and daughter will show up?" Darlene asked me.

"I hope so. I need to ask Jennifer a couple of things. Maybe I better call her." Wanting to talk in private, I headed for the kitchen, with the calico cat right behind me. Bitsy probably hoped the refrigerator door would open, and I'd deposit some fishy-smelling cat food into her dish.

Instead, I checked my phone for Jennifer's number and placed the call. "I was planning to be there," she said. "But my daughter has an upset stomach and she's clingy, missing her nana. I don't want to leave her."

"What about Jason?" I asked.

"He's not too sociable right now. And he couldn't care less about honoring Mom's memory. He's boiling mad because I've been appointed Executrix of the Will. He's older than me, you know."

"I don't mean to pry. This is only because I'm trying to find who is responsible for your mother's death. Has the will been read yet?"

"Not officially. But the attorney says Jason and I will share the proceeds when the park sells. He wants his part, and he wants it now. Like I can do anything about it."

"Jennifer, there's one more thing. Yesterday, when I was in Tampa at the service, I overheard a conversation in the lady's room. It concerned your stepmother. Are you close to her?"

"Hell no. She would have killed Mom with her bare hands if she could get away with it."

"That's about the gist of what I heard these women saying. I got their picture with my phone when they weren't watching. I wanted to show it to you tonight, so I'll know who they are."

"Why do you need that?" She sounded edgy and impatient.

"The police may need to question those women, if there's any possibility your father's wife could be a suspect in the investigation."

"Geez, I was only half-kidding when I said she'd kill her if she could. Let me think about this . . ."

"It sounded like they work in your father's company. I can leave your name out of it."

"Okay, send me the photo and, if I know them, I'll text you their names. I don't want my dad upset with me over this. He never would have killed Mom, but he really hated her. And he'll have a fit if the police question Sherry. I don't want him blaming me."

"You got it. I'll say I overheard the conversation and asked around about their names." We disconnected and I sent the photo to her five seconds later.

Rosanna and Darlene sauntered into the kitchen. Darlene reached for the door and said, "What you wanna bet Tammy hates my new look? I dread walking into our house. But she needs to get used to me doing what I want to do." She peered out a window, seeing a faint reflection. "Gosh, I hope I can keep my hair this nice."

"You'll get the hang of it," Rosanna said as Darlene eased out the door.

Rosanna turned to me and asked about the phone call.

"Nobody's coming from Tampa," I told her. Bitsy rubbed against my leg, and I bent to scratch her head. "Looks like Howard, and maybe Tate, will be the only relatives. Did you ever have a clue Marge was Howard's sister?"

"No, it never crossed my mind. They looked nothing alike. But now that we know, I can see some similarities in their dispositions."

That struck me funny, but I tried not to smile. What an understatement. They'd both been surly and disagreeable. I couldn't imagine what purpose could be served with a memorial of someone so many people disliked. But people would show up out of curiosity. And for the buffet.

***

Walking to the clubhouse, I reached for my ringing phone. When I heard Jennifer's voice, I stopped and listened carefully. "Celia, I'm texting the names of those women. They do work at Dad's office. Another thing I forgot to mention--I've been reading Mom's journal and found out her bookie's name is Jack Yancey. If you think the police need that name, now you have it."

"On that topic, the detective will be at our office in the morning. He needs to see the extra checkbook in the safe. I also told him about the journal, and he's anxious to have a look there too. Has he contacted you about that?"

"No, but he can always drive over here and get it. I can't work in another trip to Conroy right now. But let me know if anything develops on that Jack Yancey name."

I thanked her and disconnected.

As the sun dipped lower in the sky, the air cooled and soft breezes floated around me. Other people in the community were walking to the clubhouse, and several puttered by in golf carts. Parking was at a premium and the spaces filled up quickly. Some parked at the nearby shuffleboard court and walked the short distance to the clubhouse. Others parked close by in Marge's driveway.

Muffled words and soft laughter drifted through the evening air, quieter than the usual chatter heard when people gathered at the clubhouse for dances, cards, or bingo. No one appeared to be grieving, exactly. But a certain solemnity accompanies people gathering to honor a neighbor who has died. The chatter simmered down to whispers as they drew closer.

Inside the meeting room, the tables were arranged as if for a dinner or a night of bingo, but all facing the stage. One table held food from caterers, and a beverage table sat against the wall nearby.

Glory Bea stood at the end of the closest table, leaning on her walker and speaking to Darlene. Tammy was busy helping Harvey to his seat. Glory Bea leaned close to Darlene, who held her hand against her mouth looking horrified. Darlene turned away, her face red and filled with alarm.

She reached for Tammy's arm and almost dragged her away to another table. It was obvious Tammy was not used to being dragged anywhere by her sister. Her face contorted, but she went along, then fell into her seat, looking annoyed. Darlene bent low and whispered into her ear.

My curiosity was piqued, but I went in search of Whitney, wondering what was on the program. Rosanna stood with her as they skimmed over a paper with Whitney's handwriting. Devon tested the microphone and adjusted the volume. A woman I'd never met sat at an upright piano playing pleasant tunes, none especially churchy sounding, but familiar and soothing.

Whitney glanced up as I approached, and I asked if I could do anything to help. "I thought about asking you to sing, but decided that might put you on the spot," she said.

And how, I thought. Rosanna gave me a knowing smile.

"It's kinda like open-mic night. Anyone who has something to say can speak tonight," Whitney told us.

I shook my head. "I'll have a seat farther back. None of Marge's family from Tampa will be here, according to Jennifer."

The room filled up quickly. People wore curious, concerned expressions. Rosanna took a seat near the front, probably so she'd be close when she went to the microphone to reminisce about working with Marge. I bent and explained to her why I preferred to sit near the back . . . to watch the crowd more closely.

Easing my way through the people still standing, I spied Tammy and Darlene and took a seat with them. I leaned toward Darlene and asked her what Glory Bea had done to upset her.

"Maybe later," she told me. "It's too much to get into right now. Believe me."

Tammy studied Darlene. "I think she's had too much excitement. You and Rosanna are getting her all stirred up, putting things in her mind she ought not be contemplating."

Darlene glared at Tammy but said nothing. She touched her hair lightly, making sure the breeze had not disturbed the waves.

The back of my neck began to tingle with warmth, and I turned to look behind me. Milo leaned back against the wall with his arms crossed, his eyes like a telegraph line sending me messages I couldn't decipher. "Save my seat," I said to Darlene.

When I reached Milo, he slipped a hand in his pocket and drew out a folded paper. "This has the name and address of the place we saw yesterday." He leaned a little closer and murmured, "The place where we saw Marge's son smoking a joint on the boat dock."

I took the paper from him and slid it into my own pocket. "That was fast."

Again, for my ears only, he murmured, "We can talk later, but I'd wager that homeowner is a drug dealer."

With a tiny smile, I returned to my seat. I didn't ask him to join me for two reasons: First, he had chosen his exact spot in order to observe the crowd. Second, having him sit by me would set all the tongues wagging, and the evening should be all about Marge. It was hard to have a private life in a village like ours, with houses close together and full of bored and curious retired people.

The glass doors opened, and another clump of people moved inside, including Howard and Tate. Unless gossip had made the rounds already, not many people knew they were Marge's kin. The night might hold some surprises.

The meeting began with the buffet. Some may have thought that disrespectful. But Whitney announced into the mic, "This is not a church service tonight, but a memorial for our departed friend. And most of us are senior citizens, not used to eating late. I think Marge would have wanted us to have our dinner first." The crowd responded with nods and smiles.

"When I call your table number, that table can go to the buffet, then the beverage table." She reached into a plastic ice bucket full of numbers. "Table number five!" That table clapped and cheered, then looked embarrassed for their outburst, but they strolled to the tables, smug and happy. Sullen occupants of other tables crossed their arms and waited their turn.

Whitney stayed at her post, calling out the table numbers, but Devon and Rosanna offered to bring food to people with canes or walkers. Most of them were delighted with the service, but not all. Glory Bea told them, "You can bring both of us sweet tea, but we'd rather fix our own plates. We can manage." In record time, all the tables were served, and Whitney began the program.

After a welcome and some instructions about the open mic, she paused for effect, then dropped the bombshell. "We recently learned that Howard James is Marge's brother. We'd love to hear from him when he feels ready. Right now, Tate Bridges has a song for us. Tate is Howard's and Marge's only cousin."

Tate made his way to the small stage, stood behind the mic, and began to speak. "I don't have words to say. I got my feelings but they're hard to express. But I can play guitar pretty good, and Marge always loved this song I'm gonna play. She sung it a lot when we was kids, so I think of her when I hear it."

With that, he placed the mic back in the stand and lowered it enough to pick up the sound of his guitar. He began to play a folksy version of "Somewhere Over the Rainbow." The room was silent as they listened, some people dabbing at their eyes with tissues. As the song ended on a lingering note, the crowd was not sure if applause was appropriate at a memorial. But a smattering started up, then grew to whole-hearted clapping.

Tate left the stage, teary-eyed, and Whitney nodded in Howard's direction. He sat like a statue, unmoving. I was embarrassed for him, but then he stood abruptly and decisively. A robot could have walked to the stage with more enthusiasm.

Howard removed the microphone from its stand and uneasily held it close to his mouth. I don't know why people think a mic will bite them. Maybe they're worried about germs. Maybe they think it looks like they're showing off or pretending to be an entertainer. Whatever the reason, it makes folks uncomfortable, and it didn't take much to make Howard uncomfortable. And it took him a while to gather his thoughts, but his mouth finally opened.

"Marjorie Ann Coleman was born on October 26, 1938. She died at seventy-two. She worked hard to keep that a secret, but it was all in her obituary, so I'm afraid the cat's out of the bag now. I don't mind telling you I was born two years later, which makes me seventy. We used to come here on vacation with our parents when it was a fishing village. Those two weeks every spring were the happiest of our lives. I guess that's why she bought the place when she had the chance. I know that's why I came here to live when I retired. And I wanted to help her, as she had helped me over the years.

"I . . . I don't feel able to say much. I loved my sister, and I'll always love her. That says it all. I appreciate this gathering to honor her."

Howard bowed his head for a moment, then reached to replace the mic. A heavy man with pale red hair stood and spoke politely, but loud enough for all to hear. "Before you leave, can you answer a question?"

Howard looked puzzled. "What is your question?"

"Are you gonna be the new owner of this here place?"

"I have made an offer to buy Moonstone Lake Retirement Village when the estate is settled. No decisions have been made."

"I ain't meaning to cause you no more sorrow. We're worried about the future of the place, is all."

"I understand your concern, and I'll be happy to talk with you at another time, but this is not the place for that topic." Howard's voice was stiff and formal.

A woman with a heavy tan and bright-yellow bleached hair jumped to her feet. "Looks like to me, while we're all here we could get a few facts straight. Most of us didn't come tonight just to cry and get all sappy. You got something to hide?"

Howard's face turned stony, and he walked off the stage.

Whitney hurried to the microphone. "Folks, we can plan a community meeting for another evening. Tonight, we need to show some respect. Now, if anyone has some kind, respectful things to say, please come to the microphone."

Rosanna stood immediately and hurried to the stage.

I won't go into the tender speech she gave. I'll simply say it was clear she loved and missed her friend. She explained that Marge had emotional problems which caused erratic behavior. And she finished by saying if we take time to get to know someone, we can overlook some of their moods. And she vowed Marge had always treated her fairly.

When she finished, I rose and hurried to the stage. "Good evening," I said, giving everyone a warm smile and hoping to calm some of the edginess in the room. "One week ago, someone went into Marge Coleman's home and attacked and murdered her. I didn't know her as well as Rosanna did, but she was a good friend. Marge's murder should not go unpunished. The more time passes without a suspect in custody, the harder it will be to solve this crime. And I don't consider this neighborhood a safe place for any of us until the murderer is brought to justice.

"So, I have a simple and practical question for you. Will you think back to last Monday night, April fifth, and try to remember anything at all unusual or not quite right? Even if you remember something that does not seem related, or a person you would not consider a murderer, or anything out of place . . . that could be a crucial clue to point the way. Please call me if you think of something. I'll also be waiting by the door as you leave tonight, if you'd like to talk with me."

Before I could put the mic away, a bald man with a slight build stood. "Why shouldn't we call the police instead?"

"You can do both," I told him. "That makes the odds even better. But because I live here, I might see a connection they could miss. We all need to do everything we can."

A tall lady with short, gray curls added her opinion. "I stayed mad at Ms. Coleman most of the time, but I never wished her any harm. We do need to help find her killer, or else I'm not going to feel safe here much longer. I'll be moving."

I handed the microphone to Whitney and left the stage. Her enthusiasm for this memorial was wilting rapidly. She assured the residents a time would be posted for another meeting right away when everyone could ask their questions.

Her eyes searched the crowd and landed on Harvey, sitting beside Glory Bea. Who better than a retired minister to close the meeting with a sweet, old-fashioned prayer? She even carried the microphone to him so he wouldn't have to leave his chair. She made sure the mic was switched on, then whispered her instructions into his ear.

Harvey may not have heard what she said, and he certainly did not understand. He looked blank, then closed his eyes and spoke earnestly into the mic.

"Our Father, forgive us of our sins and help us to serve thee better. And thank thee for those who have gathered here tonight for–for, uh–bingo. May the winners use their money wisely, according to thy plan and purpose. Now, please be with us as we go our separate ways. Amen."

The crowd tittered with restrained laughter. Glory Bea got close to her husband's face. "Harvey, this was not bingo tonight. You said the wrong prayer!"

He shot back at her, "Speak up, woman. All you ever do is mumble."

Chapter 17

Most of the people leaving Marge's memorial exited through the double glass doors at the front of the building. I stood there hoping someone had information for me. Some nodded and said they'd think about it and get back to me. Some had already forgotten or ignored what I'd asked and paid no attention to me. One guy said he might know something but would rather call me about it when he got his facts together. So, I gave him my phone number.

I had lost sight of Milo, but I didn't mind walking home alone. Rosanna was still getting the room in order, with the help of Whitney and Devon. I chose the route home which led by Marge's house. It was like she walked ahead of me, unseen, but aware I traveled the same path. The streetlights were on, so it wasn't creepy. It was good to see the house with the crime scene tape removed.

As I passed her front yard, I heard rustling at the edge of her garage. I stepped closer and peeked around the house. Sneakers and two denim-covered legs eased backward out the garage window. I stopped in my tracks, drew in a breath, and held it. The feet hit the ground and

Riley Atkins turned and stared at me. His eyes were almost as big as his open mouth, and his arms held a heavy-looking backpack.

I glared back at him, and he held up one hand. "I can explain!"

"Make it snappy, because it looks to me like you're breaking the law."

"I just came back for these old Batman comic books. Ms. Coleman told me when we, like, cleaned out her garage, that I could have them. But I didn't have nothing to, like, carry them in. Then the cops put up that yellow tape and I couldn't come get 'em. And I thought nobody would believe me. Honest, she said they were her son's, but he left them with her and wouldn't never, like, come back for 'em." He thrust the backpack toward me. "Here, you can see."

I crossed my arms and didn't move. My heart said he was telling the truth, but my heart was stupid sometimes. "Didn't you say you knew Milo Delaney?"

"Yeah, he's the one told me Ms. Coleman, like, needed some help."

"Let's walk up to his house and see what he says about this."

"Oh no! No, I can't go there. Just take these back." He dumped them out of his bag onto the ground. "See, only comic books. I didn't, like, steal nothing."

I wouldn't budge. "If you did nothing wrong, then why not tell Mr. Delaney about it?"

"I'm leaving them here, okay? Just don't say anything to him." Riley turned in a flash and ran past me up the street as if wild dogs were after him. He was headed for the front gate, and there was no point in chasing him.

The old comic books were probably worth some money, and they sure couldn't stay on the ground all night. I bent to gather them up and saw Riley had left a small flashlight. I carried it to the open window and peered into the garage.

How would I know if anything else was missing? There were no signs of vandalism. He'd emptied his bag before he ran, so it was unlikely anything else had been taken.

I went back for the comic books and stacked them on Marge's front porch in a patio chair. Milo could advise me on this, but tomorrow I would call Jennifer and ask if Riley could have the books that he said were promised to him.

The street was empty when I made my way home, passing by Milo's front door and driveway. A light-blue Mustang sat next to his Land Rover. Milo's visitor must've been unexpected because Milo had been at the clubhouse fifteen minutes earlier. Well, maybe closer to thirty minutes. I wouldn't knock on his door and interrupt him, but he needed to know what Riley had been up to.

As I let myself in, I realized I had Milo's phone number. When he called me Sunday evening, his number was saved on my phone. I'd take a chance on calling him. If he couldn't talk, he'd tell me so.

Pulling out my phone, I moved to the kitchen window and looked toward his living room. I swear I wasn't trying to spy. It was a natural thing to look towards his home as I punched in his number.

But my fingers froze, and my breath hitched in my chest. There in his living room, on full display with lamps on all around him, stood Milo with his arms wrapped around a shapely woman, her head on his shoulder.

I stared, horrified, like when you see a bad car wreck and can't tear your eyes away. Then I snapped the blinds shut, said some very bad words, and threw my phone across the room onto the couch.

My anger was my defense. If I gave in to my tears, I'd totally fall apart. This new hurt was intense because it opened old wounds. A part of my heart had finally thawed. But, at that moment, it froze over again with an even harder shell.

Trembling, I sank to the couch and reached for the phone. It still seemed to be working, so I shut off the ringer. I couldn't speak to anyone right then, and I certainly couldn't handle a call that might come from Milo. Merely thinking of his name put knots in my stomach.

What was I doing? I tried to concentrate on what was important. We'd just had Marge's memorial. Riley Atkins had plundered her garage. Should I report him to the cops? That seemed like a minor issue now. Should I drag myself over to Rosanna and pour my heart out to her? No, the blow to my pride was too great.

All I could think about was *who was with Milo?* And how long would she stay, *maybe all night?* I could not dwell on that.

And yet, they were right next door.

I locked my doors, turned off every light, slunk back to my bedroom, and threw myself across the bed. My sandal slides fell off on the floor and I flopped over, laying my head on the pillow. I could not undress but pulled a blanket around myself for even more cover. Still, I felt naked and vulnerable.

At some point, the tears began. Warm liquid rolled from my eyes and slid down into my hair, even my ears. I lay on my back in the darkness, staring at the ceiling I could barely see.

Men could not be trusted. Men were the pits. I was done with men. Especially Milo.

Chapter 18

S tressful dreams tormented me when I was abruptly awakened by a screaming siren rushing past my house. I sat up in a daze, wondering why I was sleeping in my clothes, what the racket was all about . . . and finally, as my mind cleared, how I could have allowed myself to be dumped again. But there was no time to indulge my self-pity. That siren had stopped down the street, maybe at the clubhouse or the office.

My phone! I grabbed it and turned it back on. It was just past midnight. I had a voicemail message from Milo. To hell with Milo. I needed to call Rosanna.

My phone rang before I could enter her number. *She* was calling *me.* "Hey, Rosanna. Do you know what's going on?"

"No, but it's nearby. Could be near the office. Let's get down there and see."

Still dressed from the Monday night memorial, I slipped my sandals back on. I ran fingers through my hair, splashed water on my face, and dashed out the door. Rosanna was waiting outside in her golf cart. We chugged down the street, passing houses with lights turned on, people peering out their windows.

The night was strange, like a scene in a movie, and our hearts thudded from more than our hurried pace. We passed Howard's place on our right, where he stood in his front yard in his pajamas, craning his neck to see farther down the street. Across the street, lights were on in Tammy and Darlene's place, but no one was in sight.

My mind was a jumble: fearful about what the emergency might be, and fearful at the possibility of running into Milo. My heart crumpled at the thought of Milo. But as we neared the office and saw the police cruiser and ambulance with people milling about, a chill swept across my skin and Milo left my mind.

Rosanna found a place to park the golf cart. All the headlights shone into the swimming pool area between the clubhouse and the boat dock, so we hurried in that direction. Two police officers stood by the pool talking to Tammy and Darlene, whose faces were deathly white; Darlene was sobbing. Two soaked medics struggled to pull a body from the pool. A body dressed in a sodden blue and yellow pantsuit. Her walker stood nearby.

Rosanna recognized Glory Bea and cried out. I was stunned speechless. We walked up to the small gathering, our mouths open in disbelief.

"Stand back," someone shouted, and the two medics tried resuscitation. The motionless body did not respond. She looked like she was only sleeping, but there was no life in Glory Bea. We both sobbed, but I got my emotions under control. Rosanna introduced herself as acting manager of the community, then wiped her eyes and offered her services. We went to unlock the clubhouse.

The officers brought the Jessup sisters inside for further questioning, while we made coffee and hot tea. Tammy and Darlene took seats by the large windows in front of the reception counter. Darlene was dressed in jeans and a T-shirt, while Tammy still wore a gown, robe, and slippers. Rosanna took a seat at a nearby desk, and I leaned against the front counter, staying close to the action.

Devon and Whitney popped in shortly afterward, with wide eyes and shocked faces. Whitney quietly asked Rosanna what she could do to help. Devon stood silent until one officer peered out the plate-glass window, asking us to point out Glory Bea's home.

"Across the street," Devon answered. "I'll be glad to walk with you. Harvey needs someone with him when you break the news. I'll stay until some of his folks can be called."

As they left, they met Will Hendrix, who nodded and stepped inside. I wondered why a detective would be called to an accidental drowning. He made that clear in short order.

"I know you ladies are tired and want to go home. But we need to rule out foul play, which means I need to have some answers before anyone leaves. Now, I understand Darlene Jessup reported this accident."

"That's right," Darlene said. Tears ran down her cheeks and she stared at the floor.

"Can you tell me what happened?" he asked.

Darlene raised her head. "She wanted me to meet her at midnight at the pool. I didn't ask why. I guess she wanted privacy behind the clubhouse building. So, I went home and changed out of my dress into jeans and closed my bedroom door, so Tammy would think I was asleep. I lay on my bed and watched the clock, then slipped out just before twelve."

"Why didn't you want your sister to know you were going out?"

"She would have made a fuss and wanted to stop me. I had to know what Glory Bea was so mad about. So, I went to the pool, and there she was with her walker, standing in front of the pool and glaring at me.

"See, on the way to the clubhouse last night, I was in a real jolly mood, teasing people and kidding around. I saw Glory Bea dragging along with her walker, way behind her husband. I'd seen her out walking at night lots of times at a good clip, like she didn't even need that walker. So, I stepped up next to her and patted her on the shoulder and said, 'Who do you think you're kidding with that walker, girl? You can walk as good as any of us!' I thought she'd take that as a compliment.

"But she turned red in the face and told me I better keep my mouth shut. I wanted to know what she was upset about. She told me to meet her at the pool at midnight, if I knew what was good for me. That she knew some dirt on my sister everyone would love to hear."

Will wrote in his tiny notebook. "And what's the dirt on Tammy?"

Darlene had recovered somewhat from her sobbing. She was into the story now, apparently buoyed by the rapt attention of a small audience. At least, it distracted her from her grief.

"What's that got to do with anything? It was nothing much. But she swore she'd tell everyone if I dared to spread it around that she could walk just fine. I couldn't believe my ears! And she was all upset and kept backing up, away from me. I noticed she was close to the edge of the pool, but she was carrying on so bad I couldn't get a word in. She said she'd lose her disability, and she needed the money and so on."

"Get to the part where she fell into the pool," Will prompted.

"Well, she made me mad, threatening my sister. See, she thinks she saw Tammy going into Marge's house that night Marge was killed. So, she threatened to tell the cops. I stepped a bit closer to her, so I could keep my voice down, and straighten her out about that. Her eyes got big, and she stepped back again and went right over backwards into the pool!" Darlene's voice wobbled and caught on a sob. Her eyes filled with tears again.

"I didn't know if she could swim, but I know I can't. So, I didn't jump in to save her. I *couldn't*. But that walker was right in front of me, so I grabbed it and stuck the legs into the water, hoping she'd catch hold and let me pull her up so she could hold onto the side of the pool." Her voice trembled, and she swallowed hard. "Glory Bea sunk like a rock. She never did come up. I could see her down in the water." Darlene was sobbing again.

"Take your time," Will said, his voice gentle.

Darlene sniffed and wiped her nose with a tissue. "I set the walker aside and called 911. Thank goodness that's an easy number to re-member. And right after that, I called Tammy, 'cause I was about to pass out and I needed her." She dissolved into tears again.

Now Tammy's eyes filled with tears. She reached over and patted Darlene's arm, handing her a couple of fresh tissues.

Will spoke again. "You said Glory Bea thought she saw Tammy going into Ms. Coleman's house?"

Darlene's eyes slid to Tammy before she continued. "Wasn't worth mentioning. She did go over there that night, but not for long. She came back home fuming, 'cause Marge said we plant too many flowers in our yard. Tammy said she was going to check the HOA rules and send Marge an email about it the next day. She wouldn't say something like that if she'd just got done killing the woman!

"Besides, we both saw someone else go in Marge's front door not thirty minutes later." Darlene paused dramatically. "It was Howard. We never told anybody, 'cause we didn't want to get him in trouble. Howard's rude and grumpy sometimes, but he's not a bad guy . . . His cousin's real nice." She almost smiled.

"You both saw him?" Will looked directly at Tammy.

"Sure. I had got back to my front yard, and Darlene was outside taking her pictures. She was following Sandhill cranes that ended up in Marge's yard, and right when she snapped the photo, Howard was stepping onto Marge's front porch. He's in the picture, even though she didn't plan it that way. And the photo doesn't look like him. The hat covers up his hair."

"I believe I've seen that photo. I'm told Darlene didn't know who was in the picture."

Darlene blurted, "Oh, I'm so sorry. I didn't mean to show that photo to Celia. We were looking through photos on my camera and there it was. I didn't want to get Howard in trouble, but the truth is, he was in Marge's house after Tammy was there."

I didn't like thinking about how convincingly Darlene had lied to me, and it made me wonder if she was lying then, to Will Hendrix.

His questions continued with Tammy. "So, when you saw Marge Coleman, did she seem distressed about anything? Did she seem frightened, or did you notice anything out of the ordinary?"

"No, officer, nothing out of the ordinary. She was surly and insulting, saying I was interrupting her dinner. I couldn't get out of there fast enough," Tammy muttered. "She was the most unpleasant woman I ever met. But I don't go around killing unpleasant people. I go home and slam a few doors and get it out of my system."

I'd been watching Will. If I had to guess, I'd say he totally believed both Darlene and Tammy. In fact, his mouth was twitching like he wanted to laugh at their bluntness.

Part of me grew cold and angry. I knew something about Howard was off base. I had suspected him all along. And Darlene and Tammy would have never identified him, except to clear Tammy of any wrongdoing.

Will closed his notebook and stood. "That's all I need for tonight. Let me walk you back up the street to your house. I'd like to come back and talk to you both when you're rested."

Tammy and Darlene struggled to their feet. Darlene reached for Will's hand. "I'm so sorry all this happened. But I didn't do anything wrong, I swear. Tammy didn't either."

Will gave her a smile. "Don't worry. We'll talk later today."

Although it was still plenty dark outside, a new day had begun. I wondered how we'd ever get back to sleep before the sun came up. My insides churned with raw emotions.

I grieved for Glory Bea, and I ached for poor Darlene. Marge's killer was still unknown.

And underneath it all, I was betrayed and abandoned.

I shouldn't have let myself fall for Milo.

Chapter 19

It was time to hold my chin up and pull my shoulders back. No more trembling child. Why should I be afraid of Milo? Truthfully, I was only afraid of humiliation, but a proud person can refuse to be humiliated. I held my head up, plastered on a look of self-confidence, and marched up the street toward my house. Rosanna had stayed behind, closing the office. I walked alone, and I didn't want to run into anybody. Not until I could get some sleep.

My phone rang as I stepped inside. There was that odd number again, probably Milo. I guess he saw me pass his house. Well, he could leave a message.

I went straight to the shower, ignoring the ringing phone. I wanted to have another pity party, but maybe I was making too much out of this. We'd made no commitments to each other so far. Three nights earlier, Milo saw Will bring me home from a dinner date, and he hadn't made a big deal out of it.

Oh rats, now that I thought of Will, I realized he would come by after questioning everyone, to compare notes. Or maybe he'd only stop by because he wanted to see me, with comparing notes as an excuse. He didn't need my help in solving these cases.

Was there a homicide case with Glory Bea? I didn't think so. No one could have been more sincere than Darlene and Tammy when they were questioned. But Will would be back in the park, probably in the afternoon. I planned to be ready for him.

Fresh from my shower, I sat on the side of my bed and plugged my phone into its charger. In the pre-dawn hours, I set incoming calls to go straight to voicemail, and the phone to alarm at ten, then crawled into bed.

***

I paced the floor in the early afternoon, wondering if Howard was being questioned, or if Will had even arrived yet. He might come to my house first. I expected him any moment, and I was relieved Milo had not tried to contact me. I could not bring myself to listen to his voicemail, and I tried not to think about him.

A tap at my door suggested Will had arrived. I pulled the door open, and Milo walked straight in, his face full of concern.

"What is it?" I asked. "I'm expecting someone."

His face showed no hurt or resentment at my brusque manner. He was a man on a mission. "You have no faith in me," he said.

"You have no . . . fidelity," I told him.

He spoke softly, "You've jumped to the wrong conclusion."

"You jump from woman to woman." Though sharper, my voice trembled.

A car pulled in behind mine, and I glanced out the window. *Will*.

"I'm not inclined to believe anything you say," I told Milo. "And right now, I need to get some information from Detective Hendrix, privately."

"I *will* talk to you," he said. Then he turned on his heel and left, nodding to the detective as they passed each other in my driveway.

I motioned Will inside. He moved to the center of the living room and stood under the ceiling fan. "I wish police detectives could wear shorts and T-shirts," he said, pulling at his collar. He wore his usual shirt, tie, and slacks. At least his sleeves were short, and he'd left his jacket in his car.

I poured a glass of iced tea and handed it to him. He took a long sip and settled into my recliner, his favorite spot it seemed. "I love the way you booted Mr. Delaney out the door when I drove up. You didn't look too happy, either." Will's grin was pleased, even euphoric.

I didn't like him speaking of Milo as if they were competitors. We had more important things to talk about. But as long as I had access to Will and his inside information on Marge's murder, I would stay friendly with him.

"Milo and I can talk later. That's all I need to say on that subject."

"Certainly, ma'am. What topic do you wish to discuss?"

"Don't make me chuckle. This is all serious."

He raised an eyebrow and waited for me to continue.

"Do you think last night's drowning was a homicide? Or a terrible accident?"

"Unless the medical examiner finds bruises to indicate she was pushed, I'm leaning toward accidental death. Do you have any information I need to know about?"

I took a seat on the couch and propped my chin in my hand, musing for a moment. "At the memorial last night for Marge, I noticed Glory Bea having words with Darlene before they were seated. They kept their voices down and I didn't hear what was said. The older woman seemed furious, and Darlene looked stunned. Then Glory Bea motioned her closer and spoke lower, Darlene nodded, and they went to their seats. The only anger I saw came from the older woman."

"You say her name is Glory Be?" He held his lips in a tight line, but his eyes smiled.

"Yes, short for Glorianna Beatrice. It's a two-word name, like Mary Sue or Peggy Ann."

"I see. I'll use 'Ms. Golding' if you don't mind."

"Sure. It sounds respectful." In a shaky voice, I continued. "I took them some brownies a few days ago. Now she's gone."

"Two deaths in eight days," he said in his gentle voice. "It could be more than coincidence."

I didn't know my mouth fell open till I started to form a word. "Are you saying Darlene is a suspect in both deaths?"

"I consider all angles. You're too close to the situation, Celia. A detective needs to be objective."

"I object to Darlene being considered a murderer. Is that objective enough?"

He gave me a lazy smile. "Everything about you is more than enough."

I glanced away and changed the subject. "Can we talk about the Marge Coleman investigation?"

"I'm supposed to be asking you for information," he told me. "But what the heck, you've shared a lot with me. I'll tell you all I can."

"I never heard the M.E. report on Marge: When was the time of death, and was the lamp determined, after all, to be the cause of death?"

"Yes, the lamp crushed her skull. Time of death was between seven and ten p.m."

"So, anyone visiting her before seven could not have killed her? That might rule some people out."

"Those are the parameters we're going on," he said.

I had been so preoccupied with my problem with Milo, then the shock of Glory Bea's drowning, it was hard to keep my mind on the still-unsolved murder.

I told him about the conversation I'd overheard at the memorial in Tampa, about Jason's sorry attitude and his drug problem. "Rosanna says his mother stopped giving him any money and may have threatened to cut him out of her will. And now he's steamed because Jennifer is executrix of the will. He's the firstborn, and he thinks it should be his job. I thought you planned to be at that memorial," I said.

"I was detained at the last minute."

"Well, Jennifer still has her mother's journal, and I don't know when we'll see her again."

"I need to go pick up that journal and look it over."

If I wanted to see that journal before the police got it and locked it away in an evidence file, I needed to call Jennifer.

Searching in my purse, I pulled out a notepad where I had written names on two separate sheets. I tore off one sheet and handed it to Will, along with a print of the picture I took with my phone. "Here are the names. I took their picture and found out those two women work for Dan Coleman, Marge's ex-husband. According to their conversation, Sherry Coleman may have had a motive for the murder. And it looks like Jason did too."

"None of them would have planned to kill her right in her living room. They could've been identified entering and leaving her house," he said.

"They could have come from across the lake," I told him. "After dark they'd be harder to identify, wouldn't they? They'd need access to a boat, one at a nearby lake, maybe."

He sipped his tea and listened quietly. I was surprised he wasn't minimizing everything I said.

"On Sunday evening I took a boat ride with Milo. We saw Marge's son, Jason, on a boat dock across the lake. I have the name of the property owner. He runs a motorcycle repair shop. Jason could have visited him the night of April fifth, then later slipped over in a boat to see his mother."

"How'd you get that information?" he asked.

"Oh, I asked around. You want the name?"

"Sure. We already talked to Jason, but I can double-check his alibi."

I went to my purse again and dug out the slip of paper Milo had given me. "Can you write this in your notebook? I need to save this paper."

Will sighed and took out his notepad and miniscule pen. I rattled off the name and address while he jotted it down. For some reason, I could not give away the paper with Milo's handwriting.

"Since that photo turned out to be Howard James, instead of Jack Yancey, will you still need to check out Yancey?"

"I'll question him," Will said, "but it's not likely he'd have any reason to kill Ms. Coleman, just because he was her bookie."

"So, do you have a gut instinct about any of this?" I asked him.

"I know she was killed with that lamp. Since the murder weapon was close at hand, it looks like an impulsive act, not something planned. It stands to reason fingerprints would have been left on the lamp. And the only three we can find are those of Ms. Coleman herself, Howard's, and one set we haven't yet identified."

"Well, I have a gut instinct," I said. "I think it was Howard."

"He's her brother, and I don't think he has a strong motive." Will set his tea aside and leaned forward, all business.

"He's been arguing with her for months," I said. "She wouldn't let him help her run this place, and she wouldn't consider selling it to him. He's not a patient man and he's about as grumpy as she was. I think he lost it and whacked her. His prints are there."

"He has a reasonable explanation for his prints. She did ask him to repair the lamp. That's why he had left it on her table with the shade removed and the cord wrapped around the base. He said it was old and not worth fixing."

"Which probably made her furious. She didn't like excuses."

Will stood and carried his empty glass to the kitchen. "Thanks for the tea and the chance to sit and cool off." He flashed a big grin. "Anything else before I go?"

"That's all for now," I said, rising to see him out.

Will made another note on his pad, then smiled with those melting brown eyes. "I'll keep you posted. But don't tell anybody. I shouldn't be so free with you, but I can't help myself."

He had that look again, like he was zoning in for a kiss. I covered my mouth in a fake yawn and gave him a little wave. He winked, blew a kiss, and left.

Getting even with Milo appealed to me, but kissing Will wouldn't be right. Plus, I didn't *want* to kiss Will.

With him gone, there was a good chance Milo would soon be right back on my doorstep. How would I handle it this time? I couldn't bear to think about becoming a whimpering little weakling, hoping he would explain about the woman I'd seen him with. I'd rather push him away and let him know he couldn't destroy me over something like this. No explanation necessary. I had all the proof I needed to support the stand I'd always taken for the past forty-plus years: If he couldn't be trusted, I didn't want him. And if he didn't want me, I sure-as-hellfire didn't want him.

My cell phone dinged with a text message from Milo. I could refuse to read it. But that might bring him pounding on my door again. I took a deep breath, stalling, then gave in and read his message:

U don't want to talk. I get it. If Glory B's death is connected to Darlene, I must speak with u. Call me, or I can come over. Your choice.

Laying my phone aside, I thought about how upset Darlene had seemed the night before, when she was listening to Glory Bea. I did not want Darlene to be in any danger. What could Milo possibly know, and why hadn't he mentioned it to me before now?

Maybe because I wouldn't listen to him for more than half a second.

Getting to the bottom of these deaths and murders was more important than holding onto my resentment towards Milo. He had called earlier, and I had ignored his voice message. I looked back at the message, just to get his number.

When I clicked on his voicemail, I immediately heard his voice: "Celia, the person you saw leaving my house last night was Ricky's mother. I can explain."

Oh God, I didn't want to hear Milo's message. I only wanted to call him back. My heart was pounding, and I located his number and made the call.

"Celia," he answered.

"What's this about Darlene?"

"Can I come over there? I need to see your face."

Something in me did not want to cooperate with Milo. But there was more at stake here than my pride.

"Okay, fine!" I sputtered. "But this is only about Darlene. And Glory Bea, and Marge." I disconnected and opened the front door, knowing my jealousy and insecurities had to be set aside. I busied myself at the kitchen sink, wanting to appear unconcerned and un-interested in his arrival.

Chapter 20

A warm current filled the room. I was rinsing my tea glass, but I felt Milo enter the house before I heard his footsteps. The door shut with a click, and I turned to meet his gaze. My impulse was to run into his arms, but my pride would not let go.

"You better have a seat," he said, his brow wrinkling. "You have dark circles under your eyes."

"What's this about Darlene?" I asked, ignoring his comment about my tired eyes.

He pulled out a dining chair and sat, then motioned me to the chair where I stood. As bad as I hated to do anything he suggested, I knew I wouldn't get a word out of him until I sat. He rubbed a hand across his face and began.

"When Darlene was in high school, she was suspected of pushing a girl off some bleachers. That girl fell to her death. Darlene was questioned but never charged."

I stared at him like he was green and had two heads. "How do you know such a thing?"

"Sometimes I dig into a person's background when they catch my interest. Darlene's close to you, and I noticed at the lounge that Tammy doesn't seem to trust her. I wondered if Darlene might be a little unbalanced--needing someone watching over her, to keep her out of trouble and danger."

I thought of Tammy coming to see me, troubled about Darlene, and not willing to tell me why she was so protective.

"And why is this important for me to know?" I asked.

"Because it makes one think she might be prone to these things. Glory Bea could have been pushed into the pool. We only have Darlene's word for what happened."

"Well, I believe what Darlene has told us is exactly what happened," I told him.

"Except for the fact we have two dead women in this community in less than two weeks. We know Tammy did not get along with Marge, which could make Darlene come to her defense. And now Ms. Golding is dead, drowned in a pool she would have naturally avoided. Celia, from where I stood at the back of the ballroom last night, I saw Ms. Golding and Darlene having a conversation that didn't look so friendly to me."

I shifted my eyes, wishing I could say they were kidding around. But that wouldn't be the truth. I hadn't heard them. But body language spoke loudly, and they were not happy with one another. My mind begged, *Oh, please, don't let Darlene be a murderer. Not sweet Darlene.*

Looking Milo square in the eye, I said, "I've got to talk to her."

"I have a feeling our detective is already there. I told him they seemed to have a disagreement at the meeting."

"Darlene told him that herself, last night." We all had to tell the truth as we knew it and leave the rest up to the authorities. Still, I had to talk to Darlene.

"I know you're going straight there," Milo said. "I'm following you. If I hear raised voices, I'm coming in, like it or not. I will not see you harmed."

Bitterness rose again, and I remembered what I needed to tell him. "Yes, I'm going down there to see Darlene. But first, since you mentioned Riley's mother, and you know the boy, you should know he broke into Marge's garage last night."

Milo stood in surprise. "Say what?"

I knew Milo had some kind of connection with Riley's father. He had implied Riley was raising himself, without much parental guidance. Odd that Riley was busy stealing comic books, while his mom was up the street stealing . . . well, what I thought was mine. My eyes grew misty, and I made a huge effort to stay focused.

"Yeah, I was walking home past Marge's house and saw him climbing out the garage window. Guess he thought he could get in and out while everyone was at the meeting." I told Milo the story, about Riley justifying his actions. "When I said we'd have to come tell you about it, he dropped the books and took off up the street like a jack rabbit."

"That explains a lot. He was supposed to be waiting in the car while his mom talked to me."

I raised my hand like halting traffic. "Spare me the details."

"I listened to your details, darling."

"Don't call me darling," I said through clenched teeth.

He studied me silently, and I wondered what ran through his mind. He's so sharp, it was like a computer clicking away. Whatever it was, he must have decided not to push me.

"When you're ready to hear the truth, let me know. Meanwhile, if you're going to see Darlene, I'm going with you."

He was tearing me in half. I wasn't sure which half I wanted to cling to.

Chapter 21

With Darlene on my mind, I marched down the street toward her house, trying to ignore Milo next to me. Dark clouds blocked out the sun, matching my mood. With the cooler temperature, many houses had raised windows to let in fresh air.

When we got to the home of Tammy and Darlene, I was relieved Will's car had not arrived. I glared at Milo and said I wanted to talk with them alone. He stood within earshot of an open window and gave me a silent nod. If voices were raised, I knew he'd be inside before I could blink. He would listen to every word.

I rang the doorbell, and Tammy let me in. Her eyes were large and worried. Darlene looked as if she hadn't slept at all. She sat stiffly at their dining table, pale as morning mist, her eyes swollen and puffy.

Taking a seat next to her, I squeezed her cold hand. "Detective Hendrix may be stopping by with more questions. Like he said he would."

Darlene turned to me with teary eyes. "I didn't do anything wrong."

Tammy turned to me. "Darlene gets caught in the middle of things. That's why we had an agreement she could always live with me, and I'd keep her out of trouble, but she had to follow my rules. You see, this kind of thing happens when she gets too independent."

"What kind of thing are you talking about?"

"She had no business meeting Glory Bea at midnight, after I was asleep. She should have told me about it. But she wouldn't have hurt that woman any more than she'd hurt a baby kitten. "I know everything that happened last night," she continued. "When Darlene called me, I hurried right down to see about Glory Bea, and there she was, lying on the bottom. I can swim, but I can't pull anybody out of the water. Besides, I knew she was beyond help."

Darlene rose and started down the hallway. Tammy nodded and turned to me. "She's had several cups of coffee. I'm sure she needs a bathroom break."

"Quickly, while she's gone, what can you tell me about the death of her friend in high school?"

A cloud came over Tammy's face and she bit her lip. "First of all, that girl was not her friend. And there were no witnesses. Darlene swore it was an accident, and she did not push that girl off the bleachers.

"Darlene was different after that happened. Lost her self-confidence, became kind of daydreamy. Mother made me promise I would always take care of Darlene." She looked down the hall, making sure Darlene was not in sight. "I don't know where you heard this, but it has nothing to do with Glory Bea. Please don't mention it to the police."

"I heard about it from Milo. If he knows, the police may already know about it. If Darlene was never charged––"

Our attention was drawn to the sound of a car pulling in the drive. The nose of Will's car appeared outside the window, and I stood to leave. Darlene drifted back to the table, and I wrapped my arms around her. "Keep your chin up, girl. We'll get through this," I told her.

Will walked into the house, and I excused myself and left. Milo stood outside, leaning against a post of the carport. While I stood there, wondering what to do next, I heard Will's deep voice inside. "Ms. Jessup, I need to ask you a few more questions."

I caught Milo's eye, raised my hands in a "stay away" gesture, but I knew that wasn't likely. Frustrated, I dropped my hands to my sides and started home. Without a word, Milo walked beside me.

Darlene had been in the wrong place at the wrong time. Convinced she would never push Glory Bea or anyone else into that pool, I wanted to help her but had no idea what I could do. Milo was the most competent person I knew, but I was hesitant to ask him for anything.

We arrived back at my doorstep, and at that moment, I wished he didn't live right next to me. In his presence, I felt humiliated. I wasn't ready to make nice. I guess he could sense that coming from me.

With a nod, he simply walked away down the strip of lawn between our houses, back to his small patio where he always sat alone.

Standing at my own doorstep, I hesitated to go inside. I had to confide in someone; only Rosanna would do. For years I had relied on her to give me honest, straightforward answers when I couldn't understand myself. She'd always said, "Don't ask for my opinion unless you're ready to hear it. I won't water down the truth to spare your feelings."

She wouldn't be home from the office for another hour. I didn't want to bother her at work, where other people could hear me. But I couldn't bear my quiet, empty house right then.

I walked around the far side of her house and crept onto her back deck. A ten-foot privacy hedge stood between Rosanna's deck and mine, which blocked any possible view from Milo's deck. I sat in the shade of a small awning, resting uneasily in a lounge chair, waiting for her to come home.

With my mind spinning, I tried to organize my thoughts. Marge's unsolved murder and the questions surrounding Glory Bea's drowning should take priority. But I couldn't move forward until I could get Milo off my mind. Rosanna's deck was a quiet haven, and I closed my eyes.

***

"Celia, what are you doing here?" Rosanna's voice was anxious. I blinked and sat up, trying to get my bearings.

"Waiting for you to come home. Must have dozed off."

"Good thing I walked up the back way. Cripes, I wouldn't have known you were out here."

"I'd hear you moving about in your house," I told her. "It would wake me."

"Well, I'm ready to relax too. I'll go in and get us something cold to drink. Or do you want to come inside?"

"I want to talk about some private things." I kept my voice low, thinking of Milo and his excellent hearing. He probably did exercises to make his ears stronger, like the rest of his body.

I followed her inside, and she went straight to the kitchen for bottles of water. We sat on her couch, where she slumped down and released a weary sigh.

"You have to be exhausted," I said. "Lots of phone calls?"

"Oh yes, and the office stayed full of people. The *poolside* was crowded with people. Word got around in a hurry, and I heard the same questions over and over. Thank God Whitney was there to help. Didn't seem to bother her at all."

"Are you telling me people were swimming in the pool? That would be like having a picnic on the side of the road where your best friend died in a car wreck."

"Heavens no! They avoided the water like it was filled with 'gators. Just gathered there to talk and speculate. We've had two deaths in less than two weeks, both unresolved." She kicked off her shoes and tucked a foot under her knee. "What are these private things you need to talk about?"

I took a sip of water and hesitated. Rosanna had already been through enough that day. "Maybe this is not a good time. I know you're worn out."

"Not too worn out for my best friend. Is this about Glory Bea?"

Sighing, I ran my hands through my hair. "No, it's about Milo. I gotta get my head straight about Milo."

Rosanna turned to face me. "Glad you brought him up. You've really got me puzzled about the way you're acting."

"I don't always understand myself. But I know I'm distrustful of men in general. Especially when I get romantically involved with them."

"Tell me something I *don't* know," she said with her usual smirk.

"Well, I thought I was beyond all that, at my age. Now this slips up on me. I didn't see it coming. We haven't made any kind of commitment to each other, but I know something's there. Something real and strong. I don't have the right to a broken heart at this point, but I have one anyway."

"Celia, stop beating around the bush. What on earth did he do?"

"He had his arms around another woman! I came home last night, glanced out my window into his living room, and I saw them. All his lights were on, and I could see them clearly. Her head was on his shoulder and his arms were wrapped around her. I thought my heart would stop beating before I could get the blinds closed."

Rosanna's forehead wrinkled, and she rubbed her left temple. "Did you know the woman?"

"No. I never saw her face, but she's younger than me, tall and shapely with long, shiny red hair. Why would Milo want me when he can have a woman like that?" I didn't often bare my soul like that, and my voice trembled.

"Have you talked to him?"

"I've been too angry, too crushed. But I heard part of a voicemail he left me when I wouldn't answer my phone. It started out saying the woman I saw in his house was Riley's mother, but I didn't listen to the whole message; I was too furious. I don't care who she was, that didn't make it right."

Rosanna shook her head and told me I was the stubbornest person she'd ever known. And my own worst enemy.

"Wait," I said. "You're supposed to be my best friend. You have no idea how this has torn me apart and how much I've cried. Why aren't you on my side?"

"I love you enough to tell you the truth," she told me. "Ever since your marriage fell apart, you've been running men off and breaking their hearts before they could break yours.

"If you ever fall in love, you have to be vulnerable, y' know? It's a chance worth taking. And you're about to wash Milo right down the drain before you even listen to him. Don't let your insecurities keep you lonely your whole life."

Rosanna got up and paced the floor. She'd given me a lot to consider. And she turned to me one last time.

"Listen, you wanted the truth from your best friend, and you got it. But it's not me you need right now. And it's not me you need to be talking to."

Back home, I went over and over Rosanna's words. She was usually right. What if I wallowed in self-pity, turning Milo away without ever hearing him out? Was it worth losing the one man on earth who was truly meant for me? I was simply too insecure to admit my feelings to him.

I hoped he could be patient with me a little while longer.

Chapter 22

A smart woman would have settled things with the man she loved before another hour went by. I wasn't feeling very smart, and I didn't like admitting to myself I was in love with Milo. Did I even have the right to expect him to love me?

I was distracted from my search for Marge's killer. She'd been murdered nine days earlier, and I was still no closer to solving the mystery. My personal life kept interfering. And I'd always heard, the colder a case becomes, the harder it is to solve.

Every time I checked with Will, all I learned was one person or another had been cleared, either with a solid alibi or no known motive. Maybe I'd been too distracted, mooning over Milo, cozying up to Will, singing the blues every Friday night . . . and another one was coming up. How could I possibly concentrate on performing right now?

With my mind a jumble of questions and emotions, I gazed out my front windows at the homes across the street. If I stepped out onto my tiny, screened porch, I could look to my left and see the street leading to the lake. If I ventured onto my back deck, I could look in the same direction and see a glimpse of the lake beyond the boat dock. The lake always calmed and comforted me. But Milo lived on that side of my house. Walking out onto my deck might bring his attention, which I didn't want.

Back at my kitchen table, I sipped cold coffee and tried to organize my thoughts. I needed some index cards, the kind private detectives used to solve crimes in my favorite mystery novels. Or maybe some sticky notes. I didn't have either, but I had plenty of lined notepads in my office, which I only used for storage. I'd rather drag everything to the kitchen table and work there, with its bright light and a clear view of people passing by on the neighborhood street.

Seated once again, I tried to think, and *Milo, Milo* filled my mind. I hit "escape" on my mental keyboard and started again.

Glory Bea was most recent, so that's where I began. I wrote *Glory Bea Golding, deceased, Tuesday, April 13* (since it happened Monday after midnight.) Under her name, I jotted *Harvey Golding, near-invalid spouse.* Was he really an invalid? Glory Bea had pretended to be feeble but wasn't. What difference did it make? Darlene had been with her when she drowned. Harvey played no part in that. Was Darlene innocent? I believed she was. And unless a witness materialized, claiming Glory Bea had been pushed into the pool, it was doubtful law enforcement would bring any charges against Darlene.

On a new sheet of paper, I wrote Marge's name. The list began with her ex-husband and his current wife, some employees of the ex-husband, Marge's two children, her son-in-law, her bookie Jack Yancey, and finally, her brother, Howard James. Although I had been suspicious of the ex's wife and of Marge's son, both had alibis for the Monday night Marge was killed.

I thought of the lamp, the murder weapon. New sheet of paper, new notes. Three sets of fingerprints were on the lamp: Marge's,

Howard's, and one set still unidentified. The trail kept leading back to Howard. Tammy and Darlene both swore they saw Howard on Marge's doorstep after dark, and after Tammy had visited her. Was he her last visitor? If so, he could be charged with murder.

Who else had I talked with about this murder? Well, of course I talked to Rosanna. She'd been my best friend for years, and she was one of the few people in the community who even liked Marge. Howard, Marge's own brother, didn't appear to like her. They may have had a sibling bond, but they obviously disagreed on many things. Could he have killed her in a sudden rage? I could easily imagine it. Howard was surly most of the time, as if anger bubbled just beneath the surface.

I wrote down Candy Freeman's name. I had talked to Candy, and she lied about being home on the night of the murder. She had signed the nursing home guest book on the morning of April 5, not that evening. Why would she lie? Will Hendrix had questioned her and found no motive for Candy to harm the park owner.

Devon and Whitney often volunteered their help and never showed any disrespect or ill will toward Marge. Devon repaired the sound system wiring, and they both helped with the memorial service, as well as attending the service in Tampa. Did that make them the nicest people I'd ever met, or was it all a front for people who had hated Marge?

Trying to think of motives people might have seemed so callous. Was I only stirring up trouble? These people might not be guilty of anything.

Other names came to mind, not suspects, but maybe clues. The owner of the property across the lake, for one. I still had the slip of paper with Milo's writing: Cliff Browning, owner of Browning Motorsports, home address 340 Palmetto Drive.

My other frequent contact was Milo. I jotted down his name. He didn't like to talk about it, but he knew about killing. He'd watched his buddies get blown apart, and he'd been in plenty of fighting in Afghanistan. I believed he was honorable, not someone who wanted to harm or cause pain for anyone. If Milo ended up being the murderer, it would be the greatest shock of my life, and I would never trust my judgment of character again.

Loose sheets of paper, full of notes, covered my kitchen table.

A knock sounded at my door. It had to be Milo, and I had put off facing him long enough. I was finally ready to listen to him, to make myself vulnerable, and to admit the truth: I was in love with Milo.

When I opened the door, I looked into the face of Drew Wyndham, the man who broke my heart and divorced me shortly after our second wedding anniversary——forty-two years earlier.

"I'm sorry to surprise you like this, out of the blue," he said. "But I thought if I phoned, you'd make some kind of excuse not to see me."

Speechless, I searched for suitable words. Beyond Drew's shoulder, about two steps behind him, Milo stood gawking at me. Drew turned to see what I was looking at, and I found my voice. "Come in, both of you."

Though I never would have arranged it, I thought they might as well meet each other.

Drew stepped inside, wrapped his arms around me, and held me for a moment. He kissed my forehead and stepped back, turning to study Milo.

I watched Milo, a man who always kept his cool. He looked dangerously close to losing it.

"Milo, I'd like you to meet Drew Wyndham, my former husband." I nodded and continued. "Drew, this is my next-door neighbor and close friend, Miles Delaney. He's ex-military and a writer."

They shook hands with the same enthusiasm one might have for an IRS auditor.

"Please, both of you, have a seat." I gestured toward the living room, where Drew settled on one end of the couch.

Milo remained standing. "I came with a lame excuse about borrowing coffee. But I can talk to you later today." He turned to Drew, bit his lip, and narrowed his eyes. "Mr. Wyndham, I need to tell you something while I have the chance. You made the worst decision of your life when you gave up this woman. If you came here today to upset her in any way, you should leave now."

Drew rose to his feet, taller than Milo, and glared down at him. "I don't believe you have any right to tell me what to do. I will leave whenever Celia wishes me to leave, and not before."

"Please, guys. Pull in your claws. Drew and I are nothing more than old friends at this point. We can sit and talk, and you two can get to know each other."

"No, I'm going. Sorry to interrupt." Milo turned abruptly and left.

When the door closed, Drew spoke up. "Does he borrow coffee real often?"

"Almost never."

"Must've been a trumped-up excuse so he could check me out."

"Well, he's gone now. What's on your mind, Drew? Where is Adam?"

"Lying on a sunny beach at St. Petersburg. He's fine with me visiting you. For old time's sake and all that." Drew ran his fingers through thinning gray hair and gave me his familiar impish grin which hadn't aged at all.

"Are you happy, Drew? Have you been happy all these years?"

"Yes, I have a good life, and I don't regret the choices I made. I'll always miss you, Celia. But Adam is my soulmate," he said. "Our son, Todd, is a photographer for *The New Yorker* magazine. He's been married nearly three years and they're expecting their first child. I'm going to be a grandfather!"

"I'm happy for you," I told him. "I stopped loving you long ago, but I can't allow myself to love anyone else. If it didn't work the first time, why risk going through all that again?" What I *didn't* say was that we could have adopted children. We could both be looking forward to grandchildren if we'd stayed together.

Drew reached for my hand. He had a few extra pounds around the middle, but he looked fit and healthy, a man who could still turn heads. His eyes glistened with tears. "I could never love you the way you deserved. I thought you'd find somebody else, raise a family, have the things I couldn't give you. You're the one part of my life that hasn't worked out like I expected. I want you to be in love. I want to stop worrying about you." He released my hand and glanced out the window. "The guy who was here, the coffee drinker. He lives on that side?"

I nodded.

"He's crazy about you. Is his writing any good?" Drew was a retired professor of English literature and fine arts.

"I've read one of his books. It's great."

"Is he right for you?"

"That, I can't say. But don't let it concern you."

"Aw, why are you shutting me out?"

"Shutting you out? You're not part of my life, Drew. You're an old friend. Period. I don't resent you anymore––whew, it feels good to say that." I laughed with relief. "Now, tell me what you've been up to. Is Adam retired too?"

Drew sat on the couch again, the lines on his face relaxing as he told me how he and Adam had been traveling, remodeling their home, and spending more time golfing. "We have so many friends in Georgia, but we're considering moving to Florida where we can golf all year round."

His eyes shifted to the papers on my table. "Maybe I came at a bad time. Looks like you're in the middle of some kind of project."

I told him about the recent murder of Marge Coleman. "I made some notes of what I know so far. And it annoys the police detective on the case, but I'm trying to solve it."

Drew got to his feet and leaned over the table. He moved some papers around, scanning what I'd written. He straightened, crossed his arms, and looked back at me. "You know, it often turns out to be someone close to the victim."

Bingo, I thought. *Who's closer than Howard?* Well, her children were closer, but Howard left fingerprints on the lamp.

"I better be going," Drew said. "But we need to stay in touch. Don't ever hesitate to call me if you need anything. And tell that uptight fellow next door to treat you right, or I'll come looking for him."

"He was Special Forces in the Marines. He works out every day. I don't think you'd want to mess with him."

Drew studied my face and broke into a smile. "Promise me you'll invite me to your wedding."

I shook my head and waved him away. He knew he had me rattled, and he laughed all the way to his shiny new Hummer. He blew me a kiss and drove away.

Back inside, I gathered my notes together and paper clipped the stack. I couldn't concentrate on the murder.

Over the years after our divorce, whenever I saw Drew, it opened old wounds. I was sad for days afterwards. That day, he left me laughing. I could forget about Drew. Finally.

Milo was a different story.

Chapter 23

April in Florida is like full summer in northern states. Most of my neighbors' yards were full of flowers and color. By comparison, mine was bare. Setting out some plants or adding some window boxes would spruce things up. Maybe lift my spirits at the same time.

It also seemed like a frivolous thing to do, with all the sadness and loss in our community. But life goes on, and it would keep my hands busy and my mind clearer. I was a little rattled after seeing Drew and seeing the posturing and bluster between him and Milo. Over *me*. I needed some quiet time to let my mind settle down while my hands stayed busy. Maybe I'd think of a reason Howard might've wanted to kill his sister.

I'd bought red and white geraniums, and I had loosened the soil around my front porch. My shovel leaned against the steps like a reluctant helper. With a bandana around my forehead to catch the sweat, I worked on my yard-improvement project.

From next door, Rosanna headed in my direction on her way to the office. She wore white cotton slacks and a black, scoop-neck T-shirt.

She stopped at my side. "These are beautiful, Celia. I love the colors."

I reached for my shovel. "Trying to get it all done before the sun gets even hotter."

"Good luck with that. It's too hot already." She watched me dig a hole for the first plant.

"Have you talked with Milo?"

"Not yet."

"You're waiting too long. Don't push your luck."

"You don't even know him very well. What's all this concern about Milo?"

"I have a good feeling about Milo," Rosanna said.

"Girl, you don't know the half of it. You want to know about good feelings? He makes me tingle from head to toe with good feelings," I told her. "With only a kiss."

She smiled, her teeth sparkling. "Just like I thought. You need to see him soon, y' know? Before he gets discouraged."

"As a matter of fact, he stopped by yesterday afternoon. But he was one minute behind Drew, who dropped in for a surprise visit."

"Drew Wyndham?" Rosanna raised her eyebrows and held her hands palm up.

I had to grin. "Yeah, it's been a few years since I've seen him. Milo spoke to him briefly, and he wasn't too friendly. Drew acted like he wanted to toss Milo out the door, but I'm glad he didn't try."

"Oh no! Stop by the office and tell me the details. I'm meeting Whitney and I have the key, so I better move on."

"Sure. Save me some coffee. I'll have to put ice in it."

I settled a bright red geranium into the first hole I'd dug and packed some loose soil around it. When I got all the plants in the ground, I'd water them thoroughly and add mulch on top. With my mind on my work, I jumped when someone behind me cleared his throat.

"Miss Celia?" The male voice was unfamiliar. I turned to see a neighbor who lived up the street, close to the entrance gate. Although I often saw him and his wife working in their yard, I couldn't think of his name.

"Good morning," I said.

"Hope I didn't startle you. I spoke to you Monday night after the memorial for Marge Coleman, remember?"

"Yes, I do. Let's see, you're . . . Buddy! Buddy Monroe."

"Right. Me and Leanne always wave when you drive by in that convertible. That's how I knew where you lived––your silver Miata parked here in the drive."

I leaned my shovel against the house. Buddy wore a T-shirt that advertised a bait shop by the lake.

He shifted from one foot to the other. "At the memorial the other night you were asking for information on Marge's murder. I've thought back over the last few days, and I did see something a little weird that night. It's probably nothing, but I'd rather not talk about it out here where everybody can hear me."

"Let's go to the porch," I said, removing my gloves. "I've got the fan on, and I'll get us something cold to drink. You like iced tea?"

We were stepping onto the porch by then, and Buddy sat in a wicker chair. He grinned at me. "Long as it's sweet and full of ice cubes."

"Be right back." I slipped off my dusty sneakers and went inside.

When I returned with two frosty glasses, Buddy adjusted his cap and seemed uneasy. He took a sip of his tea and shifted his eyes to the empty street. He kept his voice low and plunged right into his story.

"The night Marge was murdered, I had gone bowling, like I always do on Mondays. I got home around ten, and I saw something unusual.

I can't say it's related to the murder, but it's all I have for you." He looked at me with dread, or maybe he was changing his mind.

"Go ahead," I urged him.

"Okay. So, I went to the kitchen to get a glass, and I glanced out the window. You know, we live right across from Vince and Candy Freeman. Well, they were out there strolling arm-in- arm down the street toward the lake——and Marge's house. I was so surprised. I thought he was in a nursing home full time. Aside from that, who takes a walk at that time of night? Folks our age go to bed right after "Jeopardy" half the time. Monday nights are hard on me, being up later than usual." He rubbed his chin and glanced around, then continued.

"You said you wanted to know about anything out of the ordinary. Well, that was sure unusual. When he was still living at home, the lights went out over there around nine. And I've never seen them out walking after dark."

Nothing about Candy would ever surprise me.

"Did you know Vince very well?" I asked. Again, Buddy looked uneasy. He stared at his feet, then slowly raised his face to meet my gaze.

"We chatted now and then. He couldn't stand on his feet and talk for long, but when he sat on his porch and saw me outdoors, he'd wave and holler for me to come over."

"Did you form any opinions about Vince from those conversations?"

"Well, yeah. I know his politics, his dim view of what this world is coming to, things like that."

"Did he ever talk about Marge?"

"I have to tell you, Miss Celia. He let me know Marge had insulted his wife time and again, and he did not appreciate it——even talked about moving, but then his health went bad. You know, I really don't think he'd kill the woman, even if he had the strength. I don't want to get him in trouble." Buddy paused a moment, and his lower lip jutted out. "But I'm not sure what that wife of his would do––so stuck on herself. Fact of the matter, she'd be trotting after *me* right now if I was loaded with money. She wouldn't let Leanne stand in her way, neither."

I liked Buddy. He was a good judge of character.

"What gave you that opinion of Candy? Just curious."

"Oh, like casual remarks she made to Leanne from time to time. And if she was out on her deck near the street, she'd wave at every passing man, if he drove a high-priced car. She didn't pay much attention to women. Me and Leanne couldn't help but notice."

"I appreciate you telling me all this. It might turn out to be helpful, even crucial. I'll let you know. Oh, one more thing: Did you find out why he was home that night? And did you see him any other time?"

"No, just that one night. But Leanne saw Candy load him in the car the next morning and went over to ask what was going on. Candy told her Vince had been upset the night before, and she thought he needed a night at home. I suppose she took him back to the nursing home." Buddy set his empty glass aside and rose to his feet. "If that's all, I better get myself back up the street."

I shook his hand, and he headed for home.

Slipping my gardening shoes back on, I thought about Buddy's assessment of Candy. And I remembered my conversation with Candy when I sat with her at the pool. She already had her eye on Howard and told me, "Even if he was married, I could get him if I wanted."

Maybe, like me, she had believed Howard and Marge were lovers. Even more reason for her to dislike Marge.

I had new information for Detective Hendrix. He needed to take fingerprints from Candy Freeman. If they matched the unidentified prints on the lamp base, she would become a murder suspect. Also, I needed to know if the detective had questioned Howard.

All in good time. Right now, I had to get the geraniums in the ground and water them. I stood, pulling on my gloves, and counted six plants still in their pots.

Someone grabbed my shovel, which was leaning against the house. I looked into the clear gray eyes of my next-door neighbor. "Where do you want me to dig these holes?" Milo asked. "Looks like you need to get out of the sun. You look hot." He grinned pointedly at my tank top and cut-off jeans.

So, he thought I looked hot, did he? A sixty-three-year-old woman? Maybe he was making a joke. Maybe it was a little of both. I was hopeful, anyway.

Both of us were quiet as we finished up with the plants. Milo put away my shovel and discarded the plastic pots while I watered my flowers. When I turned off the water hose, he invited me inside for something cool to drink. I was afraid to put him off again. It was time to talk.

I followed him to his screened front porch, where I left my gardening gloves and grimy sneakers. We continued into his living room, and Milo offered me a paper towel.

When I patted the sweat from my face, I realized I still wore my bandana, Willie Nelson-style, around my forehead. I pulled it loose while I found a spot on his sectional sofa to relax.

At the fridge, Milo turned to me with a bottle of cold water and a bottle of cola. "One of these okay?"

He walked my way, and I reached for the cola. No telling how this conversation would go. I needed more fortification than water, and there was nothing stronger in sight. He chugged the bottle of water and I drank deeply from the cola. Then we stared at each other. A burp rose in my throat, really bad timing. I covered my mouth and swallowed the air bubble.

Milo settled himself one seat away from me and began. "I suppose you have some questions for me?"

"You don't owe me any explanations," I said.

"I'll answer anything you ask. I have nothing to hide, and I care about you. If you're bothered or upset about anything, I want to relieve your mind."

I couldn't make myself speak. It seemed so small and sniveling to accuse him of being with another woman, when neither of us had mentioned being exclusive. On one occasion, he'd kissed me. It's not like we were a couple.

Milo sighed. "I'm guessing you saw me on Monday night, through my wide-open blinds. Riley's mother stopped by with problems. She ended up in tears, so I tried to comfort her."

Stubborn and skeptical, I rolled my eyes and looked away.

"Celia, please hear me out before you make judgments," he said. His voice sounded earnest and reasonable.

"Sure, Milo. I'm all ears."

He shook his head and smiled. "If you recall, Riley visits me now and then. It's because I know his father from the Marines. His dad has PTSD and has become an alcoholic--uses drugs, but I'm not sure which ones. He's not a responsible parent for Riley.

"His wife, Melanie, divorced him. She's a flight attendant and often out of town for days at a time. Living in Orlando, she has to leave Riley with Sam when she's on the job. She has no one else, and Sam is drunk and passed out half the time. Melanie is beside herself with worry for her son, and wants me to talk to Sam, or let her pay me to look after Riley."

"Sounds like a tough situation," I said.

"Well, Riley wants to stay with his dad and look out for him. But *Riley* needs someone looking out for *him*. I'm his godfather, and I don't mind if he stays with me. I don't want any pay from Melanie, either. When I made the offer, she nearly collapsed, and I put my arms around her like I would a daughter."

Telling me all this, he was so sincere I nearly cried about it myself. But still . . . "Why is she so much younger than you, if you're friends with her husband?" I asked.

"Sam's fifteen years younger than me," he said. "I was his commanding officer. When I retired, I ended up near him and his family. I knew he was having a hard time."

We were quiet for a moment. I had some explaining of my own to do.

"Milo, please don't think I'm a jealous stalker; I've never peeked through your window. But I came home Monday night, needing to tell you about Riley being in Marge's garage. I saw the car in your drive and knew you had a visitor. So, I phoned you, and automatically turned toward your house next door before sending the call. When I saw your blinds were open and a drop-dead gorgeous redhead was in your arms, I turned off my phone and snapped my blinds shut. I was in shock, and I've been walking around in a daze ever since. But I have no claim on you."

His eyes were misty, and he watched me closely.

"You can walk away from me now," I said. "I'm insecure and overly jealous. I'm appalled at myself."

Milo moved a little closer and reached for my hand. "Walking away from you has never crossed my mind. I hope you can believe me, Celia. I'm aware that Melanie is young and beautiful. Sam lost a treasure when he let alcohol ruin his marriage. But they'll have to work that out. I am not attracted to his ex-wife. I only want to be there for Riley.

He needs grandparents he can turn to, and he has none. Not that I necessarily wanted to be a grandfather, but I like the kid, and I don't want to see him ruin his life."

What he said was logical. Milo had never said he loved me. But everything I heard from him that day sounded like love.

"I feel like an idiot, just assuming you were a man who played the field. I couldn't bear to be only a casual friend when you had shown me so much attention. But I can't compete with someone like Melanie. You're a hunk, Milo. I think she wanted more from you than a little comforting."

Milo tried to keep a straight face. His mouth twitched, and I saw a tiny gleam in his eye. "You think I'm a hunk?"

"Believe me, I'm not the only one who admires you." If I kept my words blunt, I could keep my voice steady. "Rosanna's on my case all the time. She stays after me to talk with you and hash all this out. Before I lose you."

"The only way you'd ever lose me is if you could convince me that you don't want me. But I don't believe that. I keep trusting in the bond between us."

Uneasy, I pulled my hand away from him and rubbed my arm. "You know I have a long-standing distrust of men in general. I think, as men age, they still want younger women. Now, a man might love his wife till they're both old and gray, and he never really looks at her age. But why would an older, *single* man want a woman his own age when there are so many younger ones available?"

Milo's voice was soft when he answered me. "Celia, honey. I wish you could see your own appeal, your own worth. I wish you could see yourself through my eyes . . . If I had met you when you were thirteen, I would love you. If I met you when you were twenty, forty, fifty, I would want you and love you just the same. Every time I see you or think of you, I'm glad I finally found you. I want *you*. No one else. Just you."

I stared back at him, and then at the wall. "This is unbelievable. What is this strong, magnetic pull I feel from you? Do I even know what love is?"

"Yes, you do know what love is."

Milo was smart. He knew a lot, and I wanted to believe him. I trusted his feelings, his sensitivity, more than I did my own. "I could use some love. Something in me is broken and needs healing. Can you handle that?"

"I can't wait to handle it," he said, drawing me into his arms.

Chapter 24

Pages from a notepad covered the side of my refrigerator. Each sheet had a name––a possible suspect in Marge's murder case. I scanned them all again, hoping something would jump out at me.

The only two I currently considered likely suspects were Marge's son, Jason––and Howard. Certainly Howard.

My notes on Jason read: Unmarried forty-five-year-old son of Marjorie Coleman. Not trusted to be the executor of Marge's will, overlooked and surpassed by his younger sister, Jennifer. Jason had substance abuse problems, did not finish college, could not hold a job, and hounded his mother for money. Jennifer said her mother finally cut Jason off and told him to go to his father when he needed money. She often threatened to cut him out of her will. Did he decide to kill her before she made good on the threat? Was he desperate for money to support his habits? But Jason had an alibi for the night of the murder; a friend confirmed they had gone together to a support group meeting for his drug addiction.

I believed the alibi could be phony. He may have spent the night of April fifth across the lake at a friend's house.

Howard's contact with his sister, Marge, was usually emotional and filled with disagreement. Yet he seemed to share a strong bond with her, understanding her moods and the ups and downs he'd known since childhood. He wanted the park. But was it because he was jealous that she'd bought it before he was able? Or because he saw she was managing poorly and needed some help, yet refused to listen to reason? Was he exasperated enough to kill his sister? Tammy and Darlene had seen him entering her house after Tammy had been there; Darlene had unwittingly photographed him doing so.

So far, there was little evidence––primarily, the fingerprints on the murder weapon. Marge's prints had been identified, Howard's prints matched a few on the lamp, and one partial set of prints was still unidentified. The prints did not belong to Sherri or Jason Coleman, nor to Tammy. Howard had recently tried to repair the lamp, so his few prints had an explanation. However, he could have killed Marge with the lamp, knowing his prints could be ruled out.

No one else came to mind as a possible suspect. If other people had reasons to kill Marge, I had no way of knowing.

I turned from the notes and opened the refrigerator, hungry for lunch. Right in the middle of making myself a ham and cheese sandwich, my doorbell rang. I opened the door to find Detective Hendrix on my doorstep. His face was intense, his eyes large and troubled. "You won't believe this," he said, and stepped inside.

I considered offering him lunch, but he obviously had more important things on his mind. He didn't beat around the bush.

"We have identified the last set of fingerprints on the lamp that killed Marjorie Coleman." I stared at him and waited. "They belong to Vincent Freeman, an elderly man disabled with Alzheimer's. I'm coming to you before I question him or his wife. You've visited him a couple of times lately. Is he in any condition to be questioned?"

Dumbfounded, I struggled for words. "The first time I visited him, about a week ago, he was perfectly coherent. We talked about his wife and their dog." I took a seat and clasped my hands together, as if that would clarify my memory. "Three days later, I went back with a photo of Candy holding the dog, and he didn't recognize their poodle. Or remember me. I didn't stay long."

"So, his memory comes and goes." Will paced the floor. "Does he seem physically strong to you?"

"Strong enough that it sometimes takes big, burly attendants to handle him," I said. "But listen to this: On the night Marge was murdered, Buddy Monroe——he's a neighbor up the street who lives across from the Freemans—— saw Vince and Candy taking a late-night stroll toward the lake. In the same direction as Marge's house."

Will stopped in his tracks. "Why haven't you told me this before now?"

"I found out about it yesterday, and I didn't think it meant anything. Vince is an old, weak man who needed a visit back home. I thought it was a coincidence."

"We can't overlook this coincidence," Will said. We were both quiet, thinking.

"Why did it take you so long to identify those fingerprints, anyway?" I asked him.

"We looked first in a nationwide database, where we have fingerprints of known criminals. There were no matches there. His prints turned up locally because he applied for a concealed carry permit for a gun several years ago."

"So . . . fingerprints from Howard James and Vincent Freeman," I said. "Only those two, plus Marge."

"Yes, and they were only partial prints. They've been smudged, with so many people handling that lamp."

"Any way to tell which prints are most recent?"

Will's eyes were thoughtful. "That's a good question. The forensics team may be able to determine that. Something has smudged the prints . . . maybe one of them made a hasty attempt at wiping the lamp clean."

"The only person who would think about removing their fingerprints would be the killer," I said. "I can't imagine Mr. Freeman in a killing rage and still having enough awareness to wipe away evidence."

I kept staring at Will. With his logic and experience, he surely knew more about the criminal mind than I did. When he made no comment, I blurted, "However, I have no trouble believing Candy would try to remove his fingerprints . . . if her husband is, in fact, the murderer. And she would have changed his clothes before she took him back to Silver Palms. He could've had blood spatters on his shirt."

"You're right." Will nodded and gazed out the window. "I'm going to stop by the nursing home to question Mr. Freeman––before his wife knows I've identified the prints. Maybe I'll catch him on a good day. I'll come back and question Candy Freeman. Don't mention anything to her, okay?"

"You can count on it. We don't see much of each other anyway."

I stood in the doorway and watched him hurry to his car. I respected and admired Will Hendrix. In fact, if Milo were not in the picture, I might have ended up falling in love with Will. Was it fair to Milo, this close friendship I had with Will? Was I giving Will the idea I cared for him more than I did? Maybe he thought I was only taking it slow with him until the murder was solved, possibly ready for a steamy affair afterwards. I hoped not.

If I pulled away from Will, I'd lose my connection to the case and the things law enforcement had access to. I would continue to keep him close, but more like a business associate who had become a friend.

Milo. That's who I relied on and trusted to see the truth and to recognize real danger. I wanted to be near Milo more and more, maybe all the time. It grew harder to sleep alone in my bed, knowing his warmth was only footsteps away. Right next door.

***

The yellow notepad pages needed some adjusting. In fact, I didn't even have a page for Vince or Candy Freeman. Would Vince have an explanation for Will when he was questioned? Why would an old man, not even in full possession of his mind, want to murder Marge? But now I knew he'd had opportunity, and so had Candy. They were close to Marge's house, if not in it, on the night of her murder.

What could be the motive for either of them? It's true, Candy didn't get along with most women. Marge had often made disparaging remarks about her, which I always attributed to Marge's jealously and resentment over Candy's sexy, near-perfect body. Marge didn't hesitate to talk about people behind their backs, and she seemed to enjoy insulting them to their faces even more. With her poor social skills, it was a wonder she kept the retirement village full. Thank goodness Rosanna's smiling face greeted most residents when they came to the office.

So, Candy and Vince had the opportunity, and possibly the motives to kill Marge. Was Vince strong enough? Maybe, if he was suddenly angry. Rage sparks a rush of adrenaline and unusual strength. How much muscle would it take, anyway, to bash Marge's head in with the base of a lamp? Either of them could've done it. But the fingerprints belonged to Vince.

I hadn't heard from Will yet that afternoon, but I couldn't stay home waiting for his call. With my cell phone in my pocket, I headed for the park's office to confide in my best friend. Rosanna might be busy, but Whitney was manning the phone that day. Rosanna could take a break.

Tammy and Darlene's house was on the way to the office, and when I passed by, Darlene called out to me from their front porch. I waved and she motioned me over.

"Hi, Darlene," I said and opened the screen door to her small porch. "What's going on?"

"Trying to recover from losing Glory Bea . . . and people thinking I might have *wanted* her to drown. Gosh, it's like that awful experience from high school. Will I never get all that out of my mind?"

Darlene was near tears again, and I sat near her on a wicker chair. "Put it all behind you as soon as you can. I don't think you're capable of hurting anyone, Darlene. You're not that kind of person."

"Thanks, Celia. That means a lot. But Tammy and I both feel bad about naming Howard as the person in my photograph."

"Why? You stated a fact; you didn't accuse him of murder. He might be the last person who saw Marge alive. If he is, then he's also the murderer. She didn't hit herself in the head."

"No, no," she sputtered. "We know him real well. Celia, he loved Marge. He talked to us a lot about his worries for her. And, yeah, they argued, but we always thought they were lovers' quarrels. What a surprise that he was her brother! Why keep that a secret?"

"That's something we'd have to ask Howard," I said.

"We want you to prove he's innocent." Darlene took my hand and gazed into my eyes, as if trying to pull compassion from me.

"But what if he *isn't* innocent?" I asked.

"You need to prove he didn't do it. I'd stake my life on Howard's innocence." Her eyes were large and child-like.

"How can you know Howard so well? He's not exactly friendly."

She twisted in her seat. "Maybe not to you, but we're close to him. I think I wore him down." Darlene's eyes twinkled. "You know I love to bake, and I was always taking him cookies or cupcakes. He'd usually frown, grunt, and take whatever I handed him. Then one day he says, 'Darlene, enough with the cupcakes! I can't fasten my pants anymore.' I laughed till I cried, cause he's so tall and slender. He started laughing too, like it was a big relief for him. Ever since, he's treated me really nice."

I had trouble imagining him relaxed and laughing with Darlene. "Do you have a suggestion for how I'm supposed to prove Howard's innocence?"

"Of course. Find out who really did it. That will clear Howard." She gave me a smile, like she knew her encouragement was all I needed.

I shook my head at her. "I'll do the best I can. But right now, I'm on my way to see Rosanna. I'll talk to you later."

"Okay," she said. "But stop thinking Howard is a murderer. Look around for somebody else."

"A different suspect is closer than you think." I waved goodbye to her and slipped out the screen door.

Chapter 25

Rosanna was busy with data entry in Marge's old office, now converted into her own. I poked my head inside. "Can you take a break?" I asked.

"Sure, I need one. What's on your mind?"

I sat in the chair next to her desk, handed her a cold can of soda fresh from the vending machine, and began. "The last fingerprints on the lamp have been identified."

Her eyes grew round. "Who?"

"Vincent Freeman."

She was quiet, staring at me for a moment. "Vincent is in a nursing home! He doesn't live here anymore, and he's too old and senile to kill Marge."

"He was here the night Marge was killed," I said. Rosanna was speechless, so I continued. "Candy never mentioned it, but she brought him home that night for a break from the nursing home. He was upset and giving the staff at Silver Palms a hard time, demanding to go home. So, they called Candy, who drove over and got him."

"He spent Monday night at home?" she asked.

"Yes, Candy took him back early the next morning. But their neighbor had seen them the night before, taking a walk toward the lake around ten o'clock."

"Okay, so theoretically, they could have gone in to speak to Marge, and Vince could have killed her with that lamp? That's a little far-fetched, don't you think?" Rosanna's eyes were bulging.

"Yes, that could have happened. Rosanna, when a person has dementia or Alzheimer's, don't they have mood changes, and sometimes unusual fury and strength?"

"The nursing home could answer those questions." She sipped her cola, looking worried.

"Will is there now, talking to Vince. I hope he finds Mr. Freeman calm and rested. He's such a fine gentleman when he's himself, and I think he'll be honest with Will."

Rosanna rose and paced the floor. "What does Candy say about all this?"

"I don't know. We can't say anything to anyone until Will gets back from the nursing home and has a chance to speak with her."

Rosanna plopped back into her chair. "I don't believe Vince Freeman killed Marge, any more than I believe Howard did. It has to be someone else."

"All the logical suspects have alibis," I said. "Maybe some of those alibis should be double-checked." I kept studying Rosanna, wondering why she stood so firm about Howard's innocence. Was it some kind of second-hand loyalty to Marge?

I straightened in my chair and probably frowned, as I usually do when I ponder a question. "Rosanna, how can you know anything about Howard? He's so withdrawn and cold, always keeping to himself, except for his buddy, Tate."

Rosanna carefully set her cola on her desktop, away from any loose papers. "Howard often came to talk with Marge. I couldn't see what drew him to her, since he seemed more frustrated than enchanted. We didn't know, yet, that she was his sister. But he was clearly concerned about the pressure she was under, running the place." She heaved a big sigh and glanced toward the doorway. We could hear Whitney in the front office taking a phone call.

"Celia, every time he came to see Marge, he politely asked me if he could see her. He could have walked past me and straight to her office. But she had me stationed out front so I could shield her and limit her visitors. Howard was so concerned about Marge, and I never had the heart to turn him away." Rosanna fiddled with a thumb nail, then looked directly at me. "We slowly became friends. He let his guard down a little. He puts up a big tough-guy front. But he's kind and gentle. I think I know him well."

"Well, I don't know him like you do, only his gruff side," I said. "If I find evidence that implicates Howard, I won't hesitate to share it with the police."

Rosanna's eyes flashed her irritation. "I know, for a fact, there is no way Howard could have killed Marge that Monday night."

"How could you possibly know that?"

"Because I saw him go to her house that night. I was walking, and I stood outside her house and watched them through a window. I saw him gesture in the air with his arms, then turn and walk back out the front door. Marge stood in the background looking angry––but upright and alive."

"Then what?" I was surprised she would spy on them that way.

"Then I went with him to his house, asking him why they were arguing."

I wondered how she could be so naïve. "That doesn't mean he couldn't have gone back later. After you went home."

"That's just it," she said. "I didn't go home. I stayed with him all night."

***

Well, well, well! Miss Rosanna might be in love again, after all these years. Unless she was lying to protect him, Howard certainly did not kill Marge. All the facts and loose ends swirled together in my brain.

Something nagged at me. If I could imagine my best friend lying to protect Howard, maybe other alibis were shaky for the same reason. I needed to go over those alibis with Will. Or maybe not. For all I knew, Vince could be confessing to the murder at that moment, if Will was with him at the nursing home.

I trudged back up the street toward home, picturing hard-faced Howard embracing Rosanna, and it seemed unreal. Maybe he triggered her urge to mother everyone. Or maybe she finally found the right connection, like I had done with Milo.

The cell phone buzzed in my pocket as I arrived home. Will's voice spoke to me. "I'm on my way there. Had an interesting chat with Vince Freeman. Are you at home?"

"Can't we just talk on the phone?" I asked him. I was tired and wanted to relax. But I didn't want to give the impression I had no time for him. Every scrap of information from the police detective was vital to me in my efforts to find the murderer.

"No, I'd rather not discuss this on the phone," he said. "First, I need to speak with Vince's wife, if she's at home. Then I can fill you in on both visits. Do you have a problem with talking to me this afternoon?"

"Course not. I can't wait to hear everything. I might doze off before you get here. But I'll make some coffee when you show up."

I stretched out in my recliner and laid my phone on the adjoining table. Even a brief snooze would help. My chair was upholstered in a plush, soft-blue material. Settling in, I fell asleep wondering why I chose to stand in high heels and sing every Friday night, when I could be relaxing in this lovely chair.

***

A soft tap on my door woke me, and I sat up, ran my hands through hair that was smooshed to the back of my head, and invited Will in.

"Come on in the kitchen. I'll get some coffee started."

"Only if you want some," he said. "I can't stay long."

We forgot about the coffee and settled into two comfy chairs by the window. Now wide-awake and refreshed, I wanted to hear about Will's interviews.

"First of all, Mr. Freeman was in good spirits today and seemed to be clear-headed. He remembered the last time he'd been home, the late-night stroll, and how it had soothed him to be back in his familiar neighborhood. I asked him if he remembered seeing Marge Coleman and, without a blink, he told me it had been too late to go uninvited to anyone's house. He says he and his wife walked to the darkened lake and then strolled back home."

"And you found him believable?" I asked.

"Yeah, I think he's too far gone with Alzheimer's to remember a lie he and Candy might have hatched up. Amazing he remembered any of it, but he was so lucid I asked him one more thing." Will gave me his charming grin and paused.

"What?"

"I asked him if he could explain his fingerprints on the lamp that killed Marge." Will paused again, watching my reactions. "The old guy seemed dumbstruck by my question, then something crossed his mind. He said, 'Oh, that lamp. It wouldn't work. I know about electrical things, and I tried to fix it for her. But it wasn't worth the trouble. I told her to buy a new lamp. She grabbed it away from me and told me it had sentimental value.'

"Then he told me he doubted Marge had a sentimental bone in her body." Will leaned his head back and laughed. "That was so funny it had to be real."

"I have to agree with you." Will had me chuckling too.

"I drove straight here and stopped to speak with Candy––to see if their stories jibed and if she was believable like her husband. I got the same story from her: They never considered stopping to see Ms. Coleman, certainly not that late at night . . . She also leaned against the doorway and gave me some *come hither* looks, but I ignored that part, being rushed for time and all."

There was that sideways grin, always teasing me. But I didn't care who Candy flirted with, as long as she stayed away from Milo.

"I have a bit of news," I added.

"Sure, what is it?"

"Rosanna is quite sure Howard did not kill his sister. She says she has proof."

"What kind of proof?" Will asked.

"She says she stood in the street and watched through the open front window. He argued with Marge, then left her standing and unharmed as he walked back out the front door. Rosanna walked with him to his house––and spent the night with him."

Will stared at me in silence. He heaved a sigh and said, "I have no other suspects at this point. Do you?"

I shook my head.

"Well, keep your ear to the ground. This case is growing colder every day." He looked at his watch and stood abruptly, like a redwood giant springing from the ground. "I really have to go now. I'll keep in touch."

Will started for the door, then turned back around with his hopeful grin. "Actually, I'll see you tomorrow night when you're all dressed up and singing sexy love songs."

I didn't know what to say to that, so I gave him a little wave and watched him go to his car.

He'd said he had no more suspects.

But I did.

During my brief nap, I'd had a vivid dream, and I had a new suspect. I was not yet ready to share this with anyone. It needed checking out and that would take some planning.

Chapter 26

Why is coffee so wonderful first thing in the morning? I wondered. Sure, the flavor was great. But with every sip, I grew stronger, more enthusiastic, more competent. Coffee was like a buddy whispering in my ear, "You can do it! You can do it!"

I drained my cup and decided I could tackle whatever problem was at hand––like paying a visit to the folks across the lake. The place where I'd seen Marge's son hanging around the boat dock.

The day before, as I dozed in my chair waiting for Will to knock on my door, I'd had a troubling dream about Jason. I'm not superstitious, but his surly face gave me the creeps. With limp, oily-looking hair and a scruffy chin, his icy eyes made me think of battery acid.

I was told he had an alibi for the night his mother was murdered. But alibis can be manufactured lies. That's how people pulled off affairs, by lying about where they were and having people vouch for them. Maybe Jason had a valid alibi, or perhaps he was lying. Saying he was at a meeting where anonymity was almost revered . . . well, that was like throwing down a challenge. Could someone verify his attendance without breaking the traditions of AA?

He might have people willing to attest he was at the wrong place at the right time. I had plenty of time that morning to investigate my suspicions. Then I'd have all afternoon to relax and prepare for my usual Friday night gig.

With a second cup of coffee in hand, I went to my computer and looked up a map of the area, searching for the address across the lake: 340 Palmetto Drive. I printed out the map and grabbed my purse and keys. I doubted Cliff Browning would be home, since he owned a motorcycle dealership in town. Friday would be a busy day for him. If I was lucky, the wife would be home, and we could have a chat.

When I hopped in my car, I noticed Milo's car was gone. But I would see him that night at the blues bar. If he'd been home, we could have gone over my plan. Or maybe not. Things were still a little stilted between us. I had been angry and hurt for several days, avoiding him. But after our talk, settling things, I doubt he was holding a grudge.

I turned left out of Moonstone Lake Village and followed the streets and roads that would take me around the lake. Finally turning onto Palmetto Drive, I started looking at house numbers. The even numbers were lakeside houses, and I was getting close.

So many large palm trees crowded the front yard it was difficult to see the number, but there it was: 340 in large metallic numbers attached to the wall over the double garage. The house was a soft gray stucco with a darker gray roof, modern with lots of glass. I noticed a lower level built into the hillside as the ground sloped down toward the lake. I pulled in and climbed out of my car, more hesitant than I had been. But I was there, determined to get the job done.

When I rang the doorbell, I reminded myself of the owners' names, Cliff and Amy Browning. I hoped Amy was home.

A woman opened the door with a friendly smile, and I relaxed a little. I sure hoped my acting skills were up to par. "Hi! You don't know me, but I live across the lake at the retirement village where Marge Coleman was killed recently. I'm Celia Dawson, one of her neighbors."

Her face grew serious. "Oh yes, that was awful. We were at her memorial service in Tampa. I might have seen you there."

"Yes, I think so. You do look familiar. Amy Browning?"

"That's me." She looked a bit puzzled.

"Is this a bad time? I thought I might talk to you because I'm so concerned for Ms. Coleman's children," I told her.

"Sure, I have time to talk. Come on in."

She moved back and pulled the door open for me. I stepped into a large foyer and followed her through the house to a room with sliding glass doors framing the lake. We sat on white couches, and her initial friendliness began to fade.

"How did you even find me?"

"You know that Sunday of the memorial service? I came home afterward, and a friend suggested we take a boat ride and relax for a while. We took the boat around the lake and as we passed this house, I noticed a young man on your boat dock. He looked so sad, and I realized it was Jason."

"But the front of the house looks so different from the lake side. How did you know this address?"

"Oh, I used to be in real estate. There are so many maps online, and it's easy to find that information. I knew you had to be his friends, so I took a chance on finding you. It might seem weird to you, but I thought it was worth the effort, if we could help Jason."

She looked skeptical, and I watched her mull it over.

"I would have just called, but I didn't know your number. Hey, if this makes you uneasy, I can go."

Amy breathed a sigh and waved a hand in surrender. "What is it you're looking for?"

"Okay, you know when a tragedy like this happens, the first people the police check out are the family. I'm sure they've questioned Jason and his sister, and those two have been through enough. It occurred to me, seeing him at this house, that if he was here on that Monday evening when the murder took place, he'd have a strong alibi."

Her eyes widened, and she tapped her chin. "Oh, you are so right. And the truth is, he *was* here. All night. He and Cliff were downstairs in the man cave watching a ball game. I guess they'd had too much beer, and Cliff didn't want him to drive. So, Jason slept on the couch down there all night long. I made him breakfast the next morning, and he left when Cliff went to work." She sounded delighted.

I sighed and laid a hand across my heart. "That's a relief. What a wonderful coincidence. Now I won't worry so much."

Rising, I looked around me. "You have such a beautiful home. And what a view!"

Amy stood also. "I apologize if I seemed suspicious. Although I never met Jason's mother, I'm sure she'd appreciate what you're doing."

"I had to work up my nerve to find this address and drive over here. You might have slammed the door in my face. But you've been gracious and kind." I reached for her hand. "I'll go now." It was like saying goodbye to a close friend.

Amy showed me out, both of us promising to meet again someday soon, maybe for coffee. The front door closed softly behind me, and I strolled to my car, somewhat ashamed.

She thought I wanted to protect Jason. What I really wanted was to find Marge's killer, no matter who that turned out to be.

My key turned in the ignition, followed by the comforting sound of my car warming up, preparing to take me home. I backed out of the driveway, still thinking of the information I'd gained.

More than a coincidence, I decided. Jason was right across the lake on April fifth, sleeping on a couch in a room that had a back door on the lake side of the house. And down by the lake sat a canoe with oars which could take a man silently across the lake under a cloak of darkness. I had seen that deep-red canoe on the Sunday afternoon of our boat ride when it held no significance for me. And I saw that canoe again yesterday when I napped and had the troubling dream.

What would lead a man to kill his own mother? Not in a drug or alcohol-induced rage, but in a cold, premeditated plan. He might have pretended to be drunk, or maybe he was a highly functioning alcoholic, stumbling around on purpose so his friend would ask him to stay over and sleep on the couch.

Maybe he did rest on the couch all night. Maybe someone else killed his mother. But if Jason had killed his mother, he had planned it out thoroughly.

Chapter 27

How could I have been so sneaky with that earnest, helpful woman? But Amy might not have invited me into her home if she'd known my real motive in gaining information. She'd been open and frank with me, unaware that I was establishing Jason's proximity to the murder scene. For some reason, he had given the police false information about his whereabouts on the night his mother died.

Back home, I noticed Milo's car was still missing, so I didn't call him. I'd love to discuss all the new developments with him, but whatever business he might be taking care of, I wasn't about to disturb him.

Something new in me wanted him near me all the time. If I didn't see him before that evening, I'd see him at the Midnight Blues Lounge. How comforting to know he would always be there when I sang.

I didn't know how much longer I would keep singing and entertaining. It had always filled that empty, lonely spot in my heart, at least partially. But, occasionally, a customer proved to be annoying or too friendly. The bartender kept an eye on me, and a few times, my singing partner came to my rescue with some calming words, wrapping an arm around my shoulders as if I belonged to him.

Not that I'm some kind of irresistible sexpot. I think I'm kind of ordinary––certainly over the hill. But when anyone stands on a stage with a microphone, they're on display. Some guys think I'll be easy, or some kind of trophy.

One guy from our neighborhood showed up every week or so. He never brought his wife, claiming she was too busy with needlework and crossword puzzles to go anywhere. It was Russ, the lawn man for Moonstone Lake Retirement Village. I treated him like any other friendly neighbor, but he seemed to assume every smile was an invitation for his advances. I tried to avoid him as much as possible.

It was time to think about other things. Time to get ready for my gig.

I sent Neil my playlist so he could have his music in the same order. When he returned my email with a message that he'd like to wear dressy jeans with a white linen shirt, I replied that I would dress casually as well. This was a chance to show off my recent tan with an ice-blue sundress. Of course, I had to wear three-inch heels. I'm short and it gives me longer legs.

I had a light dinner, got dressed, sent a text to Milo about seeing him soon, and then left early for the "Booze and Blues." Time to switch from Super Sleuth to Silver-Haired Singer. Truthfully, even singing to a room full of people, Super Sleuth stayed on alert.

The lounge glowed with candlelight and the dying rays from a purple and coral sunset. A lone man sat at the bar, having a sandwich and a mug of beer. A young couple sat in a booth with the sunset view, and another couple occupied a table near the bar, all of them having dinner. French onion soup scented the air, along with spicy lasagna and seasoned chicken wings.

I settled my things behind the piano and set up the stand for my iPad. The entry doors opened, and Darlene strolled into the dining room with Tammy close behind. They both waved and chose the table centered in front of the small stage. Darlene's hair looked as nice as if Rosanna had styled it. Maybe Darlene was getting the hang of it at last. Tammy stared out the window, like she'd rather be somewhere else. When she looked over the menu, her fingers silently drummed on the table. I joined them to say hello.

Darlene sat across from me and bubbled with enthusiasm. "Wow, Celia. That blue dress makes your eyes sparkle. Look, Tammy. Doesn't she look great?"

Tammy smiled politely. "Yes, indeed. That's a good color for you, Celia."

I glanced at the parking lot through the windows. "Have you talked with Rosanna? Will she be sitting with you?"

"She's coming with Howard and his cousin," Tammy said with a pointed look.

"Speaking of Howard . . ." I glanced back and forth between the two sisters. "You were concerned about him being a suspect in his sister's murder. I believe information has come to light proving him innocent."

"I knew you could do it." Darlene smiled broadly. "And here you are with good news, already."

Tammy spoke up, her brows lifted in surprise. "What information did you discover?"

Not comfortable sharing Rosanna's information, I simply said, "A witness saw Howard leave, and then saw Marge, alive and well, inside her house."

"Well, whoever saw that might be the one who ended up killing Marge," Tammy said.

"Why would they give Howard an alibi, if they are the murderer?"

"That depends," Tammy said. "Who told you all this?"

My face heated up in a blush. "I never said anyone told me anything. Not directly, anyway. I get a lot of my information second-hand, from Officer Hendrix."

"Oh, another thing!" blurted Darlene. "Just because Howard left Marge alive doesn't mean he couldn't go back later and slug her with the lamp." Her big eyes stared, then darted to the side. "Wait, wait. What am I doing? I'm trying to get him *off* the hook, not right back on it. Dumb, dumb, dumb!" She leaned her forehead into her palm.

"Don't worry about it," I said. "Howard has an alibi for the whole night."

Then Tammy's eyes lit up, and she pursed her lips, suppressing a grin. I felt like a blabber mouth who doesn't know when to shut up. If Tammy put two and two together, she could assume Howard spent the whole night with someone. And that someone was most likely Rosanna.

I turned to see Neil arrive in his casual but classy outfit. I joined him at the piano as he sorted through his notebook. He liked to limber up his fingers on the keyboard, then move to the bar and have a glass of wine before we began at eight. I considered asking him if he was still seeing Candy, but I saw his eyes light up, and I knew she had walked through the door. She sat as close to his piano as possible, as if staking out her claim. Neil didn't have a great deal of income or any kind of inheritance that I knew of, but Candy was sticking with him. She'd already inherited plenty of money from previous husbands, and Vince would someday leave her with more. Maybe her attraction to Neil . . . was genuine. Who knew?

Howard walked in next, escorting Rosanna to his usual booth. Tate followed behind, and he sent a flirty grin to Darlene. Candy ignored

Howard and focused her attention on Neil with his refined good looks and bright smile. He soon joined her, planting a light kiss on her eager lips.

I suppose Tate's grin gave Darlene courage, and Lord knows the woman doesn't need much to feed her impulses. She looked adorable in her new dress and chic hairstyle. With a quick word to her sister, she nearly skipped over to the booth where Rosanna sat with Howard. Slipping in next to Tate, Darlene reached across to Rosanna as if she had a message for her; she turned to Tate, like it was an afterthought. To me, it seemed well planned. Tate looked thrilled; he finally had a woman! His left arm wrapped around Darlene's narrow shoulders, lighting her face up like a kid with a birthday cake.

Tammy, on the other hand, did not like being abandoned to sit alone at her table. She watched with a scowl and twisted her napkin. It looked like they had not yet ordered their meal. Darlene soon returned with Tate holding her hand. He joined them at their table, and Darlene's face stayed animated for the rest of the evening. No more boring dinner with only her sister.

People continued to drift in, some only coming for dinner. I saw a familiar blond head at the bar. I'd never seen Jason there, but I'd met him in Tampa at his mother's memorial service. He hadn't brought a date. Maybe he dropped in at random for a beer. I had spoken to Amy Browning that morning. Surely there was no connection. With a half hour before time to sing, I had time to go and speak to him.

Smiling, I approached the bar, and Jason turned my way. He met my eyes with an even stare and no facial expression. His eyes were unreadable, but they did not look happy. He didn't offer a seat next to him or even speak.

I leaned against the empty barstool. "Hello, Jason. I don't believe I've seen you here before tonight. How are you?"

"You're Celia," he said.

With a nod, I continued. "I've only met you once, at your mother's memorial service. I'm still so sorry for you and Jennifer."

His eyes glinted, and it looked like rage to me. "Sorry, huh? I don't think so. I want you to stay the hell out of my life. You hear me?"

His voice was low and full of venom. I took a step back and gaped at him.

Milo entered the bar, and I tried not to look at him but replied to Jason, "Then you should stop following me around."

"Me? Following you? I'm having a beer. And I won't be hanging around long enough to hear any golden oldies from white-haired grannies. You can count on that."

Milo stood next to me by then, and I sensed his hackles rising. I tugged at his hand, and we walked away. We strolled to the other end of the bar with our backs to the barstools and Milo spoke in a quiet voice. "What was that all about?"

"I confess, I've been snooping. I went to that house where you found the address for me. Jason stayed there all night––the same night his mother was killed. He's found me out, and he's not happy."

"Did he threaten you?"

"Not in so many words. But he looked like he wanted to kill me."

Milo's arm tightened around me. I slipped onto a barstool, refusing to look in Jason's direction.

"He slammed some cash on the bar and he's leaving," Milo told me. "Do you want a ginger ale?"

"Yes, I do. I need to simmer down."

We sat on the barstools talking, while I tried to think of something besides the hate in Jason's eyes. The room filled up, mostly with people I didn't know, although some faces were familiar. Milo said he and Riley had spent the day cleaning up Riley's home. The kid's father,

Sam, stayed too stoned and drunk to take care of it. He told me Sam was ready to commit to rehab. When that happened, Riley could stay with Milo when his mother was out of town.

Eight o'clock approached, and I joined Neil at his piano. We began with "Unforgettable." For a change of pace, we sang the Pina Colada song, while a few couples danced. After that, I sang "Sweet Love." Milo turned on his barstool and gazed into my eyes, soaking up the melody and the love I put into every note.

Time passed quickly, and Neil's solo act began. When he sang Elton John's "Blue Eyes," I went happily into Milo's arms to dance slowly at the edge of the dance floor. His back stiffened, and I could see why.

Russ Evers had sauntered into the room, finding an empty chair with Tate, Darlene, and Tammy. Tate's arm was around Darlene, and Tammy pointedly ignored Russ. He shifted his eyes to me.

When the song and our dance ended, the barstools were all filled. We joined Howard and Rosanna in their booth. My breaks seemed brief, and I needed to sit while I could.

Milo excused himself and headed for the men's room and, as soon as he was out of sight, Russ got up and insisted I dance with him. I told him I wanted to stay off my feet, and he slammed his fist against the table. He reeked of alcohol, and I didn't want to dance with him. But I needed to explain a few things to him before he made a scene.

So, I walked with him over to the exit, where no one was dancing. He got the wrong idea. He must have thought I wanted to step outside for some privacy and cuddling, and he tried to drag me out the door. I held back and said firmly, "I need to say a few things, Russ. Inside, not out in the dark."

His face was sullen, but he let go of me. "I'm better for you than that Milo fellow. He acts like the military police!"

"Russ. Listen to me. I will not spend time with you without your wife."

"Then why are you talking to me right now?"

"Because you were about to make a scene here where I work, in front of friends and patrons."

"Hey, you're not a little teenager. You've been married. You've been around. What's your deal, anyway?" he said, fuming.

"Here's the deal: I'm with Milo. Period. And you are a married man. I do not go out with married men, unless they're married to me. Is that plain enough?"

"You ain't had none of my kisses yet," he boasted, and pulled me into his arms while I struggled against him.

Like an eagle grabbing its prey, Milo swooped in and jerked Russ into the air by his shirt collar. Milo shoved him out the door, stomping behind him. I was stunned, relieved, speechless–all of the above. Then nervous giggles started, and I turned and almost walked into the bartender, Johnny. He stared out the door, where Milo explained a few things to Russ, then stuffed him into his car and made him leave.

Milo headed back toward us, and Johnny turned to me. "We could use a bouncer. Is Milo available?" I got the giggles all over again.

I composed myself and returned to my seat with Rosanna, who stayed quiet. Howard barely spoke to me. He probably knew by now his secret affair with Rosanna was out of the bag. I doubt he wanted her to be his alibi, thinking it would dishonor her. For Pete's sake, we were all adults by quite a few years. But I never would have stopped doubting him until we could rule him out as a suspect in the murder. I need to know someone well before I have total faith in them. And even then . . . it's not easy.

The bartender shook Milo's hand, laughed, and slapped him on the back like they were pals. Milo seemed pleased with himself, and

I couldn't stop grinning. He came back and slid into the booth beside me.

Rosanna propped her chin on her hand. "I'm glad you look after her, Milo. She wears me out."

"Hey, I didn't ask for either one of those guys to bother me," I sputtered. "Rosanna, men follow you around in the grocery store, you're so gorgeous."

Howard finally acknowledged my presence. "Are you serious?"

"Yes, Howard. You need to go with her when she's shopping." I gave Rosanna an *I-got-you-back* smirk.

My break was over too soon. It was time for the closing songs of the evening. I sang most of them, but we ended with a duet: Eric Clapton's "Wonderful Tonight."

If not for Milo, my night would not have been wonderful. One thing was certain; I had to put a stop to any kind of disturbance at the lounge, or I could kiss my Friday night employment goodbye.

Jason would not likely darken the door again, not with me there. And if Russ ever came on to me again, I would have a talk with his wife.

Somehow, I doubted Nancy would care.

Chapter 28

Saturday morning, I had coffee with Rosanna in her kitchen. Her tile backsplash and quartz countertops glistened in shades of aqua, like ocean waves. Coral pottery and dish towels reminded me of blazing sunsets.

Next to the pantry door, Bitsy patiently awaited food in her dish as Rosanna got the coffee started. I found a small packet of moist cat food, emptied it into her dish, and watched her take dainty bites. No fishy smell, thank goodness. I wanted to concentrate on that roasted coffee aroma swirling through the kitchen. Cinnamon coffee cake completed our breakfast, and we sat at the table remembering the night before.

Rosanna hadn't noticed my encounter with Jason, and I filled her in on his anger and threats. "By the way, Will had said he'd be there. I wish he had. Now I need to call and let him know about these recent developments."

"Oh, are you pressing charges against Jason?" Rosanna asked.

"No, it wasn't that bad. But I need to let Will know what I found out when I went snooping Friday morning." I went on to tell her about my conversation with Amy Browning, and how Jason had lied about his alibi. He had, in fact, been nearby on the night of his mother's murder.

"Will needs to know; I agree. And it's even worse that Jason would come to the lounge and confront you there where you work with people all around."

"Maybe he wanted witnesses around to verify he didn't touch me. I would never falsely accuse him of assaulting me, but he doesn't know that. I'm sorry if he's grieving for his mother. But people have been known to kill a parent if they think they're being treated unfairly. He could be as moody and ill-tempered as his mother was," I said. "Anyway, when I get back home, I intend to call Will with the information."

Bitsy finished her chicken-flavored breakfast and came to wind herself around my ankles in feline gratitude. Her purring sounded like a small fan motor, and I rubbed her soft fur.

Rosanna refilled my coffee mug, and I added creamer. "Howard's worried about his nephew," she said, returning to her seat. "Jason's not as bad as Marge was, but he is borderline bipolar, which contributes to his erratic behavior and tendency to have addictions. He's so much like his mother, while Jennifer is more like her father––all about business and making money. Marge had no patience with Jason. They were too much alike."

"What, exactly, are Howard's concerns?" I asked her.

"He says Marge was always suspicious when Jason needed money. She wasn't sure if he needed money for food, or if he'd spend it all on alcohol or drugs. So now Howard thinks, when he buys this retirement village from his niece and nephew, Jason will blow his half in short order and be penniless again."

"Well, with his mother gone, he might be coming to his Uncle Howard now when he needs a loan. I sure hope Howard never makes him angry." I rose from my chair. "Thanks for the yummy breakfast. I'll give our friendly detective time for a good morning's sleep on his day off, then call him when I get back from my walk."

My best friend gave me a hug, and I headed for the door. I didn't have much scheduled for my morning, but I planned to help Milo that afternoon when he got home. His extra bedroom, which was rarely used, needed to be made ready for Riley's occasional visits.

After a brisk walk around the village, I was back home and eyeing the clock. I'd give Will some time while I filled the washer with laundry, then give him a call. Minutes later, my phone rang.

"Good morning, Will."

"Sorry I didn't make it last night. Sometimes I get covered up with paperwork."

"Jason Coleman showed up, and we had a run-in," I told him.

"I heard about that," he said. "Bartender's a friend of mine."

"He heard our conversation?"

"Well, maybe not every word, but enough to know he should step in if Jason got too far out of line. What was Jason upset about?"

"I found the family across the lake that owns the motorcycle dealership here in Conroy. They're good friends of Jason's, and I saw him having a smoke on their dock on the day of his mother's funeral service.

"Friday morning I went to that house and found the wife, Amy Browning, at home. We chatted and I found out Jason, on the night of his mother's murder, had spent the night at their house. Even though he told you he was in Tampa with a friend at an AA meeting."

Will was silent, and I braced myself for a lecture about staying out of things. Instead, I heard a sigh. "It's no use chewing you out. You'll do what you think you need to do. So--I suppose they let him know about your visit, and he was furious you blew his alibi."

"That must be what happened. Although, when I talked to Amy, we chatted away like old friends. She never seemed to resent me. I told her I was concerned that Jason didn't have an alibi, because the police always seem to come after family members. She remembered that night, because the news broke the next day about Marge's murder. She said Jason had spent the night on their sofa, which she thinks gives him an alibi. It actually shows that he was close by and had opportunity and means to commit the murder."

"I should have known about this sooner," he said.

"It only happened yesterday, and then I had to go to my gig last night. I had planned to tell you there."

"The problem is, now he knows. If he *is* the murderer--he is now a murderer who is angry with *you*. I'll try to find him today and take him in for questioning. When you talked to Ms. Browning, did you lie or mislead her in any way?"

"No. I wasn't completely honest about my intentions, but no one can prove that. I told her I was a neighbor and concerned about Marge's children. Which is true."

"Okay. I'll take it from here. The guy is unstable and might've had a motive to kill his mother, at least in his own mind. Now we know he was close by on the night of the murder. At least I have something to work with."

"I'm not sure you thanked me, but you're welcome," I said.

"Celia, I appreciate all the information you can pass on. But I want you to be safe."

We said our goodbyes, and I went back to my laundry.

Around eleven, Milo joined me on my back deck, and we sat in loungers, enjoying the sun. I could never get my mind off the unsolved crime in our community.

"Do you think we'll ever know?" I moaned.

"Know what?" he asked.

"Who killed Marge."

"Of course we will. You'll stumble on it one day and feel like a genius. It's only been two weeks. I think you've already found more clues than the police detectives have."

For the time being, I was satisfied with my progress. But the urgency to solve this crime stayed with me, and my thoughts chugged ahead.

Monday, I planned to spend time at the office with Rosanna. Jennifer was scheduled to come back and look over the business again. The estate was being settled, and Howard would purchase Moonstone Lake Retirement Village from Marge's heirs, Jennifer and Jason.

It would be nice to see Jennifer again, now that she was over all that posturing around in her business suit, treating Rosanna and me like lowly clerks. I thought back about meeting her that first time, two days after her mother's death. How shocked we were to find less than sixty dollars in the operating account of the retirement community––over 200 homes.

And then she showed us the location of her mother's safe. What a surprise! I sat mulling things over, the scenes playing again through my mind. I sat straight up and blurted, "Wait a minute!"

Milo, used to my outbursts, gave me a mild look and waited for me to elaborate. I stared at him, open-mouthed. "I just remembered."

Again, he waited. "Jennifer took her mother's secret journal, and I still haven't had a look at it. I have to call her."

"Sure," Milo said. He took a few long gulps from his water bottle. A man willing to sit with me in the baking sun deserved better than water.

"I'll make some lemonade after I take care of this phone call."

He looked at me as if he longed for more than lemonade. But he only grinned and nodded.

Back inside my cool house, I searched my phone for Jennifer's number and made the call. "I've been meaning to ask, did Detective Hendrix ever get your mother's journal from you?"

"No," she replied. "I'm coming to the park office tomorrow morning, and I told him I'd leave it with Rosanna."

"Did you find anything interesting or puzzling when you read over your mother's journal?"

After a moment of silence, she said, "Probably nothing important."

"Is it private? Would you mind if I read it?"

"I want to say no and keep this to myself. You know, like a special bond with my mom. But we still don't know who killed her." I heard a sigh. "You can read it tomorrow, before the detective shows up. But don't tear out any pages, and don't write notes in it, not even in pencil. Okay?"

I promised to follow her wishes, and we ended the call. Now I had plenty to look forward to on Monday. I'd pop down to the office, ready for coffee and information.

With fresh lemons, I made a pitcher of lemonade and carried two filled glasses out to the deck and joined Milo. He downed half the glass before he set it on the table between us.

Even at ten in the morning, Florida can be miserably hot. "Why don't we go cool off at the pool?" I asked.

"I usually go early in the morning when no one's there," he said. "Just for the exercise. But I'll go. I get to see you in a swimsuit. Like *Sports Illustrated*!"

"Not quite like *Sports Illustrated*," I assured him. I almost changed my mind about going. But we should have nothing to hide from each other. Not even my not-so-young figure. "When we get back, we can make chef salads for lunch."

He did not reply. Just grinned at me like a hungry man.

Chapter 29

Monday, I strolled down the street toward the office with new-found energy.

Jennifer and Rosanna were already in the office when I arrived. I stepped inside, waved, and headed for the coffee urn. With a cup of steaming comfort in my hand, I joined them at the front desk.

Jennifer pulled the leather journal from her shoulder bag. "I know this is what you came for. Handle it with care."

"Oh, I also came to see you." I tucked the journal into my own bag and smiled at the young woman. "How are you holding up?"

She plopped down in an office chair. "I'm getting over the shock, I guess. But inheriting this business has been nerve-racking. I'm so glad Uncle Howard is buying it and getting it off my shoulders."

Rosanna, seated at her desk, reached for her cup and nodded. "I'd like to get it off my back, too. I'll be relieved to have Howard making decisions and moving forward." The morning was business-as-usual for her.

Then she set her cup down and studied my face. "You don't look as worried and nervous as usual. What gives?"

"I had a relaxing day yesterday. I was discouraged about this murder case, but now I'm hoping to find a clue in Marge's journal. A break in this case could be just around the corner."

Rosanna rolled her eyes at Jennifer, as if they both knew me so well. Jennifer knew little about me. But she left her chair and stepped closer.

"By the way, Jason is all bent out of shape. What on earth happened between you two?"

"Well, I did some checking and found out he was across the lake at his friend's house on the night your mother died. I don't like to think he could be involved in Marge's death, but he lied about where he was that night. Really, he had opportunity to paddle across the lake to her house."

Jennifer hung her head. Respectfully, I stayed quiet. Then she lifted blazing eyes to mine. "I know you say you're looking for my mother's killer. But how dare you try to pin it on my brother!" She stopped and clapped a hand over her mouth, as if smothering angry sobs.

Staring into her suffering eyes was too painful for me, so I looked instead at Rosanna, hoping for support. But Rosanna only gave me a puzzled stare.

"Look, Jennifer. Jason came to the club where I sing. He was there Friday night, furious with me and threatening. That was not the place to confront me."

"I know, I know. He's always been a hothead. But it can't be him. He was always angry with Mom, but he wouldn't make a cold-hearted plan and kill her."

"Who knows what anyone will do? I only established that he had opportunity, which he has lied about. Jennifer, would you rather never know who killed your mother?"

"If it didn't matter to me, I wouldn't let you have her journal. But it hurts to think it could have been my own brother," she said. Her eyes glistened with tears.

"I knew it wouldn't sit well with the family. It's a bad time for you, and I've made your pain even worse. Really, I'm sorry about that. But I don't think the estate can be settled as long as any inheritor can be suspected of the murder. This has to be checked out in order to prove Jason *didn't* do it."

"Well, that detective will be stopping by for the journal. Make sure he gets it today, okay?"

I gave Jennifer a thumbs-up and waved at Rosanna. "Call me later," she said, as I left her office.

No matter how reasonable I tried to be, I could tell I made Jennifer uneasy. I understood her family loyalties, and today I needed to give her some space.

Hiking up the street toward home, I saw Milo's place ahead before I could see my own home. White with black trim, his place was always orderly, but not so much ornamental. My house was cream-colored with avocado-green shutters, and plenty of flowers around the screened front porch. My geraniums were looking good, and I remembered how Milo broke the ice between us when he insisted on helping me get them planted. Warmth spread through my chest, and I wanted to see him. However, I knew he was checking on Sam at the rehab center. I would see him that night.

I had an impulse to speak randomly with neighbors, just to see where it might lead. Sometimes my impulses paid off, like when I squared my shoulders and paid a visit to the couple across the lake where I suspected Jason had spent the night. Well, okay, that wasn't a random visit. But I needed to "stir the pot" in our neighborhood.

What if I popped in on Russ's wife, Nancy? Even if he took a break from mowing and showed up at home, he wouldn't make a scene with me in front of his wife. In fact, it might make him want to steer clear of me, knowing I could tell his wife things he'd rather I didn't.

It was too far to walk in the heat, so I hopped on my bike and rode three streets over to the home of Russ and Nancy Evers. I'd have to think of some reason for stopping by, because I barely knew Nancy. I'd seen her with Russ at bingo one night, a night when I went to mingle with people instead of staying home with my nose stuck in a book. She played bingo with rapt attention, while Russ continually scanned the room, his eyes resting now and then on a woman who drew his interest. I wasn't playing bingo either; only glancing at Rosanna's card occasionally.

Watching Nancy across the room, merely out of curiosity, my eyes had met Russ's, and he leered at me. He always leered at me. I wasn't sure what the problem was between him and his wife. Maybe they'd lost their spark, or maybe he was frustrated and looking for flings wherever he could find them. I had glanced away, giving him no encouragement.

After parking my bike, I rang the doorbell and listened for footsteps. Nancy opened the door, tapped her chest with her fingertips, and said, "Hi."

"Hello, Nancy. We haven't officially met, but I'm Celia Dawson. Every time I'm out walking or on my bicycle, I notice your gorgeous gardenia bushes. I wanted to stop and tell you how much I enjoy them. You must have a green thumb!"

"No, my thumb's not green," she joked, holding it up for me to see. "But come on in. I'll fix you a glass of iced tea."

"I don't mean to disturb you. But I would enjoy the tea."

She led me into her kitchen and motioned me to a stool at the breakfast bar. She put ice in glasses and poured the tea. "In our family, it's Russ who has the green thumb," she said. "He does more than cut grass. That comes with the HOA fees, but he also takes care of shrubs and plants, when people pay him extra."

"Well, I wanted to meet you," I said. "I've seen you around the village, but mostly everybody sees Russ, mowing lawns all over the place."

"Yeah, he gets around," she said with a weak smile. She settled down across from me. "I stay home a lot. I talk to my parakeet, watch TV, and crochet afghans and coverlets. You'd be surprised how many people like a little blanket to cover up with when the AC gets chilly in the evenings."

I looked across into her living room and saw several multi-colored afghans folded and stacked on her couch. "You made those?" I asked.

"Sure. You want me to make one for you?"

"Oh, no thanks. But they look lovely."

Nancy sipped her tea and stared at the quartz top of her coffee bar. "Celia, I think you did a brave thing, standing up at Marge's memorial service and asking for information on any suspicious activity here in our neighborhood. I've almost called you several times."

I couldn't believe my luck. Sitting quietly, I waited for her to continue.

"Maybe I shouldn't mention this," she said, absently wiping moisture from her glass. "I don't think my husband loves me anymore." Her voice trembled, but she drew a deep breath and continued. "Sooner or later, I think he'll leave me. He's not mean or controlling; we simply don't have anything to talk about. And I don't want to get him in trouble, but I have to tell you this: Marge was not just Russ's employer. She was his lover."

I almost fell off my stool. If I learned anything else new about Marge, I might as well write a book about her. Wanting to comfort this straightforward woman, I reached for her hand. "Oh Nancy, I'm so sorry."

She wiped away a single tear. "It doesn't break my heart, but it hurts my pride. They tried to keep it a secret. He was gone at night a lot, and he told me he liked to play pool at the clubhouse, and then poker on Saturday nights. But I found out he was doing neither."

"How did you find out?"

"Sometimes, when he was working in our yard, some guy would stop on his golf cart and talk to him. They didn't keep their voices down and I learned a lot." Her lip curled. "What I can't figure out is, why didn't he take up with a better-looking woman?"

I made no comment. Marge didn't take many pains with her appearance, but she had been my friend.

"I'm not suggesting he might have killed her. But I think this falls under the category of suspicious activity." Nancy continued, "And it's something most people don't know. Or maybe everybody knows it and I'm the last to find out."

"This is the first I've heard of it," I assured her. This new information stunned me. And I also hated to think I might be causing this woman pain when she decided to confide in me.

I thanked Nancy for the tea and the chance to get to know her better. She offered to teach me to crochet, and we promised to get together again soon.

When I climbed back onto my bicycle and headed home, I puzzled over how Russ had carried on an affair with Marge without the nearby neighbors noticing. This was something I'd have to ask Tammy and Darlene about, since they lived right across the street.

***

Back at home, I settled at my dining table with a notepad and pen. I opened the journal and noticed Marge's slap-dash writing. Sometimes it was hard to make out her words, but I plowed through, studying every page carefully. Then it occurred to me I should go to her last entry and work backward. The journal covered the past seven years. What I was looking for was likely to be more current.

Marge's last entry was in late March, five days before her murder. Something trivial, about when a bill was due. I read back in time from then, finding nothing interesting, until an entry dated February second. Instead of her sloppy handwriting, she had printed carefully in block letters: *Found info on F.* Next to that, she had drawn a striped candy cane. The pieces came together for me. Lots of people called Vincent Freeman by his last name. The "F" could have referred to other people, but their wives were not named Candy.

I was sure she left the visual clue for her own amusement; Marge was like that. But with that clue, she may as well have written out Vincent Freeman, instead of the mysterious "F."

I tingled with this new information. Calling Will, letting him take it from there, was the best idea. But sometimes I didn't listen to common sense. Sometimes I had to blunder along by myself and find answers.

First, I wanted to see what Rosanna thought about the journal. I photo-copied the page with the candy cane and tucked it into my purse. When I walked back into the office, Jennifer had left, and Rosanna sat at the reception desk alone. She had a file folder open. I settled into the visitor's chair. "What's that you're working on?"

"The file on a resident we both know. Marge kept a file on everyone. Since you wanted to examine her journal, I figured you'd come asking about her files." She slid the folder, labeled "Vincent and Candace

Freeman," over to me. "Strictly speaking, these are private. But with Vincent being a suspect in Marge's murder, well . . ."

My eyes fell on the original form we all filled out when we moved into MLRV. On Vincent's form, where "previous residence" was requested, he had written: The Hamptons, Long Island, New York. Next to that, Marge's sloppy print had added, LYING JERK.

"Did you see this?" I asked.

"Sure did. It's the only thing I saw of interest."

"You mind if I look through it? I think she found something to hold over his head. Or maybe this address made her dig deeper. She might have been blackmailing Vince."

Rosanna nodded, and I kept turning pages. "Rosanna, does this place take in enough on a regular basis to be financially solvent?"

"Absolutely. If managed properly, it makes a large profit. Marge owned it and could do as she pleased. But she almost bled the business dry with her gambling. I tried to turn a blind eye when I worked for her, but I'm facing the truth now."

Her phone rang, and I moved to the front counter with the file. As I scanned page after page, I wondered if I was overlooking a huge clue. All I had found was Marge's obvious objection to the Long Island address Vince had given. I wrote the address on my notepad and returned it to my back pocket.

I stepped back over to Rosanna and handed her the file––and the journal. "When Will stops by later, will you make sure he gets this? He should have had this journal from the begining."

"Except it was hidden in the wall safe, and then Jennifer grabbed it. But I'll see he gets it today." She gave me a sly grin. "Bet I know where you're headed next. Tell Mr. Freeman I said hi."

***

Maybe Vince would be lucid today and I could talk to him by myself. Maybe I could bring up Marge's name to him and see how he reacted. If I caught him off guard, maybe he would spout off about her being sneaky, vindictive––even immoral enough to blackmail people. That could push anyone into a corner, make them fight back with impulsive responses. Like bludgeoning someone with a lamp.

Back home, I brushed my hair, preparing to visit the nursing home. But would Candy be there with her husband?

I grabbed my phone and entered her number. When she answered, I said, "Hi, Candy! Are you busy?"

"I'm about to leave; what do you need?" she said.

"Well, I didn't want to bother you if you're visiting Vince. Don't you usually visit him in the mornings?"

"Not today. I'm joining him for dinner tonight. What's up?"

"Just checking on you."

"Oh well, if it's only chit chat, can we talk later? I'm getting ready to meet Neil for lunch."

We hung up and I shook my head, disgusted at Candy so casually meeting her boyfriend for lunch, then spending time with her husband that evening as if that made it right. All her men had to be handsome or rich, preferably both. Neil was stunningly handsome, and Vince was loaded. She had the best of both worlds.

And I had what I needed to know.

I grabbed my car keys. The coast was clear for me to have a chat with Mr. Freeman.

A little later, I drove up to Silver Palms, found a shady place to park, and strolled inside. Candy might not ever notice who signed the visitor's list. But I always had to sign in. I hoped she wouldn't see my name and wonder what I was doing visiting her husband again. Especially on the same morning I called her, being suspiciously friendly.

The receptionist got my signature, then asked me to wait while she checked to see if Mr. Freeman was "able to receive visitors." She walked down the hall in the direction of his room, and I wondered why he *wouldn't* be free. But he could be involved in any number of things: a visit from his doctor, a nurse checking his vitals, someone helping him with a bath, or he might even be sitting in the great room mingling with other patients. He wasn't exactly an invalid. His mind might be going soft, but Candy said he did calisthenics in his room every day. And they had a mini gym where he walked on the treadmill when he could.

The ginger-haired receptionist returned and escorted me to Vincent's room. I knew where it was, but they were careful that way.

Vincent sat by his bed in his easy chair. I could tell from his smile he was himself that day. His lunch tray sat nearby on a round table. I saw the remains of broiled chicken and roasted vegetables.

"Hi, Vince. I hope I didn't interrupt your lunch."

"Nah, we eat early around here. We get up early, we eat early, we go to bed before the sun even sets. Fact is, most folks stay in bed day and night."

Yes, he sounded clear headed, all right.

"You feel like chatting with me a little while?"

"Sure, as long as you don't test me on it later. Sometimes I remember, sometimes I don't." He gave me a cheerful grin and motioned to a chair next to his lunch tray.

I talked about his little dog, and how I'd seen Candy lately. Everyone seemed to be fine. Just some chit-chat, rather than diving right into the tough questions about Marge's murder.

Finally, he gave me a pointed look and said, "Go ahead and ask me what you came for. I might fade away and get fuzzy headed. You know, sleepy time after lunch."

"Of course. Vince, I wonder if today you can recall anything at all about a night a couple of weeks ago when Candy came and got you late in the evening to take you home for the night. It was the same night Marge was murdered in her home. April fifth."

"Oh, that. I might have known. Well, I can hardly remember anything. I was upset and shouting at the nurses here to call my wife. I remember her coming to get me. And I remember sleeping in my own bed at home, and the shower the next morning. I thought we were going to the supermarket when I got in the car, but she brought me back here. That's all I can think of."

"Do you remember your walk, or going to Marge's house that night?"

He looked surprised. "We went for a walk? Candy did that for me? I don't remember any of that."

"How about this? I found an entry in Marge's private journal, made a couple of months ago, which said, 'Found info on F.' She had drawn a candy cane next to the F. Does that make sense to you?"

"That would seem to refer to me. She always called me Freeman, like Candy did. And sometimes she called my wife 'Candy Cane,' not in a kind way." He looked thoughtful and rubbed his chin. "Not sure what information she was referring to. I don't tell everyone my business, and I came to Conroy to keep a low profile and enjoy everyday life."

"Okay, I have one more question for you, if you don't mind."

Vincent nodded and appeared to concentrate, with an effort.

"Rosanna and I looked through the information you filed in the office for the Homeowner's Association. Where you listed your previous address as The Hamptons in New York State, she had penciled in 'lying jerk.' Why would that address make her angry?"

A slow grin spread across Vince's face. "Almost everything made her angry. I remember how haughty and condescending she seemed when we filled out our paperwork. I decided to make up a phony address just to yank her chain. Looks like it worked." He chuckled noisily. "Truth is, we moved here from Greece. But that was none of her business."

I told him I was sorry to put him through so many questions. He was already yawning, and I stood to leave.

"Celia, I hope you come again, and I hope I recognize you. I want you to find out who killed that hateful woman, so you can get it settled. But it wasn't me. At least, I don't remember killing anybody." He chuckled at himself.

I stood and shook his hand. "I'll leave now and let you rest." An attendant stepped inside and took the lunch tray. When the door closed behind her, I smiled at Vincent. "Enjoy your nap. Next time I come, I'll see if they'll let me bring Puff Ball."

Vincent pressed a button on the side of his chair, and it reclined gently. He gave a small wave as I left the room. In my mind, I wished him sweet dreams. That's about all he had left.

Chapter 30

Vince's lunch had been early, and mine would be late. Back home, my stomach growled as I walked inside. Before I even put my keys away, someone tapped on my door.

What a sweet surprise to see the love of my life on my doorstep. I pulled Milo inside and wrapped my arms around him, forgetting about lunch. He smelled of warm sunshine, a freshly laundered golf shirt, and the lingering scent of cologne. And something else: warm burgers.

He set the bag of food on my kitchen table and asked if I still had lemonade. We poured two glasses and dug into the food. Riley was with his mother, so we enjoyed a meal for two.

I told Milo about my visit with Vince, how lucid he was, but that his memory of April fifth was sketchy at best. He'd had no idea what Marge's journal entry could mean, but admitted he'd lied about his previous address, just to give Marge a hard time. "He says they moved here from Greece."

"I think he had business connections everywhere," Milo said. "I never understood why he chose to buy a place here."

"He told me he wanted a quiet, simple kind of place where no one would take notice of him. He'd had enough of bustling cities. Not his his exact words, but that was the gist of it."

"He could be lying," Milo said, then took a sip of lemonade.

"I can't find a way to prove it, either way. But Will has interviewed him and finds him convincingly truthful. I didn't learn anything from my new questions."

"Sounds like you're still working with Will."

"He's my only contact with the official investigation. I've bugged him from the beginning."

"I know. You never give up. Are you running out of suspects?"

"Not quite." I chuckled and finished my burger. "Remember the guy you escorted out of the Midnight Blues grill the other night, the guy who was trying to kiss me--"

"Russ, the lawn guy," Milo said.

"He's been having a secret affair with Marge for months."

"Who told you that?"

"His wife told me this morning. I never mentioned how he comes on to nearly every woman in sight. I think she knows."

Milo put his elbow on the table and leaned his forehead into his hand. "How did that even happen? Marge was not even friendly, much less sexy."

"He worked for Moonstone Lake. At the end of a long day of mowing, he might have stopped by her house to report a problem or complaint. Two lonely people with things they had to discuss could find a mutual attraction, I guess."

"I could see how that might end up with a crime of passion," Milo said.

"Still, I hate to tell the police. The affair is over, and he might be innocent."

Milo gave me a pointed grin. "He might not be guilty of murder but, in general, Russ Evers is anything but innocent."

Milo kissed my cheek and left to have new tires installed on his Land Rover. He kept that vehicle shining, like everything else he owned. I am not quite as neat and orderly, and I wondered if that could be a problem for us later. Well, he said he loved everything about me. I would have to trust him on that. I hadn't trusted a man in a long time—-most of my life, in fact. But Milo was the real deal.

With all the new developments, I needed to update my notes on the case. I had moved the notes about suspects from my refrigerator to my desk, so I strolled back to my office and switched on the desk lamp. I went over the page for each person involved.

Howard was no longer a suspect. I set his page aside—-one less person to ponder over. With a set of prints belonging to Vince, he was briefly considered, questioned, then eliminated. Both Tammy and Darlene had been checked out and eliminated as suspects. Both Marge's ex-husband, Dan, and his wife, Sherry, had been questioned and cleared, with alibis. That left Jason and maybe Russ.

I slipped all the sheets of paper into a desk drawer and looked at the two remaining. Could it possibly be Russ? I thought again about talking with Tammy and Darlene, decided Tammy would be less excitable, and looked for her number on my cell phone.

They weren't called "The Gossip Sisters" for nothing, and I hesitated to discuss anything about Russ. I wouldn't mention anything about an affair. Even if it was true, it was over now, and it didn't need to be spread around the neighborhood.

When Tammy answered, I told her I'd been wondering about Russ Evers and his business relationship with Marge. I wondered if they ever had problems. (Because who *hadn't* had problems with Marge?)

"Let's keep this just between us for now," I said. That was unlikely, but I had to ask anyway. "Since you live across from her house, did you ever see him visit Marge at home, day or night?"

"Sure," Tammy said. "He had issues with the grass cutting, I guess. He got finished late in the evenings, after the park office was closed. So, he'd go bang on her front door, and I always watched out the window. What's going on, anyway?"

"I'm not sure. I want to check everything out and let the detectives on Marge's case know whatever I dig up."

"Well, there's one more thing," Tammy said, lowering her voice. "I can't think why he'd do this, but I saw him go around to her back door a few times when it was dark. I have some little binoculars that help me see when the light's low. You don't think he was up to some hanky-panky, do you?" I imagined her holding the phone to her ear, quivering for a juicy morsel of gossip.

"That's not what I'm getting at, Tammy. Did you happen to see him around Marge's place on the night she was murdered?"

"Can't say as I did," she said. "That place was busy, though. I went over and told Marge off, Howard was there later, and I came home too angry to sit and watch her front door. I was busy typing her an email, quoting the HOA rules to her. If anybody else went to see her that night, I never saw it."

"Well, she had at least one more visitor." I heaved a sigh. "The one who killed her."

"And you think it might be the lawn guy?" Tammy said. I heard the wonder in her voice, hoping for excitement.

"I don't even know if he had a motive. But I'll get back to you when I know more."

We hung up, and I knew she'd be the last person I'd share breaking news with. But if she expected me to keep her posted, maybe she'd delay spreading gossip till she thought she had the whole story.

***

I was busy loading my washing machine when my phone rang, and I saw Will's number. He immediately informed me he'd just been to the office and picked up the journal.

"Rosanna tells me you've already been through it. And she showed me the page where you found the note with the candy cane." He sounded tired.

"Yeah, that caught my attention. Why didn't you stop by here?"

"We can talk by phone. Celia, I appreciate the information you pass on to me, and I'm happy to keep you updated. But you've made it plain we're only business associates, and I need to keep my distance now."

"I understand––and I'm sorry if I've made you uncomfortable."

He had done an "about face" where I was concerned. I was afraid he might cut off our friendship and all the updates on the murder.

"Do you have other information for me?" he asked.

I told him what I'd learned about Russ––straight from his wife––and how Tammy had seen Russ visit Marge often, day and night. This was one more connection Marge had in the community, but I had no idea if Russ had a motive to kill her.

"Might have been a lovers' quarrel. I'll have to question him. Anything else?"

"Just one more. I didn't know when I might see you, so I went to see Vince this morning, hoping he'd be himself again. I showed him a copy of Marge's journal entry. Also asked about her remark on the HOA file, where she called him a lying jerk. He had no idea what her journal note meant, but said he gave her an incorrect previous address just to annoy her." I had to chuckle. "I know you'll want to talk to him yourself, but he seems truthful and harmless to me."

I could hear scratching as he made notes.

"Yeah, I'll double check all this. But there's another one we can scratch off the list. I'm talking about Jason, the bad-boy son. I went by Cliff Browning's motorcycle dealership this morning and he confirmed Jason was at his home on the night of April fifth. He knew all about you going over to his house and talking with his wife, and he also said he could not swear Jason was in his house all night. But he assumes Jason slept on the couch in his rec room.

"And he tells me the canoe in his yard has been turned over for several months, because it needs to be repaired. It has a hole in the flooring and can't be taken on the lake. We know, at least, Jason had no way across the lake unless he took Mr. Browning's motorboat or a car in the driveway. Either way, the Brownings would have heard the motors."

"Did you go inspect the canoe and verify what he told you?"

"Yes, *Chief*," he said. "I promise I did everything right. I saw an old, moldy break in the wood on the bottom of the canoe."

A blush warmed my cheeks. "Nothing wrong with me checking behind you. I know I'm an amateur, but I'm trying to be helpful."

"Yes, I know that. Sorry. Now here's the bottom line: Jason might have been angry with his mother, but we don't have a clear motive for him to murder her. He lied about being in the area, but we can't put him at the scene of the crime. I can't consider him a suspect any longer."

We said goodbye and disconnected. I was partly relieved, mostly frustrated. We were fresh out of suspects. I'd have to dig deeper.

Chapter 31

With coffee mug in hand, I stared at my kitchen clock while I planned my day. My plans are usually vague ideas, but they sometimes involve a list.

I heard footsteps outside my door, two taps, and then Milo walked in, smiling. My heart flipped over, and I offered him a sip of my coffee. Seeing the creamy color, he declined and walked to the kitchen for a cup of straight black. Just the thought of his lips on my coffee cup seemed a bit like kissing him.

I didn't have to wait long. He blew on his coffee, took a few sips, then grabbed me for a good morning kiss.

We made scrambled eggs and toast, and I added my homemade strawberry jam. After Milo carried his dishes to the sink and rinsed them, he said he was going to check on Sam at rehab. "They limit his visitors at this point, so I can't ask you to go with me."

He drew me into his arms and held me tight. "What do you have planned for today?"

"Weed my flower beds, wash the car, do some grocery shopping."

"I won't be gone long. I can help with the weeding and car washing later this afternoon. But I'd like to take you to lunch in the boat. Remember the little bistro on Lake Borden?"

"Yes! I'd love to go there. I need a change of pace, because I'm fresh out of ideas about who killed Marge. Everyone suspicious ends up with an alibi."

Milo considered my answer, probably thinking I was obsessed with the mystery. And he would be right. I needed to think about something else for a change. I kissed him goodbye and started on my grocery list.

At the supermarket, I piled my grocery cart with eggs, bread, and fresh fruit, adding a roast to surprise Milo with later in the week. I had a short list but kept seeing things on every aisle I should buy to save a trip later. A young man in the grocery aisle almost bumped into me, made his apologies, and hurried on his way. I read the back of his T-shirt, which displayed the name of a local high school. I wondered briefly if Riley might attend the same school, then finished my shopping and headed back home.

Close to noon Milo returned, and we strolled happily down to the lake. His Bayliner sat docked at the marina, and we climbed aboard with our water bottles. Milo slapped on his ball cap. I wore sunglasses but let my hair blow in the breeze.

The sun was pleasantly warm, and the air smelled heavenly with the scent of jasmine drifting around us. We motored across the lake close to the other shore and took a leisurely path, much like the one we'd taken on our previous outing. When we passed the Browning residence, the red canoe sat on the ground with the gaping hole obvious. A few of the neighbors had canoes at their docks.

When we crossed Lake Borden, we drew near the bistro, smelling grilled meat and warm bread. Milo eased the boat in and helped me onto the dock. The bistro was not crowded, and we were seated without a wait. I read the menu to the tune of my growling stomach.

All the servers wore T-shirts, and I looked closely, remembering the boy in the supermarket. The young woman approaching us wore an unusual shirt with the logo of a golden horse with open wings. Words encircling the logo read "University of Central Florida."

"I can't remember the name of this horse," I told her, as she arrived at our table.

"Pegasus," she said, grinning. "It symbolizes *limitless possibilities*. Maybe I'll graduate with honors and become a genius."

"If that's what you work for, that's what you can achieve," Milo said.

"Thank you, sir." She held her pad and pen at the ready. "What can I get for you folks?"

We had a tasty, well-prepared lunch, and I kept thinking of the beautiful Pegasus on the server's shirt. I would always treasure my college years and the following years as a teacher.

"If I could go back to college again, guess what I'd study," I said to Milo.

"Probably crime and the law."

"What? Are you kidding me?"

"So you could be a detective for real," he said.

"No. Like everyone keeps telling me, this stuff can be dangerous. And a lot of people don't like being asked questions. It's hard work, and it stays on my mind."

"What then?" he asked.

"I'd study writing, like you."

"I didn't study writing, just always read a lot, and my mind enjoys creating plots and stories."

"Okay, but some people do study writing. I'd get a degree in literature or fine arts. But I'd still end up teaching. I could teach creative writing and related courses. If I had studied that in college, I might be a published author by now."

Milo gave me a slow grin. "So now you admire my profession more than you do Will's?"

I had to laugh. "It has nothing to do with copying you or Will. I love mysteries. I've just realized I'd rather write mysteries than solve them."

He studied me for a moment. "Somehow, I doubt that."

We finished our lunch, and Milo left a generous tip. "College students are always short on funds," he said. "I have to respect anyone continuing their education and working to pay their way."

I squeezed his hand. Every day I admired him more.

***

Soon we were back on Moonstone Lake, and my eyes strayed back to the shore as we approached the Browning residence. My heart rate increased when I remembered Jason's stormy eyes and bitter words at the blues bar on Friday night. My Lord, I hoped he wasn't visiting them now and watching us from a window.

Still, I asked Milo to stay close to that side of the lake. As we passed the boat dock where we'd seen Jason smoking, the same deep red canoe sat with the damaged underside exposed. Next door, a light blue canoe tied to the boat dock rocked gently on the water. On the bow of the canoe, a large white circle surrounded a gold Pegasus, just like the logo on our server's shirt.

I rose and stepped closer to Milo. "Just because the Brownings' canoe was not usable doesn't mean he couldn't have borrowed the one next door. It might have been bobbing in the water like today, free for the taking."

Milo nodded. "Entirely possible, but you need evidence or proof."

I thought about calling our detective friend and the two of us telling him what I suspected. However, if I brought Milo into our conversation, Will might clam up. I would call him later and speak to him alone.

Back at our marina, we secured Milo's boat and headed up the street to our homes. "Hey, I can wash my own car," I said. "I'm sure you have things to do."

"I'll help you," he insisted. Then we can watch a movie and relax."

"Okay, you'll find supplies in the storage shed. I don't want to get these clothes wet, so I need to change."

Inside, I thought about calling Will, but decided it could wait.

I joined Milo and rinsed the sections of my car as he washed them. He easily removed dried insects from the front grill of the car. I loved seeing my car sparkling clean. And I loved watching Milo, with his close-cut, flat-top hair and rippling muscles.

We put off the weeding till later. Retired people can be flexible. How lovely!

Chapter 32

Next morning, I decided to do the weeding before the air got too hot. Milo was next door in his office, working on a book. His office window only had a view of my deck, so I worked on the flower beds by my front porch. Otherwise, he'd be tempted to abandon his work and help with mine, something I loved about him. But I didn't like pulling him away from his writing.

I had barely gotten started when my phone rang. I removed my gloves and tugged the phone from my pocket.

"Hi, Celia. This is Nancy. Russ and I need to talk with you."

Oh, no! Why would they both want to talk to me? I wondered. "Nancy, I don't think I need to be involved with you and Russ, you know, if he has problems about anything."

"It's not that." Her voice trembled a bit, but she chuckled. "We've had a long talk, and yesterday we went to counseling. We're trying to work things out. And he's told me something really crucial. We need to see you."

"Why me?" I begged. I was so uneasy, afraid he'd bring up the time he tried to kiss me.

"Because you're the one who said you need information of any kind about Marge's murder, that's why. Are you interested, or not?"

I ignored the fact she had called me so early in the morning, and that my flower bed was only half weeded. "You want me to come now?"

"Please. If you can."

I dashed inside, washed my face and hands, then gave Milo a call to say where I was going. Considering how roughly Russ had treated me the Friday night before, Milo offered to go with me. But I told him it might be confidential, and Russ would be on his best behavior in front of his wife. I promised to give Milo a call as soon as I could.

When I arrived on my bike, Nancy invited me into her house. Russ mostly looked at his feet, but he gave me a quick nod as I took a seat in their living room. Nancy noticed her husband's reluctance, and she prodded him.

"Russ, you're the one with all the big news. Why don't you go first."

"Aw, Nancy. I don't know where to begin. You start and I'll speak up when I can."

This was a Russ I'd never seen before. He was always cocky and inappropriate, even worse when he'd had too many beers. I was impatient for somebody--anybody--to start talking and tell me the crucial news.

"Okay," Nancy said. "I finally confronted Russ with all the gossip I'd heard about him. I told him how it hurts to hear about your husband trying to hustle every woman in sight, even having an affair with the park owner. He thought he'd hidden everything from me, he thought I didn't care anyway. He'd given up on our marriage, and he gave up on me."

Nancy dabbed at her eyes with a tissue. "But I told him I wanted to save our marriage, to do what we had to in order to stay together and be happy like we once were."

"That's when I knew I could tell her more about Marge," Russ said, avoiding my gaze. "I have been a gnarly Tom cat. And I owe you an apology, Celia. I treated you bad, like you ought to enjoy my rude talk. But I promise I'll never bother you again." He gave me a sheepish look and adjusted his cap.

"Apology accepted," I said. "I wish you the best of luck."

"It's time I was out mowing, but I gotta tell you what I saw. And I'm telling you first, 'cuz them cops are gonna be mad."

My mind was screaming, *Spill it, for heaven's sake!*

Russ continued. "On Monday night, April fifth, I wanted to see Marge. We had a thing going and I could visit her around midnight anytime I saw her lights still on. I'd told her to expect me, so I snuck down there and went around to the back, like I always did.

"But I saw another guy at her back door, and I ducked down behind the shrubs that surround her yard. This guy was in the shadows and moved onto her screened porch. Then, instead of knocking, he took out a key and unlocked her back door. I thought she had another boyfriend, and he looked younger than me, from his build. He wore a hoodie, but he pulled it back when he got to her door, and his hair was light colored."

"You didn't question him?" I asked.

"I was keeping my affair a secret, I thought, so I had to stay hidden––he went on in the house, and I found a window that gave me a clear line of sight to the living room. He was a young guy, and they started shouting. When he turned to walk away, I hurried off to hide in the shadows by the marina.

"They kept hollering, but they must have settled it. He came back out across the porch and headed for her boat dock. That's when I saw the canoe. It had a white circle painted on the side, up near the front. There was a figure inside the circle, but I couldn't see what it was. This guy, though, he jumped in that canoe and paddled away into the darkness. And he was looking all around, like he didn't want to be seen.

"I changed my mind about seeing Marge. She would be upset and in no mood for my visit. So, I hurried home."

"It didn't cross your mind Marge might be injured or even worse?"

"No, she hollered at everybody who disagreed with her, even me. And I never heard her scream. Things just got quiet . . . then, the next morning when I was on the mower, I rode down to see what the sirens were all about. I saw them remove her body, but I couldn't speak up. I would have been a suspect, and I didn't want my wife or anybody to know I'd been at her house." He looked at Nancy and covered his face with his hands.

I had one more question. "Would you recognize this man if you saw him again?"

"Probably could. Never met her son, but that guy was young enough to be her son."

When I stood to leave, Nancy hugged me, and Russ shook my hand. "Detective Hendrix will probably talk to you later today. I'll call him when I get home. Sure hope this ends the investigation, and we can all feel safe again."

Back home, I walked over to Milo's. He asked me in, eager to know how my visit went. When I told him the whole conversation, as close to word-for-word as I could make it, Milo looked relieved and then concerned.

"Thanks for filling me in, but you have to call Hendrix right away––you know that. And Celia . . . Jason will know you're partly responsible for getting him arrested. Until he's behind bars, you may not be safe. He's not thinking clearly. I want to be with you night and day until he's locked up."

Night and day. That sounded nice. "You got it," I said, and kissed his lips.

I stood in Milo's living room and made my call to Will. I had done all the snooping I was going to do. From there on, it was all up to the police department.

He answered his phone in his car, and I repeated to him the conversation I'd just had with Russ and his wife.

Will's voice took on new energy. "If this guy had spoken up on the day we found the victim's body, we'd have someone arrested by now. Maybe Russ Evers is guilty and he's trying to pin it on Marge's son."

"I guess you've seen enough of crime to know it can twist in all directions," I said. "But the neighbor next to the Brownings might confirm that his canoe showed signs of use. It was very likely the canoe Russ Evers saw tied up at Marge Coleman's dock."

"Do you also have that address?" he asked.

"It's right next to three-forty Palmetto Drive, on the west side of the house. I can look it up on the real estate map and text the name and address to you in a few minutes. Milo and I were on the lake around noon today. We saw a light blue canoe tied up at the dock with the white Pegasus logo on the bow. That's about how Russ Evers describes the boat he saw––and Jason had access to that boat."

"Yes," Will said. "It's all adding up, finally. I'll try to find the people at home on Palmetto Drive. I'll ask Russ Evers to meet me in my office to look through some mug shots. We'll see if he picks Jason's picture out of the photo pack." He added drily, "We happen to have a few of him on file."

I heard his car door slam, and I spoke while there was still time. "Will, do you think this puts me in any kind of danger?"

"It certainly could. We'll find Jason, question him and, with enough evidence, we'll charge him with murder. But he or his friends could come after you, if he connects you with this arrest. You need to be cautious. Keep your doors locked and don't go anywhere alone."

"Thanks, Will. Let me know how things go."

I stepped back to Milo's office. He sat staring at his folded hands, not his computer screen, but he looked up when I entered.

"I think I'll be safe in my own yard pulling weeds," I said. "At this point, Jason doesn't know Will suspects him again."

Milo's eyebrows arched as he gathered his notes and papers. "I'll bring my laptop over to your dining table. Might not be necessary yet, but I'd like to be close by."

Later, squatting by my flower beds, I wondered why anyone trying to conceal the guilt of a murder would risk assaulting yet another person. That would make their guilt obvious. I pictured myself strapping on a gun and holster, like Annie Oakley. Ridiculous. *Would Milo carry a gun? Does Milo even have a gun?*

A chill crept over my body, and I began to stuff the weeds into a trash bag. I stood, looked all around at the quiet neighborhood, wondering where someone would hide if they were stalking me. Cleaning up the flower beds no longer seemed important.

I disposed of the bag of weeds and went back inside. I'd never been so uneasy in broad daylight; clicking the door lock in place relaxed me somewhat. Having Milo there gave me peace of mind as well.

Logically, there was no reason to think Jason might be stalking me already. I imagined him, strutting and cocky, thinking he had fooled us all and no one would ever know who killed his mother.

Milo looked up from his laptop. "I'm glad that weeding didn't take too long. I was about to come out and lend a hand."

"Well, I didn't finish all of it. I know I'm not in danger yet, but I'm creeped out. It's too easy to imagine someone watching me."

He stood and wrapped his arms around me. "Want to order a pizza?"

"No, you already bought me lunch. I'll broil some salmon and steam some rice and veggies."

"I'll help. Just put me to work," he said. "Then you can read what I've been working on today. I'd like to hear your ideas."

Life was normal again. Then someone tapped on the door.

Milo looked through the peephole, saw Rosanna, and opened the door.

"Hi, Milo," she said, breezing on into the house. "Celia, I see you have company. I was going to invite you over for dinner. I made chicken pot pie. Are you going out somewhere?"

"No," I told her. "We were just about to make dinner."

"I have plenty. Why don't you both come over. It just came out of the oven."

I glanced at Milo, who looked enthusiastic and wiggled his eyebrows.

"Sure," I said. "When did you find time to make a chicken pie?"

"I bought it last night from a deli, y'know, already assembled. All I had to do was bake it."

We went over to Rosanna's and smelled mouth-watering aromas as we walked in. I helped bring food to the table, and Rosanna set an extra place for Milo while he introduced himself to Bitsy. When he knelt beside the cat and stroked her head, his jeans hiked up and exposed his ankle. I saw the edge of an ankle holster. He might seem light-hearted and happy, but I knew Milo was dead serious about my safety.

As we seated ourselves at her dining table, I asked, "Why didn't you ask Howard to dinner?" After all, their relationship was no longer a secret.

Rosanna blushed. "I did. He and Tate are watching baseball on TV tonight." She reached for my plate and spooned a serving of the chicken pie onto it, rather than passing the heavy casserole dish. "Plus, he's not a people person, y'know. I'm having to get used to that."

She reached for Milo's plate, and he chimed in, "You just wait. Before long, Howard and I will be close friends."

Sheesh. That meant I'd have to be Howard's friend, too. How could that ever happen? I'd rather be his friend than his enemy, but it was hard to warm up to cool-and-withdrawn Howard.

Chapter 33

My phone rang, and I hoped it would be Will--simply because I had not talked with him in three days, and I needed to stay informed about the unsolved murder case, which occupied my mind day and night. If I called him, it might be construed as chasing after him. He'd made it clear he wanted distance between us, and I agreed--except where the case was concerned.

I recognized Howard's number. When I said hello, he moved right into the purpose of his call.

"Will asked me to fill you in on recent developments," he said. "Yesterday, he took Jason in for questioning, the lawn mower guy picked him out of a lineup, and Jason was arrested for murder." His voice trembled on that last part.

"Sorry, Howard. I know he's your nephew."

"Yeah, well Marge was my sister. If he did, in fact, murder his own mother, he'll have to pay for the crime."

"Is he still in jail?"

Howard sighed, as if he questioned himself continually. "No, he's out . . . I paid his bail. And I hired the best defense lawyer I could find. I don't want him convicted on a fluke. If he really did this, they'll have to prove it."

"No confession, huh?"

"He's adamant he did not kill his mother. He seems indignant anyone would suggest it. But I know Jason is unstable, and he lies like he doesn't know the difference between true and false--Celia, I want this whole thing settled, but I so hope Jason is not the murderer."

"I understand." I scratched my head, still perturbed. "Do you know why Will didn't call me himself?"

"He's very busy at this point. And maybe he doesn't like to think he has to report to you, when you're not part of the police department, or even my family."

There it was. That stiff, cold side of Howard that was so off-putting. I decided I'd have to get used to it. He was Rosanna's significant other, and Milo had stated his intention to become Howard's close friend. I might as well go with the flow.

"I see. That makes sense. I appreciate you letting me know. And Howard, I truly want justice for Marge and closure for you. I also hope Jason is not guilty. Your family has suffered enough."

Howard was silent. Maybe he was speechless with emotion.

I thanked him and ended the call.

***

Closer to evening, Milo received a call from Riley. Melanie was tied up in her office, Sam was still in rehab, and Riley needed a ride to a friend's house.

"Want to go with me to pick up Riley?" he asked. He'd been working on his laptop with papers spread out beside him on my couch. He probably needed to stretch his legs and go for a drive.

"How long will it take?" I asked.

"Forty-five minutes, tops."

Still stewing over the news about Jason's arraignment, I knew I'd be better off at home. "I might be able to survive without you for that long."

"Okay. You stay home, but keep the doors locked."

I patted his cheek. "If I want to talk to Rosanna, I'll use my phone."

While he was gone, I studied Milo's notes and research he left lying on the couch, and I lost track of time. My phone dinged with a text. I glanced outside and saw dusk approaching, then grabbed my phone.

Once again, I saw Howard's number. The text read: You won't believe what I've found in Marge's boat house. Hurry, it's getting dark. HJ

Just like Howard to use his initials, keeping things formal and distant.

He was waiting to show me something significant. Howard rarely called me, and this could be the very clue that solved the case. I could call him and say I'd wait till Milo got home. But I could not wait.

I took my phone and headed out. Milo would worry when he found the house empty, so I texted him I was meeting Howard at the boathouse to see something he'd found.

My mind raced with the possibilities. Howard's text had read like he was excited. That must mean he hoped to clear Jason of the crime. *What on earth could it be?*

I reached Marge's driveway in the waning sunlight and made my way around the house to the back, where I saw a light shining from the boathouse at the end of her dock. Taking the familiar path through her yard, I started past the huge tree centered behind the house––and gasped.

A strong arm from behind me grasped my neck and shoulders, and something sharp pierced the right side of my neck. Hot breath hit my cheek and words hissed into my ear. "I got you, you little bitch. Don't make a sound, or this knife goes right through your neck."

He dragged me through the deepening shadows toward the boathouse. "Jason, don't do this. You'll be caught. You'll leave evidence."

He clapped his left hand over my mouth and chin. "Shut up," he growled. "The only evidence I'm leaving will convict Uncle Howard. This is his knife, and I'm wearing gloves."

The knife moved slightly, breaking the skin just enough for blood to trickle. He probably planned to gag me and torture me to death. I wanted to kick and struggle, but the blade was too close to my neck. I imagined blood pouring everywhere, and my life draining away.

Jason dragged me farther, but his progress was slow. I heard a click, and he stopped in his tracks.

Another voice spoke. "No, I won't get the blame. I have a cocked pistol to your head. Drop that knife, or I'll pull the trigger."

"I don't think so, Uncle Howard. You won't kill me." Jason threw me to the ground and whirled around, jabbing his right elbow into Howard's throat. I watched the struggle, horrified to see Howard's gun fly from his hand. Another punch directly to Howard's nose sent the older man to the ground, out cold.

I needed to run while I could, but I froze in terror. I couldn't move or make a sound. Jason sneered at me. "Finally," he said, and darted toward me with the knife drawn back.

An explosion sounded nearby, like a cannon firing. But the bullet found its mark; blood spattered from the center of Jason's forehead, and he fell to the ground.

I sat with my mouth open, tears streaming down my face. Was Jason my only attacker? Was I still in danger?

More arms grabbed me, and I cried out. Those arms surrounded me and drew me to my feet. Milo held me close, and my body went limp. Blood from my neck dripped onto his shirt. I sobbed and never wanted to turn him loose.

"I thought you promised to say inside," he murmured, and I giggled. My nervous response has always been to giggle, always at the most inappropriate times.

I thought of Howard and turned to look for him. "I'll check Howard," Milo said. He helped me settle onto the ground, then felt for Howard's pulse. "Out like a light, but his pulse is fine," Milo said. "I'll always be thankful he showed up to save your life."

"*You* saved my life," I said.

"He saved it first and bought me some time."

By then, Tammy and Darlene were on the scene. Being the closest neighbors, they heard the gunfire and called for help. When they saw only Milo and me stirring, they hurried down to give assistance.

Darlene covered her mouth and looked away, unable to handle seeing Jason's still body. Howard stirred, looked around, and seemed relieved to see me alive with Milo by my side. Then his face crumpled at the sight of his dead nephew.

Tammy used her medical skills to check on Howard, then felt Jason's neck for a pulse.

I lost control under the enormity of the situation: how close I'd come to being killed, how tragic for Howard to lose yet another close relative, and heartbreaking that a young man's life had come to an end.

None of it was my fault, but I sobbed and groaned, as if the sound could wash away the tragedy.

For the third time in a few short weeks, an ambulance and the police arrived at Moonstone Lake. Will Hendrix showed up, looking like he hadn't slept in days. He spotted me seated in a lawn chair Milo had found for me. Looking like he'd expected to find me in the middle of the commotion, he walked over and squeezed my shoulder. "Have you been hurt?"

"Just a scratch on my neck. But Jason tried to kill me."

People from the neighborhood gathered and gawked while police officers again draped crime scene tape around the backyard area. EMTs checked out Howard, whose nose was bloodied but not broken. They cleaned and bandaged my throat.

Once the medical examiner arrived and the ambulance left, Will determined that only Howard, Milo and I had been involved in the incident which resulted in the death of Jason Coleman. With Howard's permission, he gathered us all in Howard's house nearby. A female officer got water for all of us, made sure we were comfortable, and Will began his questions.

"Who can tell me how this all happened?" he asked.

"I may as well begin," Howard said. His eyes were bruised and darkening, and his face looked set in stone. "About an hour ago, Jason knocked at my door. I was surprised to see him, and I didn't see his car in my drive. He came in and thanked me for paying his bail and hiring a good lawyer for him. It was not his usual resentful attitude, and I accepted his thanks. I don't exactly enjoy his company——well, I never did. But he sat and stayed till we were both bored, so I excused myself, saying I needed the restroom. He told me goodbye and headed for the door. When I returned from the bathroom, I noticed my phone was missing. Then in the kitchen, a steak knife was missing from the rack."

Howard dabbed at his nose with a paper towel. The bleeding had mostly stopped.

"What made you notice the knife rack?" Will asked.

"I'm a man of habits; I keep everything exactly in place and notice details. I thought he was probably at his mother's house, looking inside for something he could sell or pawn. But why would he need my knife?

"I got my handgun and eased over there as quietly as I could. When I came around Marge's storage shed, I saw Jason in the twilight, behind that huge oak in the back. My mouth went dry, and I wondered why he was hiding." Howard's eyes darted to me, then back to the detective.

"Celia came into the backyard and Jason grabbed her around the neck. While he struggled with her, I raced over and put my gun to his head and demanded he let her go. But I'm not as quick as I used to be. He swung straight back with his elbow and got me in the neck. Made me drop my gun. Then he decked me, and that's all I remember till Milo shook me awake."

Will looked at Milo, who still held me close, because I could not stop shaking. I was glad to let Milo talk.

"I had gone to town on an errand, and Celia promised to stay at home with the doors locked." He rolled his eyes at me. "I thought I'd be gone about forty-five minutes, but it was more like an hour. Driving home, I got a text from Celia saying she was on her way to meet Howard at Marge's boat house. It said Howard had texted her to meet him there." Milo patted his right ankle. "I grabbed my gun and had it ready. When I jogged around that house into the backyard, the first thing I saw was Jason Coleman rushing at Celia with a knife raised over his head. I had to act, and I shot him to save Celia's life."

Will turned to me, his eyes looking puzzled.

"I thought Howard sent me the text," I told him. "He had just called a few hours earlier about Jason being charged with murder. So, when the text came from the same phone number, signed with his initials, why wouldn't I think it was Howard? It wasn't quite dark, and I knew Milo would meet me down here with Howard."

"You can confirm that Jason had a knife to your throat and tried to kill you?" Will asked.

Tears welled up again, but I nodded and leaned against Milo.

Will reached forward and shook Milo's hand. "I'm proud to know you, Milo. You were at exactly the right place at the right time. Celia's lucky to have you." Will turned his eyes to me, paused, and cleared his throat. "I also know you're lucky to have her . . . just, please––try to keep her out of trouble."

With hands on his knees, he pushed himself upward. "Now, let's all go home and get some rest. I'll call you tomorrow about coming to the station and giving your statements."

Will turned to Howard. "You need an ice pack for all that bruising. Didn't the EMTs give you an ice pack?"

"Yeah, it's in my freezer. I'll use it when everyone leaves." Howard looked relieved when we all rose to our feet. He was a solitary kind of man, desperately needing his privacy.

I took both of his hands in mine. "Howard, you made a sacrifice for me. I'll never forget that you risked your life to save mine. I will always love you for that."

His arms wrapped around me, and he hugged me like a brother. Then he turned his back and covered his face with his hands. Will, Milo and I slipped out the door and left him in peace.

Rosanna stood outside, waiting to go in and comfort Howard. Anyone else would have annoyed him, but Rosanna was exactly who he needed.

***

"Your house or mine?" Milo asked. He helped me inside his SUV, parked on the lawn where he'd left it in his rush to get to me. His door still hung open, and I struggled into my seat while he steadied me. When he started the engine, I touched his arm, and he turned his pale gray eyes to me.

"My house, please. We can stop at yours and get what you'll need, but I can't bear being alone right now."

"I'll hold you in my arms all night long," he said with a catch in his voice. "I almost lost you."

We drove in silence the two blocks to Milo's, then lingered in his car, with more to say. I hung my head and squeezed his hand. "You asked me to stay at home with the doors locked. I fully intended to keep my word. But the text I thought was from Howard coaxed me out of hiding. It wasn't logical Jason would come after me so quickly."

"Probably not logical he'd come after you at all. It wasn't quite dark, and he took a big risk. But when someone is dealing with OCD, they often ignore logic."

"He thought, since he used Howard's phone and texted me with Howard's initials, he could then kill me with . . . with that kitchen knife." I stopped and almost gagged, appalled to think how close I came to dying with a slashed throat. "And all the clues would point to Howard." My shaking had returned, and Milo pulled me close.

"You might need a mild sedative to help you sleep. Would wine relax you?" he asked.

"I'll try the wine. Sleeping pills make me dream wild and crazy things."

Milo nodded. "Come inside with me. I'll pick up a few things, then we'll walk over to your house and have a peaceful, cozy evening."

"Will I ever feel peaceful again? I'm so wound up I think I might jump out of my skin."

Milo helped me out of his car, and I leaned into him as we went inside. "All you need," he said, "is the man who loves you snuggled close. You'll be fine."

As usual, he was right.

***

During the next few days, Milo answered many questions from Conroy Police detectives, who had to make certain Jason Coleman's death was a justifiable homicide. Howard and I were the only witnesses, and we backed up Milo's honest accounting of events.

The investigation into the murder of Marjorie Coleman was finally closed. Howard's bruised face was on the mend, and he sorrowfully attended the funeral of his nephew. Jeniffer asked him to inform me that my presence at the funeral would only add to the family's grief, so would I please not attend. Frankly, I had no intention of attending the funeral of a man who almost slit my throat. And yet, I wished him peace on the other side. I believe his life was warped by mental illness. No one had recognized how sick he really was.

Chapter 34

Four weeks had passed since Jason's death. Howard purchased Moonstone Lake Retirement Village from Jennifer, the sole heir. Howard and Rosanna were officially engaged. With Rosanna at his side, they made a good team running the place.

My stress had lifted since the attack. I only had a thin scar on my neck, but I struggled to fight off the heart-pounding memories. The daily pressure of an unsolved murder was no longer on my mind. The relief was a breath of fresh air, yet my mind drifted, unfocused.

I sat staring at page ten in a favorite novel by Agatha Christie. I'd been staring at page ten for the last half hour.

Milo never missed a thing. "Maybe you need to get a cat."

"No, I'm happy just to visit with Rosanna's cat."

"You could start writing a novel of your own."

I sighed, not wanting him to fret over me. "My brain's too tired to write a book right now. I'm not sure what I need." I closed the book and set it aside.

"Want to go out to lunch?" he asked.

"No, I made chicken salad with grapes. It's in the fridge."

"Okay, then. I have an idea."

"Another one?" I loved Milo with all my heart; he was never short of ideas.

"This is my best one yet. Why don't we do karaoke tonight?"

I sat up straighter and gawked at him. "What on earth are you talking about?"

He gave me an innocent grin. "You know, karaoke at the clubhouse tonight. Where they usually have bingo."

"No, I don't know. We've never had karaoke at Moonstone Lake. Are you kidding me?"

"No kidding. Tonight, they're trying out karaoke to see how the residents like it. Might be fun if we go."

I was dumbfounded. "I hate karaoke. Some of the people who sing are pretty good, but there are so many who have no idea they're not even on the tune. They're tone deaf. Are you sure you want to do this?"

Milo rubbed my chin, then gave me a quick kiss. "Yeah, I really do. If they have enough attendance, they'll have it on a regular basis. This place could use something new."

"Where is this coming from?" I asked him. "You used to be such a loner, and now here you are wanting community karaoke. Do *you* like to sing?"

He chuckled and headed out. "I never said that. Hey, I'll pick you up at 6:30 and we'll walk down together. Okay?" He turned back to meet my eyes, and I turned my hands palms up in surrender.

Again, I got that impish grin.

He sure had changed. When I first met Milo, he sat alone on his patio most of the time, at least when I took my evening walks. I never saw him anywhere else. He was even a bit withdrawn when he first asked me inside to share his fresh-cooked soup and muffins. Now he seemed to like being with people. Even though he consistently spent time writing, he got out and about a lot more.

Well, I'd go with him to karaoke and see how he reacted to some of the laughable singing we'd be sure to hear. Maybe I was taking it all too seriously. People like to unwind and have some fun, find out what it's like to be onstage. I made up my mind to go with Milo and enjoy myself.

***

True to his word, Milo tapped on my door at 6:30 when the sun was low in the sky. I opened the door, and he beamed at me, checking me from head to toe. "Glad to see you haven't changed your mind. Else you'd be dressed in a nightgown already."

I wore a knee-length khaki skirt and a white linen blouse, ready to go, like I'd promised. "I don't look forward to a long, tedious night listening to people who can't sing. But you've piqued my interest." I tried to be charitable. "We might be surprised at the great voices some people have." There were always one or two. But some people's voices were torture on the ears, like a squeaky shopping cart at the supermarket. I grabbed my small purse and hung the strap over my shoulder.

Just weeks earlier, I'd narrowly escaped being murdered. It was hard to put something so jarring behind me. But it was time to turn the corner, focus on the here and now.

We ambled down the street with Milo's arm around me. The evening had cooled, although night would not fall for a few more hours. The sweet smell of gardenias drifted in the air from Tammy and

Darlene's yard. But the smell I loved most was Milo's cologne, as fresh as ocean waves. He squeezed my shoulder and asked, "What are you going to sing for us tonight, Celia?"

I turned to him, searching his face for playfulness or sincerity and saw both. "I'm not planning to sing anything. They'll be mobbed with singers signing up. It'll be fun seeing who participates."

"Some people here don't even know you're a professional singer," he said. "The ones who *do* know will expect you to sing." He grinned and gave me a light hip bump.

"I'll think about it. But some people at karaoke are shy and insecure. They might find confident singers intimidating. Anyway, this is not about me . . . why don't *you* sing something?"

"Ha!" he said. And we left it at that. I'd never heard him do anything more than whistle a tune while he washed his car.

The clubhouse bustled with people. Milo was right; the MLRV residents were as excited over karaoke as they were about bingo.

Two monitors on stands stood on either side of the stage, to prompt the singers and keep them on track with song lyrics, and a spotlight shone down on center stage. A slender fortyish woman, wearing a cowboy hat and snug jeans, stood in front of the stage on the lower level behind a long table which held her equipment. A banner hung on the front of the table reading, "Kaley's Karaoke."

Kaley's rich brown hair hung around her shoulders and down her back as she laid out several thick notebooks full of song titles. People swarmed around her, choosing songs from the books and adding their names to a sign-up list.

Milo gestured toward a round table for eight, positioned the second row back from the stage. Rosanna and Howard had chosen the same table, and they beckoned us to join them. I nodded at Howard and took the empty chair next to Rosanna. "You singing tonight?" I asked her with a teasing grin.

"Hey, I don't even sing in the shower." Rosanna looked at me like I was crazy.

"There's always a first time," I said, poking her with my elbow. At least we could laugh and cut up a little.

Howard's face told me otherwise. He wore his usual distant, preoccupied look. But his face relaxed when Tate showed up and settled beside him.

As they began a conversation, I glanced across the room and saw Darlene and Tammy. Darlene's eyes sparkled, and she waved at me. They headed our way and Darlene made herself comfy next to Tate. He paused in his conversation with Howard and gave her a dreamy smile. Her face turned pink, and I could almost see her heart pounding.

To my amazement, Candy showed up with Neil. Everyone there knew she was married, with her aging husband in a nursing home. But Candy flaunted her disregard for convention any time it suited her. They sat across the room, and Neil went straight to the front table and browsed through the song selections. I couldn't imagine him singing without his own keyboard accompaniment, but he found something he liked and signed the sheet. He swiveled his head toward me, widened his eyes, and gestured at the list. Bunching my eyebrows, I shook my head. Most of the people there did not know Neil. If I sang a love song with him, they'd get the wrong idea.

Anyway, I did not want to sing. Period.

Milo and Tate took off together and came back with an assortment of cold water, soft drinks, iced tea, and coffee. They even brought a carafe of coffee for refills.

Music played on the sound system as seven o'clock drew near, and Darlene focused on me. "Celia, you're going to sing, aren't you?"

I gave her a smile and shook my head. She was clearly disappointed.

"Well, darn! I should have stayed home." She turned to Tate, whose broad smile must have changed her mind.

Kayley started the evening with a song of her own to warm up the crowd. With a rich, sultry voice, she performed "Little Rock," a song by Reba McEntire. Able to entertain on a slow evening if she had a shy crowd and few people wanted to sing, she was also a feast for the eyes; most of the guys watched her every move, not caring how she sounded.

As she ended the song, she took off her hat and waved it to the crowd, waiting for the applause to die down. She announced that the sign-up sheet was filling up, and she called her first singer to the stage: A white-haired lady who asked to stay on the floor because of her walker. Kayley turned the screen of her laptop around so the woman could see her lyrics, then handed her a mic. The first strains of "Crazy" began, and the woman leaned on her walker and belted it out. Her voice was low and surprisingly strong. After a round of applause, Kayley called the next singer.

None of the music was too loud, and people chatted at their tables between songs. It was more entertaining than I had expected, and the evening moved along at a good pace. Soon Neil took the stage. He won the crowd over with the first sound of his velvety voice singing "Unchained Melody."

Tammy seemed horrified when Darlene scampered to the stage, all excited. She sang a song by Taylor Swift, which I didn't recognize and can't recall. Her voice was sweet and right on pitch, but the rhythm gave her some trouble. The applause was long, and Tate held his thumb and index finger between his lips and whistled loud enough to rattle the table. Darlene smiled like a kid and pranced back to her seat.

I was laughing, happy and relaxed, when Milo rose from his seat. He took hold of my wrist and lifted me gently from my chair. "Come on, Celia. Sing with me."

On my feet, still laughing with Darlene, it dawned on me what he'd said.

"What are you talking about?" I whispered through clamped teeth. "I've never sung with you."

"No, but you've sung with Neil, and I know the song. Please, trust me, Celia."

He'd already pulled me over to Kayley, who smiled like a conspirator. She handed a mic to Milo, then placed the other one in my shaking hand. I wanted to return to my seat. But if singing was what Milo wanted, I'd make the best of it, then laugh it off as a joke. I would be a good sport.

As we mounted the steps to the stage, I whispered, "What song did you choose? Are you sure we both know it?"

"You'll see," he said.

It was like I'd jumped off a rooftop, trusting him to catch me.

The music began, and I looked at the monitor. My breath caught in my throat, and his rich baritone led into the first verse. *When I fall in love, it will be forever.* His voice was deep and strong, like Elton John's. While he finished that verse, I fought for composure, but tears filled my eyes. I wiped them away as my verse approached.

When I give my heart, it will be completely. I sang my verse in a soft, tentative voice, but it grew stronger as I sang every word directly to him. We sang the words I needed to hear with my heart. I'd already had a love that was short-lived. Two-years-worth. I never wanted to try again––unless it could be forever. Milo knew that.

By the third verse, we both sang, swapping lines and filling in harmony behind each other. The key had moved a little higher, and the tempo picked up. This was the version Celine Deon and Clive Owen had recorded. As if we had rehearsed for hours, the vocals soared, and harmonies were tight and perfectly blended. Milo's eyes were bright with emotion, and I didn't bother to wipe away my tears.

The powerful song slowed to a soft, tender ending. The room was silent as the last note of our blended voices hung in the air. Then the crowd exploded into clapping and cheering with a standing ovation. The cheering continued and I looked around, puzzled.

In front of the stage, Tammy and Darlene stood facing the crowd, holding a banner stretched between them. The side facing the audience said the same thing as the side facing the stage: *Will You Marry Me?*

I burst out laughing and held my hand over my mouth. Milo stepped closer, sank to one knee, reached into his shirt pocket, and pulled out a ring. I was stunned, but I reached for the ring he held before me and bobbed my head in agreement.

Applause started all over again, and Milo stood and drew me into his arms. I never felt more at home.

Rosanna grabbed me when I got back to my seat beside her, and we held onto each other, giggling and sniffling. Even Howard managed a smile and offered his congratulations. Tate grinned and leaned across the table. "How long have you guys even known each other?" he asked, raising his eyebrows.

"Long enough," I answered. I leaned against Milo's shoulder.

We still had another hour left for karaoke. One would think more singing would be anticlimactic, but the opposite was true. People were in a celebratory mood and sang with happy smiles on their faces, dancing around the stage like pros. Before the evening was over, Whitney took the stage and sang "I Will Always Love You," sounding a lot like Whitney Houston, who made the song famous. We suffered through a few singers with tin ears and voices unfamiliar with following a tune. But everyone got applause for doing their best, and it was an undeniable success.

When karaoke was over, Kayley and her boyfriend packed up her equipment, and the crowd spilled out both exits. The moon had risen, and the sky had darkened into night. People swatted at mosquitoes and called out to one another as they strolled into the evening air, some walking to nearby homes, and others puttering off in golf carts. Again, Milo's arm rested on my shoulders, and my arm slipped around his waist. I kissed the diamond on my left hand, then lifted my face to kiss his lips. They were more precious than any jewel.

"You sure know how to grab my attention," I said.

"Your attention was worth waiting for."

"You got my attention weeks ago, when you invited me in for homemade soup. I didn't recognize my emotions that night, but that's when I fell in love with you."

"Well, you were just catching up with me," he said. "I loved you 'from afar' long before that. You made my head spin." He stopped to squeeze me and kiss the top of my head.

We walked in silence for a while. "My head was spinning when you dragged me up on that stage. Why didn't you tell me you could sing so well?"

"I saved it for a surprise. One more thing we can share." His eyes twinkled in the moonlight.

"I thought I would faint on that stage. Then you started singing, and it was like magic. You sounded so good, so alive." I looked up into his face. "This is the best night of my life."

"It's not over yet," he said, his breath warm against my cheek.

He unlocked my front door, and the moon shone even brighter as we slipped inside.

Chapter 35

We sat in my living room on a Thursday afternoon, basking in the normalcy of life. I turned to Milo. "There are no more mysteries to solve. I can think about us now."

"Oh yeah? Well then, let's seal the deal. I thought I had waited too long to get married, and it would never happen. But you're the one I've always hoped for. I can't wait for you to be my wife."

I threw my arms around his neck. "And I want you to be my husband. For the rest of my life, every single day will be better because of you."

Then my mind went straight to details; that's just how women are wired. "Milo, where will we live? Here, or in my house? We have two full sets of furniture."

He gave me a dreamy smile. "I'm thinking we'd enjoy a bigger house down by the lake."

"Oh no, not Marge's house!"

"Certainly not. I've been looking at a house I think you'll like. It's still in the retirement village, but it's larger and has a great view."

"Can we afford it? My retirement fund is modest, to say the least."

"I have full retirement from the military," Milo replied. "And I'm making more on my book sales than you might expect. We can easily afford this house . . . or any house you want."

"Who gets to decorate?" I asked. Then I wondered why I was asking all the questions. Maybe I should simply state what I would and wouldn't do.

No, I would not be confrontational with Milo. There was no need.

"We'll do it together," he said. "All I really care about is my study. I'll leave the rest in your hands. I'm sure it matters more to you than it does to me . . . and you know I'll help with cooking. I love to cook."

I must have died and gone to heaven. How could my life suddenly be so perfect? In the few weeks it had taken to solve a murder case, Milo and I fell in love and decided to spend the rest of our lives together. At our age, we had no time to waste.

"What else have you dreamed up to pamper and spoil me?" I asked.

Milo left his chair and settled next to me again on the couch. He reached for my hand. "I finally found my soul mate, and I want you to be happy in every way. I like dogs, cats, birds, frogs, whatever. You want pets? We'll have pets. We won't have children, but you can mother our pets. I have Riley, my godson. We can spoil him like a grandchild. And if you like trips, cruises? We'll do all of that." His warm shoulder nestled against mine.

"When I see you smile, when I see your love––that's all that matters to me now," he said. "And my writing, of course."

I had to laugh. I might just take up writing myself.

Meanwhile, Milo wanted to show me the house farther down on the lakefront. We both grabbed bottles of cold water and headed for his Land Rover. We drove to a different section of MLRV with larger homes.

Milo pulled into the shaded drive of a Mediterranean-style house surrounded with flowering shrubs and palm trees. A real estate sign in the yard displayed a phone number. I hoped we could call and get someone to show us the inside that afternoon. In my mind, I was already decorating the place.

The house was not occupied, so we explored the yard. We admired the pool in back with a lanai connecting it to the house, and a fountain trickling nearby.

We strolled down to the dock and gazed across the gently moving turquoise water. I pictured Milo's boat docked there, thought about the fun we could have with guests at our pool, burgers sizzling on the grill.

We scanned the plants growing near the dock, and I craned my neck, hoping to see ducks paddling about.

What I saw was a white sneaker caught in the reeds.

Milo had seen it, too. I turned my head, and our eyes met.

"Someone's sneaker probably fell overboard. Sometimes they float," he said.

"Yes, that's probably what happened." I still stared at the sneaker while questions tumbled over in my mind.

We both looked around at the trees, the sky, the driveway. Anywhere but the reeds.

Milo whipped out his phone. "Let's go back to the front yard and call the number on the sign. I'm ready to see inside, aren't you?"

I nodded and squeezed his hand. We walked back to the house, back to the front yard, back to take a closer look at the house. Just a happy couple, in love and ready to embark on a new phase of our lives.

But I would be back later to examine that lonely sneaker.

*

About the Author

Ellen Pritchard Holder is a writer and freelance copyeditor who loves to read. Originally from North Carolina, she has been a Florida resident since 1999. She and her husband have also been successful entertainers since 2008, performing dance music all over Central Florida. Ellen attributes her growth as a writer to voracious reading and the help received at various writing critique groups. Her flash fiction has been published several times in The Florida Writer online magazine and in various literary journals. From 2018 through 2023, she was published yearly in the Florida Writers Association Anthology. She often quotes Natalie Goldberg, who said, "Writers live twice." Ellen enjoys her real life but, when she writes fiction, that second life can be anything she imagines.

Howling Wolf Press

Stories that howl through the night...

At **Howling Wolf Press**, we publish bold, imaginative fiction with heart. From whimsical fantasy to haunting adventures, our books are crafted to enchant and endure.

JOIN THE PACK

Discover unforgettable stories or share your own.

HowlingWolfPress.com

Follow the call.